Witch

J Orton

J Orton

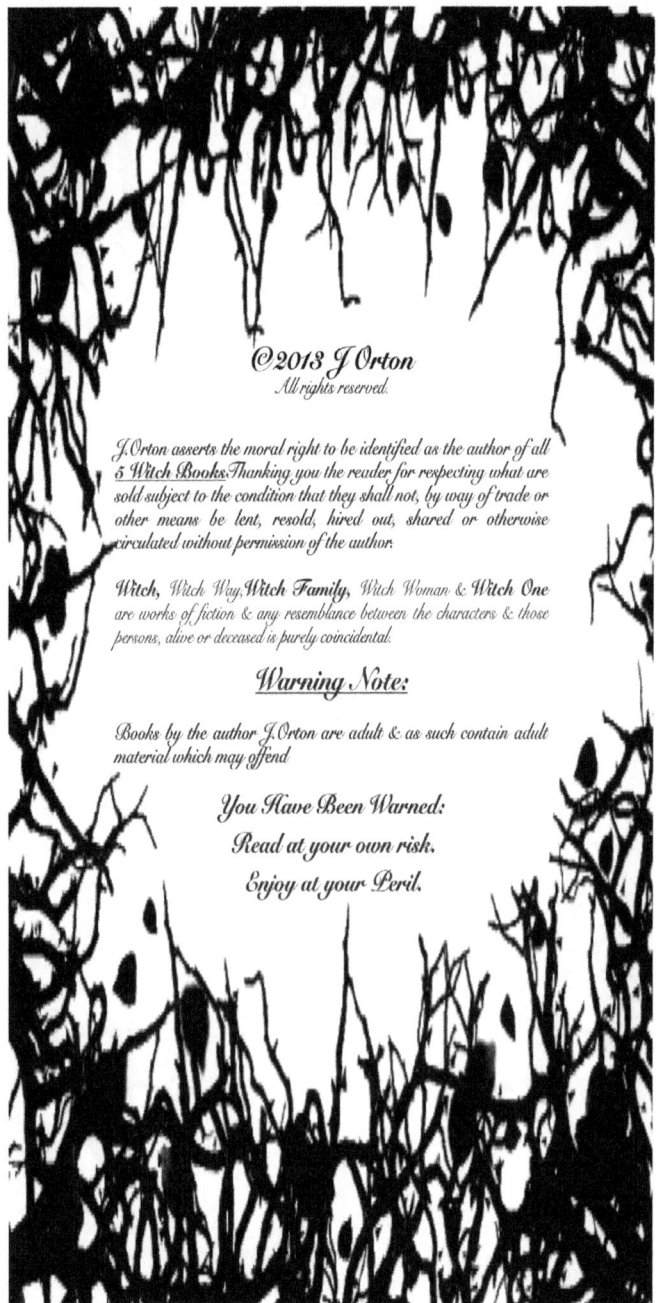

©2013 J Orton
All rights reserved.

J.Orton asserts the moral right to be identified as the author of all 5 Witch Books. Thanking you the reader for respecting what are sold subject to the condition that they shall not, by way of trade or other means be lent, resold, hired out, shared or otherwise circulated without permission of the author.

Witch, Witch Way, **Witch Family**, Witch Woman & **Witch One** are works of fiction & any resemblance between the characters & those persons, alive or deceased is purely coincidental.

Warning Note:

Books by the author J.Orton are adult & as such contain adult material which may offend

You Have Been Warned:
Read at your own risk.
Enjoy at your Peril.

Introduction

Long layered fabrics in dusky shades of black & grey, unkempt, not clean, dishevelled & dysfunctional, perceived to be the characters created within fairytales, where good fights against evil, causing even the pessimists to fall in love with the baddy.

Portrayed as being the baddies dressed in black with traits brought to life by character creators to exaggerate the darker, more sinister side of feminine nature. Strong, determined, dominate, seductive, controlling, fearless & carefree. Misunderstood by many & seen by most to be poor in etiquette, intelligence & moral understandings.

Having no need or want for material possession, expensive trinkets, or extravagant rewards. Each possesses powers to out-weigh that which makes mere mortals healthy, wealthy & wise.

Old wives tales dictate that each is old, stubborn, spooky & feared, possessing more knowledge than the wisest old owl, each carries disfigurements to hide alongside the ability to disguise what is actual. Living alone within the shadows, they hunt for eternal youth, having discovered age to be their only true enemy.

Unfortunate, many survive unforeseen circumstances under which mere mortals would crumble, lovers to have lost their one true love before becoming lost. Losers, Left to fend for themselves. Alone, many are considered to be ugly in mind, body & soul, making each unworthy of a second chance. Unhappiness covers them in the form of a heavy black cloak & a broken heart prevents them from ever loving anyone else. Magical, mysterious, untouchable, & allusive, each is protected by being feared.

Abandoned, discounted & disowned, most are said to be spinsters & widows, abandoned wives, unwanted daughters & unruly sisters. The female versions of the families black-sheep. Always the bridesmaid, but never the virginal blushing bride, they learn how to be independent whilst becoming self-sufficient within what is their personal realm.

Living within whilst surviving on, what is provided by mother nature. Retreating from the masses, hiding away to continue a never ending existence of secrecy, mystery, magic & myth. Living in amongst the shadows, each protects herself from what is everyday life. Rarely sighted in daylight. <u>The Witch</u> is said to thrive as she strives to discover, uncovering the truth about what is seen not to be natural. Unusual & strange

Cold, dark & damp, a hidden house which is never a home, not welcoming. Uncomfortable & ill equipped for modern day living. A shack disguised to appear abandoned as it sits in-amongst tall, dark shadowing trees with heavy trunks, sprawling branches & sharp protruding roots. Dirty, smelly & unloved, uninhabitable & often unpleasant. Isolated, spooky, dull, dust filled & dismal. The home of the witch is a place

Witch

emptied of any character, stripped of all colour & starved of any atmospheric warmth. A place where those to pass never wants, intends, or wishes to stay. A space where it is said one should always pass quickly, a place if able to leave, one should never return.

A black cloak, a pet cat & a pointed hat. Do people truly believe in witches? Is what people call black & white magic able to provide a lonesome female with the ability to make & cast spells. Can it be that witches are true living beings, born from a female deprived of any true emotional ties. Are spells the curse of the bitter, twisted & unkind. Can spells be cast & curses placed, by those who are jealous, cruel, revenge filled, bad to the core & devilishly evil because life left them to fend for themselves, or is it fate & the true work of mother nature; which when necessary, sees to it, that all wrongs are righted & the guilty made to pay.

Outcaste from communities for wanting to live off the land. Ridiculed for attempting to be non-reliant on what civilisation provided, each worked & developed what was their own land. Laughed at, targeted & picked upon for daring not to be the same as everyone else.

The descending generations of the wealthy Sapphire family would suffer the taunting rants & more at the hands of those unable to understand, what they refused to see.

Enter if you dare,
into the witches lair

J Orton

Introduction

1: Myth
2: Innocence
3: Torture
4: Lonely
5: Illusion
6: Go
7: Shadows
8: Legend
9: Hidden
10: Broken
11: Two
12: Arrival
13: New

J Orton

1: Myth

*R*umbling clouds and a dark night sky illuminated by intense flashes of light. Clouds rolling like waves, turning what was above; into what many below perceived to resemble the wide open waters of a raging sea. *'A storm?'* The date was meant to be one of preparation, a time to rejoice and give thanks for the harvest while making safe what would be needed for another year to prosper. *'Halloween?'* The thirty-first night of October, how could things continue happening, when so much had already happened? Some said what happened would take a lifetime to put right. Why had they done what they did? Rain so heavy it soaked everything it touched. *'Floods!'* Rivers rolled faster, growing deeper and breaking through the steepest of slippery riverbanks. *'Fierce!'* What normally stood stead fast, moved and in some places crumbled, as all, every man, woman and child to have ventured out to welcome the onset of. *'All hallow tide.'* Attempted to find shelter. Could it be that the onset of All Souls' Day had come early? *'Was this the end?'* Some questioned what it was they'd done, while others saw the bad weather to be the result of them having upset the witch? Mysterious and misunderstood, what a tangled web we unravel when searching for the reason for everything?

*O*utcastes? Ever since the beginning of time people have feared what they don't know. Feared for being different, used and abused by those who see what isn't like everything else; as being something in need of being destroyed. *'Survival?'* Fights were fought and battles lost and won. Good against evil, those coming together saw themselves defending good, linking forces in a bid to drive out what each saw to be bad. Villagers standing alongside neighbouring townsfolk because they felt threatened and unsure. *'Could anyone or anything be so bad he, she, or it deserved to be destroyed?'* Armies and committees, in the main it was menfolk who took it upon themselves to govern the land and lay down the laws. Not afraid to use the power of the laws they made, men saw fit to outcaste all women seen capable of taking things into their own hands. Accusing strong independent females of committing acts of evil, men throughout the land called upon their laws, to hang any and everyone proven to be a witch. *'Why upset a witch?'*

Shadowing trees with leaf filled branches spreading far and wide, dark and light green foliage forming a natural canopy over pathways and hidden trails. Sprawling branches and growing stalks weaving over, across and through uneven ground, shrouded with a varied mass of shrubbery. Beneath what grew tallest and stood strongest was where nature created a maze of misdirection. *'Where had she gone?'* Long and short, wide and narrow, straight and wavy walkways littered with natural plant life led to clearings large enough to allow the growing of grass. The wood, a forest, natures' garden? That which divided the town of Erebus and the village of Déspoina was reported by locals as being a place where no mere mortal should stray. *'Not since the witch took up residence'*

Home to a bubbling brook; gently trickling its' way down into a spiralling stream before leaping out into a sprawling lake. Drowning was seen to be the least brutal of ends met by those to enter what belonged to the one they betrayed. Bordered by all things manmade, by day there was much to explore and hundreds of picturesque scenes to see. By night, the place known as Ebony Wood was said to be a place best avoided. Once a space inhabited by those to be outcaste and unwanted, legend told of how the sprawling wood withheld secrets much too heartbreaking and horrific to ever be told. *'A wild wind able to blow a person off track.'* Legend recorded how the waters of Dolour Lake contained the tears shed by those left to live and die alone. *'The cries of the abandoned & shouts of the lost, trapped within a breeze.'* Some had no place to be. *'Unwanted?'* For some there was no space. *'Outcaste.'* While there were some who ran, most were driven out for not being like everyone else. *'Lost?'* For those who sought refuge within the trees, life was said to be short and far from sweet. Tall dark trees encasing a maze of pathways creating a billion places to hide. *'Why was the witch in hiding?'*

Swirling winds extinguishing hand held flamed torches. *'Why hadn't they allowed a couple in love, to be happy?'* Aware of how it began, those to have taken the law into their own hands worried about how it was going to end? *'Could what they started be stopped?'* Could it be in attempting to protect themselves; they were the ones to create the first Witch of Ebony Wood? A dark night sky illuminated by flashes of lightening, clouds rumbling and rolling, clouds meeting with a loud deafening clash before rushing apart at speed. *'A storm?'* Rain so intense and heavy; everything below became drenched, with many a plant wilting under the strain of what it relied upon to give it life. From upright and bright, everything turned dark and limp, from colour filled to grey. *'Nature turning on, what was natural.'* Running and rushing, like a herd of runaway stallions; the growing volume of raging water caused riverbanks to shatter as if made of glass. Crumbling, what was fierce caused rocks to move like they were hollow. *'Floods?'* Growing deeper and moving faster, low growls and loud rumblings of the fast moving stream turned to a roar when allowing its' waters to break free. *'What had they done?'* Animals of all sizes sought shelter; with the young, weak and elder failing to reach higher ground in attempt to survive what threatened. Extinguished, those to have carried flamed torches found themselves struggling to reach safety through what was attacking them and everything it touched in the dark. Blown by howling winds, blinded by bright sheet lightning, deafened by thunder claps and weighed down by torrential rain. *'Some wouldn't make it.'* A rough night, all anyone could do was to hope for a brighter morning. *'A freak Storm?'* All not involved in what happened, wondered what had occurred to disturb that which normally lay calm? *'Surely no one would have dared upset the witch, not again?'*

One year earlier

*P*ushed up against the exterior wall of the detached barn, she gasped in wanting anticipation of what she knew was about to happen. His hands, his body, his whole self, her man; having made her his woman. Happy to be where she was and lucky to be with the man she loved, a man who adored her, with him she was never afraid to surrender her everything.

"You tease." Strong and handsome, well bred and rich, many accused her of knowing what she was doing and what she was doing was driving him wild. From the bedroom to the barn, from the garden and out into the surrounding woodland. *'Why shouldn't they explore what belonged to them?'* Not afraid to let her man know what it was she wanted. Up against the stone wall of the barn she giggled, adventurous, young and both were more than willing. *'Married.'* From inside to outdoors, when animal instinct took control; she was a woman who took whatever her well educated man had to give. "You tease." He accused her of leading him astray as without further hesitation she wrapped her arms around his neck and linked her feet, wrapping her legs up and around his strong hips. *'Man & wife.'* Kissing passion filled kisses, lips on lips, lips separating lips to allow teeth to nibble, tongues to touched and lips to do what ones' lips did when meeting lips, open and closed kisses. Kissing ones' lover meant giving and receiving sweetness fuelled by passion. *'Young & in love.'* The fact she was naked beneath her skirt and petticoats made his entry quick and direct. Kissing her neck, he took what she permitted him to take. *'In love & happy.'* She told her husband his kisses tasted of love and he said hers' were saturated with temptation. *'The temptress taking his power.'* How could what felt right, ever be wrong? Alone, the two allowing household staff to join fellow villagers and townsfolk in giving thanks for the summer on the eve of the day before winter began, meant them being home alone.

What some saw to be a true life fairytale, was frowned upon by others because he was rich and she merely managed to get by. One born into wealth, the other had to work hard to keep her head above water, locals said such bloodlines should never be mixed. A marriage born from true love, not convenience, the young Master born to be Lord felt fortunate his father wasn't a stickler for what many saw to be the unwritten rule around who and who would not be acceptable as a daughter-in-law. Some said they could never call the one to have been the innkeepers daughter a lady, not a Miss. Unacceptable, the young and in love twosome paid no heed to what other people said and thought. If honest; the two hadn't noticed the disapproval of others, until them noticing, was too late.

J Orton

How they met

*I*t happened so fast, in a place so small it wasn't named on any travellers map. In a place where life was basic and people easygoing, the innkeepers daughter Rosa Ruby Tinker was encouraged by her widowed father Renfred to flaunt her womanly assets, to smile and to take from thirsty punters their hard earn cash when supplying alcoholic beverages, simple food and card tables. A father and his daughter, the keepers of Tinkers Tavern could and would provide basic rooms on a bed and breakfast basis if offered the going rate. Hard working, in the absence of another female, from the age of thirteen years; Rosa became both housemaid and barmaid. *'Look. Do not touch.'* While he was happy to have his little girl learn the trade which was the family business, Mr. **Renfred Rocky** Tinker, never permitted his only child to be manhandled and would reward all overly amorous punters with a swift and sometimes brutal kicking out onto the street, should they over step the mark.

Long black hair and ruby red lips, her pale complexion was a natural consequence of Rosa living a life inside. The bar, the basement accommodation, guests rooms and the stables, rarely did the maturing female have the time, or the energy to venture beyond what was her home and livelihood. Polite, helpful and friendly, the daughter and only living child born to the busy innkeeper was quick to acquire the interpersonal skills needed to serve her, her father and the family business well. Maturing fast, turning from a well developed teenager into a voluptuous womanly woman, Miss Rosa Ruby Tinker was an asset and added attraction the local tavern couldn't be without. From *"Thank you kind Miss,"* And *"What a beautiful smile."* A woman? Over the years the efficient housemaid, busy barmaid learned how to take the harsher comments and abusive words; alongside the gratitudes and pleasantries.

"You teasing tart." By some the maturing Rosa was seen to be a tantalising witch. *'Not proof enough to put off a man to have lost his heart.'* Reece Ray Sapphire knew little about the place where he and his family owned properties alongside businesses and land. *'The perfect gentleman,'* His private education equipped the young gentleman with all the skill needed to manage the vast estate which would one day be his, but the all male establishment responsible for his academic knowledge had given little to no warning about what Master Sapphire should do, when faced with someone able to steal his heart with one smile.

      Thick dark hair and eyes of emerald green, the youngest son born to the Lord of Déspoina's grand Mansion Manor House was a man many a single female would be looking to catch the eye of. Master Reece Ray Sapphire and his all male family were proud landowners and thriving businessmen. Richer than rich, the Sapphire's wealth was seen to grow with rapid speed when the building of cottages on what was their land created a healthy income from weekly rents. Landowners, the family estate was split into both private gardens and open areas accessible to the public; including Ebony Wood. *'A place where the thick tree top canopy caused many inner areas to appear so dark & black, it inhibited ones' ability to see further than ones nose.'* The vast and varied woodland was what separated the town of Erebus and village of Déspoina. Neighbours to have never been anything but neighbourly. *'Dark & mysterious?'* Ebony Wood was a space which kept the curious guessing; while creating both morbid interest and mythical fear. *'A place which was easy to become lost in.'*

Having completed his private education, Master Reece was home to see what would one day be his. A gentleman of wealth and high values, he wasn't usually a man to acquaint himself with village taverns, but found his curiosity getting the better of him when his need for refreshment brought him into the village of his family home. *'Sapphire Manor House & estate stood on the edge of Déspoina village with its' boundaries ending inside Erebus town.'*

    "Will your horses require watering Sir?" The hair of a raven and the skin of a snow queen, upon greeting the horse drawn carriage known to be used by the upper classes; Rosa was her polite and welcoming self. Friday the thirteenth was seen by many to be unlucky. Friday or not, the thirteenth day of August was for Rosa her twenty-first birthday. Birthday or not? Friday for Rosa was just another working day.

"Happy birthday," A single father doing the best he was able, a man left on his own, doing what should be done by two parents. Wishing his adult child all the best, on her twenty-first birthday there was no man more proud. *'A woman?'* "Make a wish." Cake washed down with a mug of fresh coffee, her special day had begun with her father waiting on her, but it being her birthday didn't mean she wouldn't have work to do. *'Never too old to be his princess.'* Having decorated a cake with a candle to be extinguished with one single exhaled. *'What hard working female wouldn't wish to rest?'* Loving her father dearly meant her being happy, often enjoying the help she gave, but not being able to remember the last time she had a day off and time to herself meant the gift of a book to read being added to the growing library and list of things she would get around to doing one day. *'Maybe?'*

On the morning of her twenty-first birthday; the only daughter born to the innkeeper of Tinkers Tavern had blown out her burning candle and wished for nothing more than a little time to herself. August thirteen, the building heat of the summer meant thirsty punters and thirsty punters with money to spend meant rest not being an option.
 "Happy birthday Princess," Rosa would always be her fathers' pride and joy. *'There for one another,'* Mr. Tinker relied upon his only child for help as much as she relied upon him for everything.

 "My driver can take the horses to the stables." His gaze couldn't disguise his shock at meeting someone with the looks of a goddess alongside the kindness and grace of an angel. Insisting the young, beautiful female didn't trouble herself with such a physical chore, the birthday girl blushed when directing the handsome stranger to the main entrance of the popular village establishment to double as her home. *'Busy?'* From the kitchen to cleaning guest rooms, from housemaid to barmaid and stablehand, wherever Rosa cleaned, poured drinks or served food, she did so with a polite smile and a willingness to please. In the absence of paid staff, Mr. Tinker and his girl worked hard to uphold the tavern to have been in the family for generations.

"It is this way." She led the driver and his loyal mares to where they could receive what was needed to cool and shelter them from the intense rays of the afternoon sun. Unhitching the fine animals from restrictive harnesses; carriage driver and head groom to the Sapphire family Mr. **Donald Dixon** asked if he could use what he saw as being available to rub down his tired mares.

"And for yourself?" Rosa asked with a nod, telling the young male the stable and equipment was his for the use of throughout his stay. "Would you like a drink?" She asked; having brought and given pales of water to his four legged companions. "Lemonade, my own recipe," Sensing the male's reluctance to accept refreshment which may incur a cost not permitted by his employer; the smiling female assured Mr. Dixon his drink would be on the house. *'Truth being it was incorporated within the charge for the stables. A ploy giving visitors something to talk about, creating good word & month which in turn led to attracting new clientele.'*

"Thank you." While those inside the bar area requested the finest in food and refreshment, Rosa fetched Dixon a jug of her homemade lemonade along with a roll of freshly baked bread, a chunk of well matured cheese and a slice of her birthday cake.

"You're new." Aware of the constant need to expand the tavern's popularity, Rosa shown interest and always offered her most excellent hospitality to those she saw able to spread the word on her behalf. While her father served and made polite conversation with the young gentleman unfamiliar to such humble abodes, the female in the Tinker family gained the information sought from Mr. Sapphire's loyal employee.

"Birthday cake," Dixon questioned when noticing the iced and fruit filled sweet treat being offered.

"Twenty-one today," Rosa blushed for a second time as along with his gratitude, the stranger revealing how he could become a regular, wished her all the best.

Landowners and landlords with a fleet of cargo ships displaying their fine family name. Rich, the Sapphire's worked as merchants of whatever needed transporting, his having struggled to find his sea legs saw Master Reece happy to leave any and everything on the oceans' constantly moving waves to his elder brother Master **Roman Rich Sapphire**. Priming his youngest son to take over the running of the land based estate, Lord Raymond Richard Sapphire intended to split his fortune in equal part between brothers' whose talents, expertise and interests had taken each in a different direction. *'No father could be prouder.'* Roman would earn his living from the sea, his assets being the fleet of seven cargo ships, a dockside warehouse and a city based apartment home. On his thirtieth birthday, Reece would inherit fields, pastures, properties, businesses and Ebony Wood. Wealthy, that which each fine gentleman would oversee, would incur earnings enough to sustain the rich lifestyle they were use to. If they planned right; the Sapphire men would forever be able to sustained the upper class status they were born into.

Master Reece's personal portfolio would soon include the local village church of St Julian and the busy market square along with a multi storey cotton mill in the town of Erebus and the families historical manor house. *'A wealthy, healthy, handsome man of means.'* What female wouldn't be interested? Having heard much about what was to become his; when thirty, at the age of twenty-five the youngest Sapphire brother travelled from the city to town and into the village, eager to investigate the place purchased by his parents' before he was born. *'A dream?'* Having made many a long term investment in what he saw to be an attractive up and coming area, Lord Sapphire bought for his good lady wife Victoria-Jane the grand ten bedroom mansion style home they called Sapphire Manor.

Encouraged to redesign and refurbish what was to be their family home, Victoria-Jane said no woman could be happier. *'Young & in love.'* The couple blessed with one son, soon learned a second child was on the way. *'A family?'* Girl, or boy didn't matter Healthy and happy, the expectant parents believed their lives and family would soon be complete. *'A family of four?'* A life cut short led to changes no one could imagine, as those left behind lost control. *'Sad?'* What should have been a happy homecoming; was filled with reminders of what turned from a longed for event, to a devastating tragedy? Promising not to disturb what his late mother designed and put together with enthusiasm, excitement and love before her sudden death, Reece wished he could erase what for his father; was a memory he tried to forget.

'Tragic?' Dying in childbirth, the gravestone beside that marking the final resting place of Lady Victoria-Jane was inscribed with the words. *'Dark Angel,'* Not wanting to know the sex of the child to have taken from him his one true love. Born without life, doctors said they'd done all they could, Victoria-Jane hadn't been strong enough to deliver into the world, that which was unable to help itself. Dragged from her womb, her husband never wanted to lay witness to that amount of blood ever again. Unable to stop what began bleeding, Raymond held his wife's hand when she gurgled her last words and held her body close to his when she took her last ever breath. A widower, Lord Raymond Sapphire had kept hold of his wife's deceased body until others stepped in, to tare it from his loving embrace, releasing her from his tight grip. *'Gone?'* The father of two, insisted the coffin containing the body of his wife remained with him until lay to rest within the grounds of Sapphire Manor. *'A man*

bereaved,' Raymond insisted he do everything he could for his second son, but wanted nothing to do with what he would always blame for the tragedy to have occurred. *'Twins?'* The tiny body of the one who never was, was never seen by the man who refused to acknowledge the fact he was father to three. *'His twin?'* Only one person knew the sex of the baby lay beneath the Dark Angel nameplate and that person was the doctor paid to wrap the lifeless corpse in bandages so no one would ever lay eyes upon what Lord Sapphire believed to be evil. *'His special boy?'* Raymond saw Reece to be a survivor.

Protecting his family, Lord Sapphire had a private chapel built so the body of his wife could lay in the shadow of its' protective steeple. In amongst what was a tale of sadness and tragedy, the grieving widower told how he remembered the way the woman he loved used the last of her strength to kiss and so give their second son her blessing. *'A second son?'* Reece was told a billion times of how his mother said he should be loved and looked after, never made to feel guilty for what his father saw to have been the fault of his twin. *'A good, kind & caring businessman,'* Reece was seen to be the one best prepared to take charge of all things land based. *'Frilly, frothy & soft?'* Unaccustomed to getting his hands dirty, Reece was the brother most at home when in amongst people. *'Social & approachable,'* The twenty-five year old male knew how to conduct himself in private and public, but was unaccustomed to having his head turned by a member of the opposite sex.

*H*air as black as a raven's wing, ruby red lips and sapphire blue eyes, a snow queen shinning bright in the sunlight. His first glance had stunned and caused intrigue, his second had taken his breath and a third had left him never wanting to look away. Entering to ask if her father required assistance; she appeared to float with gracious ease, her whirlwind like energy carrying with it a confidence only gained with experience. Leaving no detail to chance, the stunningly beautiful female served customers, took payment, cleared tables and socialised seamlessly in amongst those happy to pay for the hospitality supplied. Seen to be of a class well below that of Master Sapphire, Miss Tinker nevertheless captured his eye and melted his heart. *'Love at first sight?'* Not a whirlwind romance, her first ever romantic encounter, when they eventually got together, for both it was first love. *'Two people finding one another.'* There were many who disagreed with a man of such high standing mixing his bloodline with a woman they saw to be common and not worthy. A female without the influence, or guidance of a mother; was seen to be a woman lacking femininity, elegance and domestic skills. Reece couldn't disagree more.

Clean and immaculately dressed, having followed the female he couldn't get out of his head into the village graveyard, he asked.

"Who?" Having watched as she placed two hand tied posies of wild flowers before one stone inscribed with two names, he apologised for his intrusion, but was unable to hide his interest.

"My mother and twin brother." It seemed the two shared something no other could relate to. *'Deceased twins?'* Rosa's brother Rock Red, lived to the age of two years, but like Lady Victoria-Jane, Mrs. Ruby Rose Tinker had also failed to survive the trauma of giving birth to two babies on the same day. *'Survivors?'* It being her twenty-first birthday meant her brother Rock being twenty-one too. "The missing part of me." Rosa felt shocked when her unexpected companion said he understood.

"Happy birthday," His information came via his employee and as he tipped his hat to walk away, Rosa felt a feeling she never felt before. Glancing to the headstones stood representing the last and final resting place of both her mother and brother, Rosa felt the great gap to be left by their passing; beginning to close. *'An odd couple.'* The wrong couple, Reece refused to listen to anyone but his father and his father believed love should be allowed to guide those falling under what he called its' breathtaking enchantment and magical spell. *'Meant to be together?'*

It started when Master Sapphire moved into his families manor, ignoring the warnings. At the age of twenty-six, Reece continued to acquaint himself with the Tavern, enjoying the friendly warmth and free flowing hospitality whenever he found the time. It began with him spending time in the company of Mr. Tinker and continued when he asked the proud father of one, if he could court his daughter. Happy and in love, his heart had been hers' at first sight. The innkeepers daughter and the next Lord of the manor, it is said by some that we can't control who we fall in love with, but there were many who believed his control was all hers'.

Strong and handsome, when first the two met, it was Reece's employee who caused the young barmaid to blush. Married to the Sapphire's head housekeeper Mr. Dixon apologised for what was his natural charm and jolly conversation; when the young single female pointed out the fact he was wearing a wedding ring. There was and would be many more times when the one all called Dixon found himself being his masters' voice. Knowing Master Sapphire the way he did, meant Dixon knowing when Reece began showing signs of wanting to settle down. *'Not a place for the sophisticated?'* Reece popping into Tinkers Tavern to sample the fine ales whenever he got the chance, caused the appreciative innkeeper to question which it was he had his eye on? *'His business, or his daughter?'* Reece assured the concerned father; his feelings towards both were honourable.

"Sorry," Like her father, Rosa apologised, not because she didn't understand, because she didn't know what else to say. "No," Not taken or betrothed. Rosa was a hard working member of the lower classes, loyal to her father, her upbringing and lifestyle left no space for her to learn polite niceties, or know anything about how to be fancy. When he first asked, Rosa said no, because she wouldn't fit into his world and saw Reece as being someone who could never understand her and hers'. *'Not willing to be a rich mans bit of rough.'* Tavern gossip told of well to do gentlemen on the lookout for those they could use for practice; before marrying one of their own. Accepting, but never deterred, Reece was advised by his elders to be in the place's she went and to allow time if he truly wanted to win her heart, allowing her to hold his safe. *'We all fear what is different.'*

Days felt like weeks and weeks like years when all the young eligible bachelor wanted to do, was to take the woman he'd fallen for, out on their first date. *'The first ever date for them both.'* Smiling when she heard he'd turned more eligible suiters away, shocked when he turned up to show his support for the annual fete in the village square. Laughing when he rolled up his shirt sleeves to win his fair maiden a coconut from the coconut shine. A community coming together, Reece and his father were seen to throw themselves whole heartedly into what each said had been a joyous occasion allowing town and village to join in a day filled with laughter, smiles and fun. Smiling, Reece was told the fact he caught Rosa watching him; was a possessive sign. Joining in when he could, sat drinking ale, playing cards and inviting Mr. Tinker to accompany him and his father for a days fishing and drawing up a business plan allowing the innkeeper to poach and forage on Sapphire land. A business agreement which suited all, Renford agreed to relishing the opportunity to vary his offered menu while gaining his produce from the offered local source.

Passing in his carriage, offering to take her home and assisting with her heavy shopping, every time she stumbled across him in a place she didn't expect him to be, Reece sensed her acknowledgment of his presence becoming warmer. The Tavern, the market square and every event to be held within the town and village. When visiting her brother and mothers' grave; the bright bouquet of flowers revealed his being where she stood, first. *'Thoughtful & kind?'* Two different people with much in common, over a year on from when they first met, when Reece spoke, Rosa began to listen.

'Three years & much had happened.' In three years things had changed, but nothing altered the fact the two to have fallen head-over-heels were falling deeper and deeper in love. Friends for life becoming family for all eternity, when their children became a couple, Lord Sapphire and Mr. Tinker couldn't be happier. Proud parents, one was single father to his only daughter and the other a lone gentleman with two grown sons, both a businessman in his own right, both widowers to know the meaning of true love, neither would force apart what was destined to be together. Having suffered personal loss, heartache and the severest of heartbreak; each male told his child it was them, their love and their happiness to matter most. Paying no mind to those who approached to their daughter was better suited, from richer stock and able to bring to any marriage; much more than stunning looks, quick wit and a generous nature. *'love would conquer all.'* The Sapphire men defended the female whose own community turn on, when accusing her of being a devious and enchanting witch. *'Not possible?'* Few believed the marriage of the next Lord Sapphire and the

innkeepers daughter to be a relationship born of true love. *'Lust?'* Both were mocked when seen to be affectionate, stepping back when others approached, Rosa saw many a wanting, well to do female throw herself at her man. *'Understandable?'* Rosa continued to be polite, even when accused of having put a spell on the affluent gentleman so to separate him from his power and money. *'Married.'* Those who mattered, supported and blessed what many witnessed the good lord join together in holy matrimony. *'The soon to be Lord of the manor & the innkeepers daughter became man & wife three years after they met.'* A young couple in love and a married couple loving life together.

Not right, while some in the village and many more in the neighbouring town saw the coming together of the barmaid and the next Lord as being wrong, Lord Raymond and innkeeper Renfred blessed and supported what was the union of their children. Able to see the devotion in the eyes of his youngest child, the eldest and most worldly wise of the Sapphire family was able to feel the love his son held in his heart for the one he took to be his wife. Ignoring those who informed him of better suiters for his heir, Raymond welcomed Rosa and Renfred with open arms.' *The best family Christmas,'* Free to acquaint themselves with the grand ten bedroom manor whenever they wanted, there were occasions when Rosa and her father overheard the not so nice comments made by the visiting higher classes, many of who mistook them for being staff. Sometimes comments were cruel, but Reece always knew what to say to help Rosa feel better. Two incomplete families becoming one, them discovering they had much in common, only went to tighten their bond.

The first Lord of Sapphire manor and the innkeeper of Tinkers Tavern uncovered a liking for much more than a taste for good whiskey, forming what for one would be a life long friendship, the men from different worlds were seen fishing, shooting and sharing more than the odd drink together. *'Friends becoming family,'* Two people marrying who, each wanted to marry. A union creating a group of people happy to be in one another's company. *'Why wouldn't others leave them alone?'* Why hadn't others left those who never caused harm, to be happy and content?

A tantalising witch, while accepting invitations to the traditional wedding, many were heard whispering about what for the newly weds was a joyous occasion. *'A spell?'* Some accused the female seen to be a commoner of using witchcraft to capture the heart of the most eligible bachelor for miles. *'Lucky?'* There were some who saw the marriage of the barmaid to the son of a Lord, to be a romantic fairytale. Beauty and the beast in reverse. He was the Prince who kissed a frog and turned her into his Princess, the age old tale of rags to riches. Few saw mixing such bloodlines as being a good thing. *'Not permitted to create a monster.'* Afraid the couple would create an unstable, unstoppable force, many set out to destroy the relationship formed by those living as one. *'Married?'* Many saw and believed the time to save them, their village and the town from the evil destruction of a wanting woman, was running out. A couple was a strong bond to break, but breaking up a family would be impossible. Those in the village of Déspoina and town of Erebus saw themselves as having no choice but to take the law into their own hands. *'What had they done?'* Whatever the personal opinions, there was no one who didn't agree with the fact that on the biggest of big days, the bride looked stunningly in white, enchanting.

Like an angel, Rosa wore white and like any true Prince Charming, Reece stood handsome and strong. *'Happy?'* The proud husband told his new wife not to worry about others. Reece loved his lady and both male's to have lost their wives' agreed love was what mattered most.

'Happy & in love?' Doubters lay witness to what on the surface appeared a strong and unbreakable bond. Aware the love between two people can sometimes weaken and die over time, those with true concerns believed there was no time to wait. A traditional white wedding, she was twenty-four and him twenty-eight. *'No rush,'* Those agreeing they had all the time in the world; said there was no reason to wait when feeling sure. The glorious day turned out to be as sun filled as the first day they met. The fifth day of September, traditional yet simple, those happy for the bride and groom; said it couldn't be more perfect. With no bridesmaids to give support, it was Rosa's single father who told her she never looked more beautiful. Like he so often did, Renfred assured the blushing bride; her mother would be proud. *'Renfred couldn't be more proud.'* The invitation was open to all and all including those who disagreed, attended to participate in the merriment, enjoyment and taking of Lord Sapphires generous hospitality.

From the private chapel there was an indoor banquet for family and close friends running alongside an outdoor hog roast for all wanting to stay and celebrate the joining together of Reece Ray Sapphire and Rosa Ruby Tinker. A traditional ceremony conducted before the eyes of God inside the Sapphires' private chapel. Visiting friends and loyal employees of the family sat to the front of the chapel on the right, while alongside the father of the bride, friends' and regulars to Tinkers Tavern sat on the left. Good friends and family, Roman stood as bestman. *'A perfect day.'* That which was respected and renowned for bringing people together was conducted by the local man of the church and witnessed by all and everyone who wanted to see. *'A couple in love being joined in holy matrimony.'* There was no doubt some were there expecting to see the witch walking on sacred ground turn to dust, but there was no denying the fact the couple looked happy.

Witch

*M*erry making, Business ventures were won and lost, a couple getting use to being man and wife, time never stood still and for those to have become family, time was filled with all the things each enjoyed and had to do. *'No place for a lady,'* When asked, Rosa was happy to assist her father and Reece proud to be there to meet her when she finished work. Unpaid, her leaving to be a wife; released funds for Renfred to take on a part time employee, but no one did what his daughter had been brought up to do like she did. Enjoying one another's company, good whiskey and the odd cigar; Raymond hid what were his growing ailments from his sons, turning to his daughter-in-laws father for advise and support. Two years married, from what had been seen to be an extravagant celebration, the next time so many found themselves together within what was the vast grounds of the manor house; saw a village and town in mourning.

Two years of happy marriage, what was going well was disrupted by an illness taking from Lord Raymond Richard Sapphire his life. Ageing and concealing the fact he was growing weak, within days of taking to his sickbed, news broke that the first Lord Sapphire had died. *'Why?'* Some saw what happened as being strange and sudden. *'How?'* Focusing on their own reasons, the fact Rosa Tinker had been permitted to marry his son was again seen to be wrong. *'A spell?'* The tantalising female was rumoured to be the only reason why the strong and prosperous family suffered sudden misfortune with some wanting her taken to court and accused of murder. *'A murdering witch?'* Her accusers lacked evidence. Aware her father-in-law was ill; Rosa nursed him to the end. *'Devoted.'* A good wife, those who were there, relatives, staff and the local doctor refused to see, or agree as to how the new Lady Sapphire had done anything she shouldn't. *'Rosa did nothing wrong.'*

Dressed in black Mrs. Rosa Ruby Sapphire supported her grieving husband out in the open where everyone could see. Planting her feet firmly on what was hallowed ground and watching the body of her dearly departed father-in-law being lowered into a deep dark hole. Mrs. Sapphire caused doubters to question what were their doubts? *'No proof?'* Suspicion and speculation, few looked to find the facts which were clear indications of why a man to have spent much of his adult life traveling the seas and visiting foreign lands would return home in ill health; eventually losing his battle for life at the age of sixty-six. *'Bad luck?'* Burying their father's body in the families' private burial plot beside that of their late mother and the grave marked. *'Dark Angel,'* Sapphire brothers Reece and Roman took the reins of what each had, and would inherited from their loss. *'Unfortunate?'*

With no experience of the changing environment outside the area each lived their life, local's again blamed an unlucky choice in wife, when newspapers reported four of the Sapphire's seven cargo ships lost at sea. Seen to be the unlucky charm on the next Lord Sapphires' arm, Rosa was blamed when the cotton mill inherited by her husband; was forced to close. Bad luck, and not what was happening in a world growing bigger and expanding quicker than anyone could keep up with. Those living in the village of Déspoina **and the neighbouring town of Erebus**; blamed the female to have been permitted to join the strong all male family; for any and everything which went wrong.

Rosa and not the economic climate, not the pending unrest, the said witch; was blamed for the loss of work and growing financial instability being experienced by those living and working in and around what belonged to the Sapphire family. *'Not happy?'* The couple happy to be together, felt bad for what was out of their control. *'Doing the best?'* When Raymond Sapphire died, those he left behind needed time to grieve his passing. *'Unhappy*

& *sad,'* Rosa, Reece and Roman felt the loss of placing another family member to rest in what was fast becoming the families' private graveyard. *'Unlucky?'* \

Chairing meetings, making deals and fighting on behalf of his tenants, the new Lord Sapphire; did all he could to keep and protect his workforce, but was met with opposition, mistrust and misunderstanding at every turn. Offering to purchase homes from those struggling through lack, or loss of employment. His promise to allow ex-homeowners to remain in their houses as paying tenants at affordable rates; saw him accused of being a trickster. *'A ploy?'* Only those with no other choice, took up what on the face of it appeared too good to be true. A good, kind and caring businessmen, aware he was the exception to the rule, Reece didn't hold anything against those to mistrust his good intentions. *'Why did other men blame him for wanting to protect his wife?'* Living in the large house, when his father passed, Reece earned the right to become Lord of his families manor, but few would ever regard Rosa as his Lady. *'Unpopular?'* Rosa and her husband continued to work hard, assisting when they could. *'What could they do?'* Would things be different if they did nothing?

*F*lamed torches and hood covered heads, Reece's own brother was heard to support those to advised he ditch the witch, with a sacrifice being seen by many to be the only sure solution and only way of stopping the evil eating away at the town, the village, it's residents and their livelihood. To offer up something or someone, was for many believed to be the only option. *'Animal sacrifices?'* Those who believed in an eye for an eyes tried, but failed when attempting to offer the lives of goats, sheep and pigs to the Gods. *'The witch must die.'* Those to have failed, made no secret of the fact they were making enquiries about how to kill what they saw to be evil? *'Seeking a witch hunter,'* It soon became clear witch hunters required riches to do what it was said mere mortals couldn't. *'Not interested.'* While agreeing his sister-in-law was bad, Roman refused to help finance what many believed to be needed to end all suffering. *'Roman was a man who looked after nothing & no one, before looking after himself.'*

Name calling, stone throwing and vaduhlisum, with money running out and tempers running high, Tinkers Tavern became the first target for those blaming the innkeepers' daughter for what they saw as the curse on Ebony Wood. Boycotted, the continuous break-ins and smashed windows forced Mr. Tinker to flea in fear of losing his life. *'Frightened & tired.'* The ageing innkeeper asked his daughter and her wealthy husband to take the reins and purchase the business he was struggling to keep afloat, sad to leave the home he no longer felt at home in, Renfred wanted enough money to leave and live a more peaceful life away from where others saw his daughter to be the cause of all misfortune. Sorry he couldn't stand by his little girl like a father should, the man entering his mid sixties saw himself as no longer able to protect his Rosa and it was with a heavy heart the man to have brought up his daughter alone, admitted defeat. Seeing his only choice being to take the money offered and run, Rosa's father handed over the safekeeping of his daughter and family business to Reece. Saying goodbye, Renfred told both to keep one another safe *'They understood.'* Reece and Rosa agreed to reinstate the tavern when they could, each telling Renfred their door would forever be open. *'Renfred would always be Rosa's dad.'*

Like when infected from a bite;
once in ones' bloodstream
there is no escaping the wrong
which feels so right.

2: Innocence

*P*ushed up against the wall; as he pushed into her she accepted all of him, as their passionate love making began she surrendered her everything and he gave his all. Passion filled, she told him yes and he held onto her for all he was worth. *'Excited?'* Before long the two were at the point of no return, husband and wife. *'In love?'* Their encounter was wild, yet them coming together was never just sex. *'Always sweet,'* Whether impulsive or planned, when the Lord took his Lady, he did so with a passion he couldn't control. Whenever Mr. and Mrs. Sapphire came together, each became stronger, their love growing deeper as each felt more loved. *'In love & happy.'*

"Yes, Yes, Yes!" Agreeing with what was happening she felt breathless, excited and lost in the moment. "Yes," She was getting what she wanted and he was doing what he knew would please. Together, passion filled, their erotic and wild encounters were always romantic. *'Still young & in love?'* The couple wrapped around one another and caught up in the moment, were suddenly dragged apart. *'Shocked!'* Ripped from one another's embrace, he fell to the ground, watching as she was lifted up and taken away. Held back by those who stood before and behind him, he saw his wife taken. *'What was happening?'* Disappearing into the darkness, a night filled with calm was suddenly laced with chaos and pain. *'A halloween prank?'* Those happy to keep themselves to themselves were aware of what were the celebratory traditions of the eve when all were warned to beware the dead. Swooping down without warning, three of the six to have arrived uninvited were seen to take Rosa from her man before heading out of the grounds belonging to the grand manor house.

"Stop!" Attempting to stand; he was knocked to the ground. "What are you doing?" He asked and was told to keep quiet. "No," No longer able to see or hear the woman he loved, Reece warned those to have invaded his privacy that each would be charged with trespassing. "This isn't funny." The stunned male struggled to understand the truth and make sense of what was happening? "Don't." He attempted to plead with those whose faces lay hidden within full and shadowing black hoods. "You can't, you mustn't, you shouldn't." He told all to beware and warned of there being consequences for those he saw as being answerable to the authorities. When told he shouldn't have wed a witch, Reece asked why neither was concerned about suffering at the hands of the one they saw to be possessed by the devil. *'A Goddess of evil? Such women should never be taken by a man wanting a wife.'* "Stop." He called, but those leaving were already too far to hear. "You mustn't." He repeated his warning. Informing those he struggled to recognise; they didn't know what they were doing. "Stop!" His second attempt to stand was again prevented by those determined to keep him down. First a fist and then a foot, a fist to the face and a booted foot dug into his ribs, the stern warnings to stay where he lay were hard and harsh. "You shouldn't." He begged those leaving to heed his words and return what they'd taken, as lifted from the ground; his only choice was to succumb to his capture.

Shocked, shattered and injured, the male whose injuries caused by a beating prevented him from breaking loose, found himself taken kicking and protesting from where he lay, over and into his estates' private chapel. Dragged in through the main double doors of what was family owned, the young male seen to be naive and weak, was instructed to beg his Lord God for forgiveness and told to turn back to the light. Shocked, shattered and injured, Reece asked what it was his and his wives' captures wanted? He had money, he could provide them with work and housing, but those unwilling to accept he was happy and content with his bride; said they wanted to save him. Not for the first time, all in the village of Déspoina were aware of how the defiant male was unwilling to comply and heed their countless warnings. Not the first time, Reece warned his captures if they hurt his wife, this would be the last taste of freedom each would get. *'Kidnap & imprisonment was punishable by law.'* Reminded of how his head had been turned and his heart stolen by a witch. Those he threatened, warned him to stay clear of Miss Rosa Ruby Tinker.

"Rosa is my wife." The one to have inherited what was his families' vast fortune, asked for proof of what others accused. *'How could something so pure & beautiful be dark & evil?'* The innkeepers daughter had grown up strong because the environment in-which she lived was also the place where she worked. Accused of being gullible and called a fool, his mind was made up and his head not for turning. *'In love with the woman he took to be his wife.'* Defenceless and becoming delirious, Reece Ray Sapphire asked that his and the life of his wife be spared.

Witch

Flamed torches, faces shadowed by oversized hoods and hoards of angry people. *'The traditional costume party?'* When desperation took over what was common sense, a discontented village joined forces with a failing town in attempt to destroy what all believed to be bad luck, born from an inappropriate marriage. *'Seen to be evil.'* In marrying a witch and becoming Lord of the Manor, it was declared Reece Sapphire had awarded Rosa Tinker powers which should never be bestow upon someone able to take and use such strength for wrong doing.

Long cloaks with oversized hoods, none of those wanting to put right what each saw to be wrong was willing to have his, or her true identity revealed. Faces kept in shadow, each was strong because each stood together when using the sometimes fatal element of surprise. Cowards? *'Rushing this way before running that?'* Under the cover of darkness, Reece and his staff had, had dealings with those wanting their opinions heard on numerous occasions before. Grown men and mature women holding flamed torches and coming together to threaten those who when alone; each would show respect and politeness. *'Wanting & needy, no individual was brave enough to be seen.'*

Alone, having pulled him this way and pushed him that, having forced him to his knees before the statue of our lord and demanded he pray to God, two held his arms outstretched while the third ripped his shirt and whipped his back with more than one leather horse whip. Bruised, what was made to bleed was fully exposed before being doused with holy water. *'What had he done to them?'* Landlord, or employer? Were those intent on having him seek forgiveness; men who when not wearing cloaks would be beholden to him for his, or her livelihood and survival? *'Why wouldn't they leave him & his wife be?'* Where had they taken Rosa? Left bleeding out and in pain, when his returning staff starting banging on what those inside had locked, those who knew they were outnumbered, left via the chapels' rear door. Freed, he needed to find those believing they'd captured a witch. Released by Dixon and his loyal workforce, the one weakened by what was inflicted, told those to have found him, they needed to help find Rosa.

Searching both the town and village, it seemed everyone had lost control. Running around, chasing and racing, disoriented and confused, that which was normally peace filled erupted with the disturbing sound of frustration and anger. *'Why was everyone out?'* From darkness to bright flickering light, the dancing, heat filled flames from the hand held torches being carried high for all to see, shown how the masses believed fire to be the ideal means of both attack and defence. Arriving and walking in-amongst those wanting him to leave, wandering amongst those appearing and disappearing from out of and into the shadows, unsure what was happening? Some found themselves running for cover while others took advantage of what was both mindless and lawless behaviour. Why destroy what they said they were fighting to keep? How could one man and his handful of loyal employees stop what amounted to hundreds of townsfolk and villagers running wild? Igniting the building to have been home to the witch and her father, setting fire to the village tavern abandoned by its' owners, a business closed because no one wanted to be associated with the establishment responsible for housing a woman capable of evil. Running this way and rushing that, with many not knowing where to go or what to do? Vigilantes set out to banish evil because they believed evil was to blame for everything going wrong.

If found roaming free, none would allow Reece to continue his search. Unable to discover his missing wife in amongst the mayhem and confusion, Lord Sapphire was encouraged to return home to keep himself safe. Running around, chasing and racing back and forth, as those to hide their identity slid back into the shadows, others grouped together in attempt to fight the flames engulfing what had been the stables adjoining Tinkers Tavern. *'On fire!'* Burning, Dixon assured his employer he would do everything he could.

"We will rebuild." When urging the one to have regained his freedom to get to safety; head groom Mr. Dixon helped and hoped with all hope Rosa and no other had been inside the wooden structure turned from a stable into a smouldering shell. Why attack a building? Why burn what had stood tall and strong for years? The oldest building in the village, what had been thrown at the roof of the main structure had hit but rolled off, leaving behind nothing but ash, its' bright sparks had flickered and flashed before falling and setting the neighbouring stable alight. Fire! People called out for assistance, but few came in time to save what turned from solid to an unstable skeleton; through what was the night, turning to day.

Arriving home alone, taken into the kitchen and given a blanket along with something warm to drink by housekeeper Daisy, all Reece wanted was his wife back by his side. Happy, two people in love, a twosome willing to help others. *'Wild!'* When Rosa Ruby Tinker stepped into the shoes of Mrs. Reece Sapphire, staff to include Mrs. Daisy Dixon, reported them never having encountered anyone like her before. *'Fun loving & free,'* Rosa gave her husband a reason to smile more than a thousand times a day. Loyal and true, those to work where she lived, understood what it was Reece saw in the young woman to treat everyone how she said she preferred to be treated. *'Always respectful so to earn respect.'* Grateful to those looking after and out for him, unsure if Tinkers Tavern had been saved, Reece needed to know if his wife was safe?

3: Torture

*P*leading her innocence, the accused female struggled. Unable to prove her ability to capture the heart of a man like Reece was anything other than witchcraft, the one to have been taken, could do nothing but bow her head and say she was sorry. *'Sorry others didn't believe in true love.'* A commoner with a Lord, a rich man falling for the charms of a poor woman. When standing up for his wife, Reece's comments about Rosa's unique beauty, magical charm and kind heart only went to prove how she had him under her spell. Captured and told to ask his Lord God for forgiveness, weak and weeping silent tears, Reece cradled the mug containing his nighttime coco with added brandy, holding it within his shaking hands.

When in the chapel, Reece had prayed; not for his own life, or to ask God to save his soul, with his head bowed and his eyes closed, Reece had prayed for the safe return of the woman he loved. Asking God not to allow any harm to come to his good lady wife. *'The Prince wanted to rescue his Princess.'* The King wanted his Queen back. How could those who relied on him and his vast fortune for their livelihood; threaten and take from him what was his? When locked inside his family chapel, Reece believed he wouldn't make it out alive, but he had, he was home and hoped his wife would make it home too.

Witch

*C*aptured and threatened with torture, tied up and told she must be sacrificed, Rosa pleaded to be allowed to prove her innocence, but not even the female's ability to be in the same room as lucky stones, horseshoes, crosses and sickles without suffering any ill effect; could sway those believing her to be a witch. Captured and taken from the sanctuary of her large, rich comfortable home to be stripped naked. Her skin was searched for telltale sign of evil wickedness. *'The devils' bride?'* Unable to uncover so much as a pimple on her smooth flawless skin, those to have failed in their quest, accused the frightened female of hiding what they were looking for on, the inside.

Inside her mouth and inside her ears, determined to leave no stone unturned, those on a mission searched as deep as they were able; using whatever they could. Unwilling to stop what they started, they opened her legs to search places described as being deep and dark. *'Tortured.'* The female with no choice but to endure what was being inflicted, was told if she failed to give those searching what they wanted, she would be sacrificed. *'Doomed.'* Frightened and unable to believe how those who were her neighbours' and friends' would take things so far. *'Would she survive?'* Her being strong willed, didn't equal her being physically tough enough to take what was happening, when one male and then another searched for what he was looking to find. Chanting what was said to protect all from evil, it being the night said to open the gates allowing spirits both in and out, was the reason none wanted to be recognised. The night when the dead were said to walk amongst the living, those stating it as being their right to destroy evil, made circles of salt, lit candles and recited words said to be taken from a book written by a true hunter of witches.

Begging each to stop as they used fingers, hands and an assortment of long hard implements to delve deeper than was comfortable. *'Please stop.'* Her words and silent tears were ignored. *'Was her fate sealed?'* The innkeepers daughter, Rosa never did anyone wrong and only ever did her best to please her father and serve those to acquaint the family run establishment into which she was born.' *The birth of Rosa Ruby & not the birth of her twin brother Rock, was blamed for the death of her mother. Like Dark Angel, Rosa was born last.'* Housemaid and barmaid, absent of a female role model, she grew fast. *'Headstrong?'* Rosa's lifestyle meant having to learn how to look after herself and stand on her own two feet, but none of what others saw to be the rough and tumble of life in a tavern, prevented Miss Tinker from maturing into a stunning and beautiful woman.

A well established hostelry supplying good food and refreshment to weary travellers and thirsty locals, Tinkers Tavern was no whorehouse and Rosa had kept herself pure prior to becoming a wife. Hardworking and loyal to her father, her only aim was to make Renfred proud. Why was it wrong that the young woman whose father had been approached by many a suitor for her hand, had taken the offered hand of a man who loved her and who she had grown to love? Having lost his only son to the fever at the age of two years, Renfred encouraged his little girl to be her own person; meaning it was with pride he'd stood by her when she married for love. How could she prove she was nothing more than a loving and devoted wife? *'Where was Lord Sapphire's wife?'*

Witch

From the deep, cold echoing basement up to the artefact filled attic, each and every room in the large manor building was searched and searched again by loyal employees led by Dixon. All were sorry and many were confused as each failed to find Rosa inside any of the ten bedrooms, numerous outbuildings and stables. From double checking the main house through the large reception lounges to the library, small study and vast dinning room, to venturing back into the family chapel. When called; by Dixon to assist, all living and working within the Sapphire Manor came to their employers aid, but found nothing. *'Rosa Ruby Sapphire was gone.'* Taken from out of his arms, Reece would blame himself if anything happened to his beautiful wife. Looking, searching and Hunting, Reece agreed to the use of dogs when what was taking place within; moved outside and away from the house, told to leave no stone unturned, instructed to go to the very centre as well as the outskirts of Ebony Wood. Advised to be careful, each and every bark was met with wanton anticipation and a need for any silence to be broken by the news that Rosa was home. *'Be careful.'* Gardener **Morris Minton and his son Miles** agreed to knowing the surrounding land better than most. Filled with flowerbeds, bushes and trees, both said they would leave no rockery or bush unexplored. Called brave to separate and go out to search alone, Miles told his father to take their dog Spirit, as both relit their handheld torches for what was the second time in as many hours.

Silent and black, what was outside called for little to no artificial brightness at night, no installed exterior lighting the call went out, to put every internal house light on and to use what required candles. Busy, while female staff illuminated the patio areas with what flickered in the breeze, the men took flamed torches to see what each could find. Silent and darker than what permitted natural vision to see, the chapel and the burial ground appeared encased by a thick swirling mist. A ground cloud? What was believed to fall from the sky at dusk wasn't seen to be uncommon within and around areas where few ever ventured?

Bodies lay to rest within the shadow of the tall steeple, Miles wasn't sure why his attention drifted to what in daylight was kept tidy and flower filled. Dark, there was something moving, but what? An owl? Sure he was able to hear the sound of feathers and wings, the young male expected what he believed to be there; to fly overhead as he approached. An owl or other night bird, was bound to fly away when disturbed. Should he shout out? Had what only came out after dark heard him approaching? A fox? The eyes he saw looking back were the wrong shape and much too small to belong to any owl. Two legs and not four? What Miles was seeing, was something he had never laid eyes upon before. Who and what were they doing? Rosa? The male to feel his heart jumping out of his chest; couldn't say whether what he was seeing was male or female? Dark, black and smaller in height than himself, the feathers he heard; were wings, large, black wings. If asked, Miles would say he'd seen laid eyes upon the one buried as Dark Angel. Good, or bad? Virtuous or evil? Was he in danger, or was the one born beside Reece, out to assist their twin bother in his hour of need? Had what was buried beside parents' been the one to have taken what Reece loved most? Too stunned to scream, Miles turned to run, sure what he saw had taken to the air and was behind him, he fell as with a swish, what had stood before him, flew up into the night sky above and was gone. *'Where? Where was Rosa?'*

Witch

Bricks, sticks and stones, threatening words and devices designed to inflict torture. Bound by thick ropes and tied with strong knots, trapped within a wooden structure she failed to recognise, Rosa was beginning to surrender to what she saw to be her fate. *'Wanting her dead?'* A mere mortal couldn't take what others saw fit to inflict on those perceived to be witches. Pricked with pins and scratched by those blaming her for their personal discomfort and misfortune. *'Wounds left to bleed out.'* Sleep deprivation, each and every time she was on the brink of passing out, Rosa found herself splashed by water, hit by cold, sharp stones or shaken until her eyes reopened. *'Not going to leave her alone.'* Told she was to face pressing, followed by dunking, before being burned at the stake. *'Frightened?'* Rosa had nowhere to go.

Threatened and tortured by men; some of who were twice her age, the captured female begged they stop. Aware of how some acts being carried out on her naked body caused some in the room to gain sexual gratifications, the defenceless female accused her torturers of being perverted, dirty old men. Examined inside and out, the one being put through what no one should ever have to endure, shouted No! No, she didn't want what he was doing, when one man insisted he taste what made her a woman.

"No!" Unable to stop hands touching and fingers prodding every part of her naked form, she flinched. *'Examined inside & out.'* Unable to move, Rosa begged her attackers to stop. Wearing hoods, their faces were in shadow, what they wore didn't stop the one time barmaid recognising the voices of those she'd serve with food and drink. *'How could they?'* Married men with children. *'Why would they?'* If they truly intended to burn her at the stake, why wouldn't they stop what had turned from torture, to sexual assault? Had night turned to day? *'All had homes to go to.'* Rosa and her husband owned some of the homes housing her attackers and their families. *'Enough?'* Numbed by what at times caused immense pain, the place in-which she was being held remained dark; right up to the time her eyes were blinded by a bright white light. *'Was she dead?'* Was this the light said to lead ones soul up to and through the gates of heaven? *'What was happening?'*

What had taken place had included everything which could possibly take place with the exception of actual sexual intercourse, fingers, tongues and who knew what manmade objects had been used, inserted inside, prodded into and scraped over her naked skin, Hit, punched and in places bitten, no man had entered her with his erection, *'None would dare?'* Hard and excited, she saw as each walked away to sit in the corner of the room and relieve what needed relief, some by themselves, some left together. *'Tied down?'* Whether what she lay upon was a table, bench or stripped bed, she didn't know. *'Why & what was happening?'* Was she dreaming? With all vision blurring as a result of her exhaustion and pain, Rosa saw those around her were naked. A man kissing a man, men touching men? *'What?'* Was their taking her captive; the excuse needed to do what they were doing? *'Dreaming?'* Drugged? Was what she was interpreting to be an all male orgy, nothing more than an hallucination?

Sat touching themselves on their own, some were in couples and there were some whose hunger and passion for what was happening reached out to share themselves with as many as were willing to share themselves with him. Men kissing men, if not actual, why would she imagine such unimaginable scenes. *'One, two, threesomes & more?'* While able to see those to have disrobed, the one numbed by her inner and external pain, was unable to see who continued to explore her weakening and injured form. *'Why?'* Why not kill what none wanted living? Daylight, or flames from a fire? The light to appear like the rising of the largest and brightest moon, was overshadowed by something dark with large wings flying by. Day or another night? Sunlight, having entered her fixed starring eyes, the light illuminating where she was, wasn't clear enough for her to see when her tormentors left. *'Weak?'* Even if she wasn't tied down, she wouldn't have the strength to escape. Broken, bruised and bleeding. Rosa questioned her reasons to live, when right then and there Mrs. Rosa Ruby Sapphire wanted to die.

One night and one day, as the sun to have risen at dawn, set and made ready to bid the world goodnight, Reece felt defeated. Having asked everyone and searched everywhere; the Lord of Sapphire Manor hoped the offered reward would encourage someone to seek out, find and return to him, his missing wife. Twenty-four hours, as a day of searching dissolved into night of worry, threatening words, raised fists and flamed torches were again carried through the village. A group intent on destroying what they believed to be bad, determined to finish what they started. With the skeleton of the stables belonging to Tinkers Tavern withering into ashes, it was the large dominate structure to stand beside it which the villagers and townsfolk targeted next.

Unable to persuade the stubborn Lord to disown his wife, the plan was to run the two out of town. With no place to be, the Sapphires would have to go and so for those prepared to stop at nothing to rid their lives and land of the one seen to be sent by the devil to do his work, the village tavern was the historical structure which had to go first. Believing the witch wouldn't be able to stay; if she didn't have the safety of what was her true home the destruction of Tinkers Tavern was planned. Shouts, screams and disruption. *'A storm?'* No one to hear, realised the volume increasing rumblings were being caused by those to arrive under the shadow of darkness.

Fire setting to scare, it wasn't their intention to cause life threatening damage, out to create concern and doubt in those blinded by the witch. When those hired to work for the Sapphire family set out with Reece to defend what others wanted to destroy, each discovered their efforts to save everything and everyone had come too late. *'How could people be so thoughtless?'* Extinguished by the sudden gust of wind, the loud clap of thunder sent those to have set the building alight, running for home. *'Burned to the ground?'* Had the sudden thunderstorm not released the contents of its' heavy clouds; much more would have been lost, *'A sudden rain fall?'* Rain the likes of which no one had seen before, rain so intense and heavy its' volume and weight aided the few who fought to save the vast property from being destroyed beyond repair. *'Safe?'* When the flames turned to smouldering ashes, the only room to have perished was the scullery. *'Ruined?'* The room in-which Rosa and her father had lived and worked side by side; was occupied by one finding life on the streets more scary and uncomfortable than he ever imagined. *'A young boy?'* A life taken unnecessarily? *'A terrible accident?'* Wittinesses reported the fire to have destroyed both property and life to have been started by a lightening strike. Nature, the unpredictability and fierce power of the weather was what would be blamed for turning what lay beneath a wooden roof to ashes and rubble. *'A freak fireball?'* What was said, could be true? *'Gone?'* The only one not to have survived, was someone who shouldn't have been where he was.

Sleeping by himself and attempting to keep himself safe, the innocent male was just thirteen years of age. A teen to have had a disagreement with his parents. *'His father was amongst those carrying flamed torches.'* When recognising her son, his mother struggled to hold back her tears; as all around strived to understand why young Thomas Riley had been where he was. *'Why hadn't he escaped?'* Lost and alone, all saw it as sad to see how flames had engulfed his young fragile body and taken from him his future. *'What had they done?'* Darkness, strong winds, hot flames, deafening thunder, heavy rain and confusion. Some to have arrived in attempt to stop the flames; reported seeing a large bird in the night sky. Having taken all able bodied staff to assist, the few fighting to save what was burning, felt pleased to have their efforts assisted by the rain from what all saw to be a freak storm. *'Could the wings of Dark Angel start strong winds?'* Was it the death of a local and the suffering of his relatives which led to Rosa being released?

Exhausted and distressed by the fact they hadn't been able to do more, those returning to Sapphire Manor were thanked for everything they'd done and told to get themselves a well earned drink from the families personal wine, beer and spirit cella along with whatever they wanted to eat from the kitchen; before going to their beds. *'No early start,'* Reece instructed his employees to take two hours paid leave prior to recommencing what were their usual daily duties; following what all hoped would be a well earned nights rest. Bidding one another goodnight when walking to their individual dwellings in the vast grounds of Sapphire manor, Morris told his son to keep to himself what he was saying he'd seen and Dixon heard something disturbing the horses in the stables, before someone called everyone over to the barn.

Hurt, injured, disheveled and abandoned, inside the barn she and her husband had been outside of when attacked. *'From where?'* Relieved to see his wife back where she belonged, Lord Sapphire refused to believe Rosa had been where she was found; all along.

Witch

*E*ncased in darkness, lay bleeding with her wounds stinging, bond by ropes and held down by leather straps, the vanishing of those intent on torture and telling her, she must die caused what had been noise filled to fall silent. *'Had she fallen asleep?'* Tied up and strapped down. *'Was she living or dead?'* Left alone, the space to have been illuminated by the sun was overshadowed by darkness in what felt like the blink of an eye *'Had day become night?'* From the light and heat of the sun, to the cool darkening night. Shocked, when opening her eyes with a start. Alone, the place she failed to recognise suddenly turned from black to bright and white, a lightening flash bringing with it a clap of thunder shocking her back from wherever it was she went. *'Wind, thunder, lightening & rain.'* A storm? Her captures had failed to return, how could men intent on torturing a witch, be afraid of weather? *'How had Rosa gotten free if she wasn't a witch?'* The female to have experienced what she described as being in hell, couldn't recall how she got from where she was, to arrive back at where it all began. *'Taken, or hidden?'* Wittinesses said the Lady of Sapphire manor had coward in the barn so not to be caught setting the fires responsible for causing what were the injuries she gained, when running from what she left burning.

𝓑ack home and being accused of attempting to burn her childhood home to the ground. *'Too weak to argue.'* Bathed and nursed back to health by both her husband and housekeeper Daisy, Rosa told no one of what she'd been through. *'Ashamed,'* Pleased, relieved to be back with her husband, Rosa felt she should have been able to do more. *'Blamed?'* Responsible; she blame herself for the death of the young boy seeking refuge from a family quarrel. *'Weak?'* None thanked the good lady for attending the burial she insisted she and her husband pay for. *'Guilt ridden.'* Few looked in the direction of the female taken with the intent of torturing to death. *'Secrets to keep?'*

Rosa said she and her husband should find a law abiding way of making those she recognised pay. *'Redundancies'* Rosa disagreed with doing what would see wives begging on the streets and children out of school, insisting the babies were never to blame, the Lord and his Lady spoke about introducing a refuge; should males falling on hard times abandoned their women or disown children; when those they lived alongside received pay increases to assist with what would be a minimal rise in housing costs.

Fearful to fall asleep, Reece took on security to patrol the manor and surrounding area, day and night. *'Anything to protect the woman he loved.'* If it was up to him, those responsible for what happened wouldn't be living within what he saw to be his; town and village. *'Not an unreasonable man?'* He wished those wanting to harm his wife, knew it was she; who was keeping them from suffering more than a little financial inconvenience.

Witch

*P*anic, someone had seen something, someone was where he or she shouldn't be. *'No!'* Miles couldn't go and warned his father he should remain indoors. Three employed in the role of private security officers, when the alarm was raised, all males living within the Sapphire manor was ready to do whatever needed to be done. He walked because the gates were locked, having climbed over what was a high stone wall bordered by tall thick trees, he saw no reason to apologies for having entered his childhood home. Alone, the tall dark figure standing by the graveside of his parents' and Dark Angel; said he was there because he had someone he needed to bury. *'Of course.'* Sad to hear of his loss and concerned to be told of his struggles. Opening up the gates to allow the carriage carrying the body of Kyle Benson to enter, Reece assured his brother he would always be welcome.

'Not a relative?' The body to be buried in the families private burial ground was someone Roman called his special friend. A young man with no family and no other place to be. Staying the night and more, *'Welcomed for as long as he wanted.'* Before returning to what was his busy life of traveling the world, Roman Sapphire spent his nights drinking the finest whiskey in the company of his brother and crying into the pillows on what was the four poster bed in the room to have belonged to his late father. Hurt and heartbroken, when pulling back the curtains to reveal the early morning sun, Roman vowed he would never allow himself to be hurt, or his heart to be broken, ever again.

4: Lonely

Under constant surveillance, walking into what in the Sapphire manor was known as the blue, or boys lounge, because it was the reception and entertaining area to have a large drinks cabinet and small card table, Rosa told security officer Albert Potters he was free to join the others employed to look after the house and keep everything secure at their appointed posts outside. Stood watching, her unimpressed brother-in-law asked if she should be where she was; when taking himself a glass of the most expensive whisky he could find.

"Reece won't mind." He smirk and Rosa agreed of course not. "Should you be in here?" The male who hadn't yet revealed for how long he would be staying, reminded the female of the nature of the room in which she was making herself comfortable. Entering with a wool rug to cover and keep his wife warm, Reece informed his elder of his wife's need to be comfortable and feel safe.

"We can drink, play card and do whatever we need, with Rosa in the room." Roman said he didn't, when asked if he had any objection to the Lady of the house being with them.

"No," When Roman asked. Rosa said she didn't play cards, happy to sit and read. When his brother left the room to fetch a second bottle of his preferred brand of whiskey, Roman made comment on what his sister-in-law had endured. "I hear what they do to find the mark of the devil on a witch, can be barbaric." Not wanting to talk about what she wanted to forget; Rosa didn't reply. "If I was my brother, my knowing what they did would result in my never being able to go be near you." He continued. "I don't there will be any children."

Witch

"You would never go near any woman." In a bid to have him stop, or at the very least divert the upsetting line of conversation, Rosa made it clear she, if no one else, was aware of her brother-in-laws truth. "Kyle?" Her eyes asked what the absence of more words failed to say. Coughing, nervous and becoming twitchy, Roman repeated what had been his story; Kyle Benson was a cabin boy who died at sea, an orphan with no family and no place to be. Rosa told Roman the kind of heart which beat inside his chest, didn't do what he was calling his good deed. "Not without good reason," She asked if she should have their gardener plant flowers or evergreens by what was his friends' burial plot? "So you don't have to put yourself out bringing flowers." The look Roman sent and she returned, told both, each had said more than enough on the subjects neither wanted to broach.

"Sorry," Roman said he shouldn't have said what he had and Rosa told him people often don't think about what they are saying, when they are sad.

Unable to sleep because she was scared to close her eyes Rosa had heard Roman crying in his room, sobbing late into the night. From the window where she stood in attempt to avoid her own nightmares, Rosa had seen her brother-in-law leaving the house under the shadow of darkness to spend time by the grave of the one he called a good boy. More than a good friend, assuring him that her words weren't meant as a way of asking when he would be leaving? When he returned; Roman told Reece he would be leaving the day after next. *'Drink makes one melancholy.'* Saying he had ingested more than his fill for one night; Roman refused the offered second nightcap, telling his brother, what everyone needed, was a good nights sleep before nodding to Rosa as he left to retire to his bed. Wishing him a restful night and sweet dreams, the two agreed that the passing of time would return to all, what had been taken in way of health and routine.

Her birthday, how had it come back around so fast? Aged twenty-eight, it being Rosa's big day meant it was Rock's celebration too, visiting the village cemetery to lay flowers on her twin brother's grave. *'Vandalised?'* The constant upturning led Reece to make enquires about how to move the bones of those who would've been his brother and mother-in-law, to be laid to rest within what was the expanding site of his families private burial ground within the stone walls, high gates and boarding trees of the Sapphire Manor House. *'A kind thought.'* Renfred told his thoughtful son-in-law he believed what was happening would stop and asked he didn't disturb those lay resting; unless left no other choice. Paperwork to look through, his wanting to make his and his wives life more peace filled; was why Reece was sat reading through books and checking documentation inside the large library while she set about tidying her mother and brothers' grave.

Her birthday, woken with breakfast in bed and asked to wear a blindfold; Rosa was taken into the village, where Reece surprised her with the completion of a project he'd kept secret. Showing how the place to have been her home was repaired, rebuilt and refurbished. Hidden behind protective fencing, those to have done what needed doing had come from the city, hired because they were the best of the best. Told to keep what was original, real wood was rubbed down and revarnished while bricks and stones were cleaned and relaid. What was changed had been changed for the better, indoor water closets, Rosa revealed how the emptying of the chamber pots had been her most hated task, happier to muck out the horse manure and bag it to be sold, or swapped with those wanting its' revitalising qualities for vegetable patches and flowerbeds in return for whatever service or product they could supply? Once her eyes were able to see all, her being encouraged to explore what was shinny and new while feeling familiar, caused her smile to grow brighter. The bar, barrels, bottles and jugs, Reece said there were people willing to sell what they brewed for fair prices. Booth style tables for dinners, benched gaming and card tables for drinkers, whilst nothing had been removed, everything had been renewed via varying treatment and flawless repair. *'Best birthday gift ever.'* Not only back to how she remembered, but improved to how Rosa and her inn keeping father had always wanted it. The Tavern: A back room with large tables for gatherings and a place to hold meetings, the updated kitchen was to be shared by both residential and hospitality business. Up on the first floor, four double bedrooms adaptable for guests; meant the residential living accommodation moving from the basement to the loft space, where those whose architectural skill knew no bounds when incorporating not one, but two Juliet balconies, one leading out from the lounge and the second from the main double bedroom, both to the front of the building now standing three storey's above ground. Reece said those to work hard, should be able to see and watch over, not live below and hide from those they were there to serve. *'Wonderful,'* Outdoor benches to be used by youngsters left to wait for adults needing refreshment, two ropes to swing on and another two with a wooden seat between, hung from the branches of the trees to have been used by many a generation for both climbing and hiding. When stepping out onto the grounds acquainted with what was the oldest building for miles. *'Tears of joy.'* Rosa called the vine covered walkway leading from tavern to the new stables, enchanting.

Stables to have burned to a black and crisp skeleton shell had been resurrected using a mix of stone and wood, standing within the exact footprint of what stood before, those whose skills shown creativity and foresight, constructed what was able to offer shelter for both horses and grooms. Stalls to one side and single bedded rooms to the other. When walking between what she saw to be beyond her wildest dream, Rosa wanted, but resisted the temptation to ask her husband if they would be the ones to run what her family owned.

"Yours," Like he read her mind. Reece told his wife the paperwork was all in order and Tinkers Tavern was again hers' to do with, whatever she pleased. Aware her father would never return to live permanently, Rosa couldn't wait for Renfred to visit and see what he feared would be destroyed, being brought back to life. *'Forever grateful,'* Knowing her husbands' breeding meant him being a man who would never miss out on a money making opportunity, Mrs. Sapphire felt overwhelmed to be told Tinkers Tavern was her birthday gift.

What had been her home and workplace, on the day she turned twenty-eight, was gifted back to the innkeepers daughter; told to enjoy her new venture and what was her first real business venture, *'Happy & excited?'* Rosa appreciated all Reece was doing and everything he'd done. *'Protecting her future,'* Not wanting to live under threat of what had happened, happening again. *'Out to disprove the existence of witches.'* The loving and loyal husband of the one being blamed for anything and everything to go wrong, had done nothing but attempt to refute the existence of evil and convince local villagers and townsfolk his wife was one of them.

Together to explore the renewed tavern and standing side by side to lay flowers and wish Rock a happy birthday, they decided to separate when Rosa said she wanted time to tidy what others disturbed. Apart? *'Her birthday being the day they met, made it extra special.'* Being man and wife, meant Rosa and Reece being there for one another, standing strong and being supportive in everything each wanted, or needed to do. The Lord loving and trusting his Lady, meant his agreeing to give her time with those she missed.

Witch

Alone, she was sure there was someone watching, having told Dixon to wait by the gates of the graveyard on his return from taking Reece home, Rosa said she would be out when finished. Kneeling to speak to her brother; something told her the one she was sensing, wasn't anyone she knew. *'Rock?'* Not a believer in ghosts, the female left alone within what was a maze of headstones, plants, trees and memorial benches; told the one to have lost his life, she was happy. *'Eight months on,'* The strong, independent female shrugged her shoulders when feeling a shiver run the full length of her spine. Aware that not even the news she revealed in a whisper; contained words strong or magical enough to bring a corpse out of his grave. *'Would she tell anyone else?'* Aware her husband should have been by her side, the planned candlelight dinner seemed a more fitting environment to tell the man she loved what it was she had to say. *'Waiting for as long as she could.'* Rosa questioned her waiting longer, when asking Rock and her mother to keep her secret. Happy, with a smile; she hoped her news would make Reece happy.

Busy reading books said to be filled with facts, caught up in checking and rechecking the paperwork being prepared to present to those governing the law of the land. He never noticed those who ran by the large windows, not when relying heavily on his dim table lamp for light. *'Sleeping?'* Unsure when or if he and his wife would come under attack again, Reece too had found sleep difficult to enter and almost impossible to maintain. *'Dreams turning to nightmares.'* When lay beside his wife in their martial bed, the one to have failed to protect her, imagined what she said, she could never put into words. *'Lay side by side, not knowing neither wasn't sleeping.'* Tired mentally and worn out physically, drained, both Lady and Lord Sapphire were exhausted. Agreeing to spend the day doing what each needed to do, the two were looking forward to them coming together for a relaxing birthday and anniversary meal. Neither needed any more pressure, both wanted to do what was right, while never neglecting what was the day they called their most special date.

Witch

*R*ustling trees, August wasn't a month known for outbursts of unpredictable, changeable weather. *'Was it raining?'* Rosa hadn't thought to bring a coat or umbrella because the thirteenth day of August was a day known for its' soaring heat and dryness. The month when green fields turned yellow, if the few high floating clouds were about to release their hydrating cargo; local farmers would give thanks. When sensing a movement indicating an atmospheric shift, the one wishing her deceased brother many happy returns; felt something wasn't right. Who? What? Where?

Watching as what stood straight, tall and strong began rustling before beginning to sway and bend. Questioning the presence of an approaching hurricane? *'Not native to where she was.'* A storm, with the horses waiting to pull the Sapphires' carriage home becoming restless, Dixon climbed down to steady them with his calming words having pulled up the hood which would keep his returning Lady dry. *'No?'* Not dark rolling clouds, what Rosa saw in the skies when heading towards the large iron gates of the village graveyard; was the floating of long black cloaks; their wearers carrying flamed torches as each ran into the grounds, along the road and up to the Sapphire Manor house. *'She shouldn't have left him alone.'* Rushing, when what was dry turned wet, it became slippery. Running over what turned from solid to soft, soil changed to mud and what was light went dark. Never having seen clouds like the ones rolling in low and strong, blocking what was the natural illumination of the sun, Dixon felt unsure what to do?

Watching what had been a bright day; turn into what resembled a dark storm filled night. How? Going from blue to grey before arriving at pitch black. *'How?'* Was this the end of the world? Why was the gate to which Rosa was heading, moving further away? Why had what was open suddenly slammed shut? *'No!'* How was it possible for a root to protrude where there was no tree?

'A hand?' Had the hand of someone buried beneath what was turning from smooth to mush; emerged to take hold of the ankle of the one attempting to escape what was being locked down; a root or a hand? Something caused Rosa to trip and fall? *'No!'* Unsure how, or why she fell. *'Holding her stomach.'* The gate being locked meant the male waiting outside being unable to get in to help. *'How would she get out?'* Why? How was he sleeping inside a room filling with smoke? *'Wind, thunder, lightening & rain?'* Another storm and another fire said to have been started by a stray lightening bolt. *'Had the lightening hit her too?'* While the man of the church and local grave digger assisted Dixon in carrying Rosa to the waiting carriage, other Sapphire employees' brought Reece out of the flames, his young body unscathed, the healthy male had inhaled much too much smoke for his internal organs to survive. When fire started and took hold of what was the Sapphires' large book filled library, the heat filled flames engulfed; before taking what was the life of Lord Reece Ray Sapphire. *'Gone?'* Rosa woke to discover her husband no longer there. *'A widow?'* No law in the land would punish a grieving woman. *'Loss was punishment enough?'* A wife preparing to bury her husband, Rosa felt she should have been able to do more. *'To blame?'* She felt responsible and would never stop blaming herself for what happened. *'Minus the love of her life,'* Rosa couldn't stop herself wishing she'd been the one to have lost what would be her future. A funeral? *'Married three years.'* Together for six short twelve month periods, the happy couple hadn't spoken about death and dying, because they were young. *'Forever side by side.'* Alone with no one to turn to, Rosa sought guidance and advise from Dixon and wife Daisy.

When questioning the answers given by the manor house staff; investigating police officers, heard gardeners Morris Minton and his son Miles say they'd done everything they could to fight the flames alongside Butler Arthur

Ambers and footman James Watt. *'Fighting to save the library.'* Chambermaid Sarah Lynch had gotten burned while security Jon Holt. Kenneth Kelly and Albert Potters said they hadn't seen anything. Distracted by the horses becoming distressed due to the sudden storm, those hired to keep the manor and all in it safe; had rushed to the aid of stablehand Sol Green; while cook Miss Josephine Hazel said she never seen or heard anything like what she called the opening of the gates of hell. *'Employees turned friends.'* Fear and desperation, caused the grieving widow to struggle; when deciding what would be the proper and right thing to do?

With her husband gone, Rosa begged her father to return to support her in her hour of need. Having built for himself a new life. Mr. Renfred Tinker advised his only child she should do the same. *'A woman saying a final farewell to her man.'* Aware of how she would suffer if she was to remain in Déspoina; Rosa wanted to take her husband with her; wherever she decided to go, something she knew she couldn't do. *'Gone, if he couldn't go with her, she couldn't leave?'* Why him and not her? The facts about what happened; only went to strengthen the belief that the witch; Rosa was and forever would be able to protect herself with magic.

Sorry, her staff and father expressed sadness when telling the grieving widow they were sorry for her loss. Sorry they couldn't do more, unable to save Reece, none knew how to help and some felt fearful about continuing what were their posts' serving the female who attracted trouble resulting in tragedy. *'A service?'* A few words said within the walls of the families' private chapel. Standing in the place where she and the man she loved had been joined together in holy matrimony, sat listening to the voice of the man to have pronounced them man and wife forever. Rosa hid her tears behind a heavy black veil; when what was happening confirmed how from this day forth, two would be forever one *'Death did them part.'*

Two had become one, sensing the eyes of others burning deep into her back, the Lady of the manor knew most would be expecting to see her reduced to ashes or turned to stone. *'A witch shouldn't be able to step on hollowed ground.'* The fact the chapel stood on ground which upon the death of her husband became hers, meant many concluding how the witch amongst them had cursed what would automatically be passed into her hands. *'A Lady inheriting limitless wealth?'* Rosa would give it all up, to have the man she loved back by her side. A service filled with words of kindness and praise for a man who only ever wanted to do what was right for others. *'A fair man.'*

Reece Ray Sapphire was a good man. Kind, caring and sharing, he would and did do everything he could to stop all the things which within his home and business life was going wrong. *'A rich widow?'* Continuing to call Rosa a witch, meant those who were responsible for her husbands' death; switching the blame onto her. Murdered in his own home, a freak accident caused by wild uncontrollable weather. That which was created by nature, was what officials held responsible for the death of the second Lord Sapphire. *'Why him & not her?'*

Witch

Many believed it was because she was protected by the devil himself.

"This is mine." In the absence of a wake Mr. Roman Rich Sapphire chose to confront his bereaved sister-in-law directly following the service. *'There to bid his brother farewell.'* "All of it!" Outside the main doors of the chapel; the elder brother of the dearly departed stood firm to prevent the grieving widow from following the coffin leaving to be laid to rest inside the deep, dark hole waiting to keep Reece encased within what was the Sapphires' private burial ground. Stopped, stunned by his outburst. *'Rosa needed to be with her husband one final time.'* Obstructed and prevented from following the body being carried to its' last and final resting place, Rosa asked Roman not to spoil things. Angry and upset, the last known surviving member of the Sapphires' pure bloodline; wasn't going to let the day end without having his say. "All of it!" He repeated. Demanding she hand back what had been in his family for centuries.

"Roman," Warned by her late husband never to give into his elder brothers' demands, Rosa thanked him for coming, before saying she was sorry and understood his loss. *'Alone?'* Both he and she had lost someone they loved dearly. *'By himself,'* Roman had never married. *'A player not a stayer?'* Maybe it was Rosa knowing his truth, which caused him to be hostile and uncaring at her time of need? There to challenge, not to support, there to regain what he believed to have been taken.

"You can't keep what is rightfully mine." Aware of what he was saying, she was truly sorry, but the fact was, Roman and his brother had each been awarded their personal inheritance prior to their fathers' early death and everything which had been signed over to Reece; was now legally hers' to keep. *'Not the time for arguments?'*

"Sorry," She didn't want what she had without her husband by her side but both Reece and his late father had asked she promise never to allow Roman to be awarded what was left of the Sapphire estate. *'What had*

Roman done with what had been his fortune?' Rosa assured him she would look after what had been left in her care. Leaving the chapel to oversee the burial of her husband, accompanied by her father, Rosa told Roman he was welcome to join them.

'Earth to ashes & bones to dust.' Watching as the one who should be standing alongside her; above, was lowered and laid to rest in the ground, the widow needed the support offered and given by her father; as she fought the urge to join what had been taken. Lay beside the graves of his parents, his unknown twin sibling and the male said to have been a good friend to his brother. Her silent tears pleaded Reece to return. *'Gone?'* Why him and not her? How would she survive alone? *'What the good Lord had joined together, no man should have torn apart.'* Prevented from falling to the ground by the strong arms of her father, Renfred promised his frail daughter; he was going nowhere until she was strong enough to continue what would be her new life?

"Come back with me." He said there was always space enough for her to live with him and assured her she would thrive in the seaside town he chose to make his home. Both father and daughter knew them having gone their separate ways; meant them being destined to live different lives forever.

"Marry me?" Interrupting the private conversation, Roman demanded his brothers' grief stricken widow betroth herself and her gained fortune to him. "It is up to me to look after you now." He attempted to justify his need to move into the big house and become Lord of the Manor, but Rosa told him No. *'She wouldn't.'* Rosa could never marry someone she didn't love. *'Happy for him to have the title of Lord Sapphire, she would never be his Lady.'* "I'm not leaving." Preventing the female dressed head to foot in black from returning into what was now her large, cold, empty multi roomed dwelling; Roman was asked by Mr.Tinker to have some respect and leave his daughter alone. "You owe me." Approached by those considering the new terms and conditions of their employment. *'Out numbered.'* Roman agreed to remain calm as all there to pay their respects were invited to partake in coffee and cafe on the patio.

Coffee and cake, Rosa offered the assortment of spirits kept in her late husbands' collection, but none including herself accepted what most saw to be a bribe. *'None except Roman.'* Afraid of loose lips, none from the town and village wanted to be heard saying the wrong thing. Coffee and cake accepted out of respect for the deceased, those who remained, stayed out of curiosity, with few seen to make eye contact with the one all suspected to be aware of what was the truth of what had happened. *'A bad intension gone wrong?'* Another death caused because no one saw someone being where they believed there would be no one. *'Reece should've been with his wife?'* Many feared, the witch discovering what each was hiding.

Whispered conversations, sly remarks and silent stares, none looked comfortable with what was tradition following a burial and Rosa wanted it made clear her dearly departed husband was to blame for nothing.
"Short and not so sweet." Roman made comment when the last of those who weren't staff or family, left what was the quiet celebration of his younger brothers' short lived life. *'Less than an hour,'* He said he thought Reece would have been more popular as Renfred asked his daughter if she was all right? *'No,'* Rosa doubted she would ever be all right again. *'Yes,'* She assured him and all keeping watch over her, she could handle Roman. "I'm destitute." A gambler and heavy drinker, his words neither shocked nor caused concern when approaching his brothers' widow for the second, maybe third time. "What is it like?" He asked. Looking out onto the land surrounding the Sapphires' grand house; Roman asked what it was like to live in what should have been, but

never was his family home. *'Boarding schools & holidays supervised by hired nannies.'* While being well educated, Roman told Rosa how he and his brother had been denied a childhood inclusive of true family life. "I have next to no memories of this place." He signed. Too young to recall the day his brother was born and his mother died. Little over a year older, the pregnancies being close was believed to have added to the complications experienced by the female whose second twin baby died before having chance to live. *'Boy, or girl?'* Roman said he didn't know the sex of the one whose life ended at the exact time of Reece's birth. Dark Angel? Their father allowed the babies body to be buried because he heard his wife telling him how everyone make mistakes. *'His entire family deceased.'*

Lay side by side, gone, his mother, Dark Angel, his father and his little brother. Gone to a place they could never return from, Rosa said she was sorry; when informing him how she was doing what his deceased family members had asked she do. *'Save him from himself.'* When telling Reece they were unlucky, Reece had told Roman how in the absence of their father, each was responsible for creating his own luck. "Taken from this place before we had a chance to appreciate it, this should be my home." Rosa told her brother-in-law it wouldn't be right for the two of them to live together under the same roof. "This is my family home." He insisted and she asked if he was financially stable enough to keep it.

"I can't help you." Rosa said she would look after things, when Roman said no, aware the drinking male was becoming unreasonable and obstinate, the widow requested staff escort the drunk off, what was now her property and land. *'Not driven out of town?'* Rosa was merely doing what her late father-in-law and recently departed husband asked she do, she knew he would be back and assured her watching father not to worry. Of course she would allow him to place flowers and spend time at the graves of his family and good friend. Of course she wouldn't see him come to any harm, but Rosa needed space and time to think of how best she could help, without breaking her word.

Widowed: A woman left alone, a woman in mourning, a woman in black. *'A witch?'* All official documentation stated that as the lawfully wedded wife of Reece Ray Sapphire, Rosa Ruby was entitled to inherit everything which her dearly departed husband legally owned. *'Rich?'* Seen to be a woman of means, Rosa knew there would be more men to come calling, but for her there would only ever be one; she wanted to share her life. *'A businesswoman?'* The status awarded, was one seldom heard of being held by a female alone, with many a man believing all things financial should and could only be dealt with by men, Rosa knew her being left to get on with things; wouldn't happen. *'What should she do?'* Having stayed on, to help and support his daughter, Renfred agreed, when she said the paperwork alone was a lot for her to get her head around. *'Not educated.'* Rosa was no fool and insisted she would appoint those she wanted, to assist in the running of what without a Lord, became her Sapphire Estate.

All shinning like it was new, Renfred agreed some things would have made his and his daughters' working lives easier. *'Registered to forever be named Tinkers Tavern.'* When looking at what Rosa wanted him to see, her father agreed to thinking a billion if only's?

"Couldn't you give Roman something." Aware of his constant harassing, having seen him plead and heard Mr. Roman Sapphire beg for what he believed to be his, while saying he, couldn't return, Renfred attempted to help sort for his only child, what was uppermost in her mind. *'Not a believer in ghosts,'* Rosa had encountered dreams where both her deceased father-in-law and recently departed husband told her No! Dreams which saw her back in the arms of the man she loved, turned to nightmares filled with warnings of what would happen if she was to break what had been her word. If handed to Roman, the Sapphire estate would crumble until it no longer existed, first the manor house, then the homes rented by others and eventually all businesses would die. Auctioned off to the highest bidder, Rosa saw her brother-in-law losing more than his pride when sitting around the card and roulette tables inside the casino he would introduce baring his family name. *'No,'* Shaking her head, she told her father she couldn't do anything more for the man unable to help himself. Agreeing to cover his expenses, happy to pay for his hotel room and ticket home, the one wealthy enough to buy whatever her heart desired, said she would allow her husbands' brother to take up residence in one of the estates' cottages, rent free. Attempting to help, Rosa warned others not to give Roman hard cash. No, she wouldn't allow a man known not to be able to handle his drink to run her Tavern and no, she couldn't allow someone she saw as unstable and unpredictable to live where she lived.

No investments, no money making schemes, the lone female ignored hard luck stories and put everything in place so Roman was never allowed close enough to gain control of what was hers.
"You're a good girl." When she explained, Renfred said he understood. Promising Roman would never be homeless or go hungry. "A good girl," The cheque she presented to her father, was money enough to allow him a peaceful retirement in his new home by the sea. *'Enough for him to buy himself a fishing boat.'* Always the host, Renfred Tinker had purchased a building large enough to rent out rooms to those whose livelihood was governed by the sea. *'A visionary?'* Noticing the need of visitors to do something more than lay in the sun and build sandcastles when spending recreation time by the coast, Renfred saw himself taking rich folk out to fish on the ocean waves for sport. "A good girl," Rosa wished others could see her to be a good person.

"Buy one of my ships." Approached by Roman on his final day with his daughter, it was clear someone had told the last true Mr. Sapphire about what Renfred planned. "I only have the three left, but they have nets for fishing and plenty of cabin space for cruising." Not what the older male was looking for. Renfred said he was sorry he couldn't help. "It's my money." Roman accused the father of his brothers' widow of assisting her to rob him of his inheritance.

"The harbour I live by wouldn't accommodate a ship."

"Then move. Live on the ship." Roman accused the one trying to be reasonable of making weak excuses. "How much did she give you? I'll take whatever she gave." A desperate man, Renfred told Roman he was sorry. "She really is a witch. The two of you planned this." He accused the father and daughter of robbery.

"I think it's time you left Mr. Sapphire Sir." Having seen and being able to hear what was his raised voice, Roman said the arrival of those hired in the role of security; proved Rosa's mystic capabilities. Telling an ageing Mr. Tinker his strange daughter wouldn't always be around to protect him, the last Mr. Sapphire was led away and escorted off what had been his' families land.

"Everything all right Mr. Tinker." Watching as his colleagues escorted the one to have been threatening; off the premises, Kenneth Kelly asked the father of his employer, if there was anything he needed.

"Someone strong enough to look out for my daughter." When realising Rosa needed someone to help, Renfred also saw himself as too old, too weak and no longer the one she needed. *'A witch?'* Having brought her up the best he could, independent and strong didn't make her bad. Waving her father goodbye, the Lady of Sapphire manor wished him well and he in return wished her luck.

A widow, the woman left alone; turned to Dixon and his wife Daisy for assistance. Being the ones to run and keep the manor house going, its' Lady looked to those to have been her husbands' most faithful and loyal employees to help her with what was her plan. *'Unable to stay.'* To go away and leave those who she blamed for the untimely death of the man she loved was something she had to do. Those seeing her to be the true culprit for any and everything to go wrong held their tongues and said nothing. *'A given time of mourning.'* Allowing the bereaved a given time to grieve. *'Given time to sort what needed sorting.'* From the thoughts inside her head, to all things financial, when alone, the female seen to have the world at her feet; spent her nights looking through paperwork and reading one legal documents. Aware time was running out and knowing how those determined to continue in their plight, would soon return to outcaste what they saw to be evil.

"We can't take this." While Dixon saw his years of loyal service to be worthy of the large sum of money being offered, his wife felt panicked by the responsibility such riches would bring. Seeing the large manor house as much too big, those to have put the needs of another family before them having a family of their own. Agreed when told they should convert one of the barns by the stable block to be their full time, rent free home. The stud and stabling of horses was a business the couple were told to make their own. *'Caretakers?'* Mrs. Rosa Ruby Sapphire asked Mr. Donald Dixon and his sweet wife Daisy to take care of what she had no choice but to leave. *'Help?'* Aware her discontented neighbours would never allow her to rest, Rosa knew she wouldn't ever be accepted. *'Outcaste?'* While doing her husband and father-in-laws' bidding, the one left with no one to turn to, couldn't be cruel. *'Only as cruel as the law would allow.'* Enlisting the professional help of the men to have been her late father-in-laws' advisors, his bank manager and his solicitor. Agreements were made which for those known to be influential in the organising of behaviours to have resulted in damage, harm and death; meant a substantial increase in charges to include rents and any work benefits. Wanting those she saw as being responsible for her loss; to pay. Those found to be Sapphire tenants or employees, would soon find themselves signing new agreements to include clauses making each liable for all repairs, redecoration and any improvements needed on the properties they called home. Not evicted. Those she blamed for taking her husband would find living the lives each took for granted more difficult. *'Their choice to move out of what Rosa provided.'*

"Of course." Mr. Thomas Sheldon and Mr. Stuart Holt agreed with most of what their wealthy client asked. Yes, they could assist with the things she wanted putting in place. Making sure Roman made it back home safe, one of the first things Rosa did was to arrange for her brother-in-laws household bills to be met using money provided by profits accumulated from what many saw to be the extortionate rent increases. *'A kept man?'* Far from happy, instead of being grateful, Roman made no secret of his want for more quickly moving from his one room bedsit into a two bedroom flat overlooking the dock where the last of his fleet were spending much more of their time.

"Yes," When told of Roman's new residence; Rosa agreed to his household costs being covered, buying the large multi storey property divided into six, two bed flats form its' landlord and adding what her brother-in-law lived in; to her property portfolio. Rosa told those taking care of her business and the Sapphire Estate, all Roman's living costs should be met along with a food parcel sent to him weekly. No money or anything he could sell, Roman was reluctant, but signed what said any financial assistance would be withdrawn should he feel the need to move home again.

Tougher living conditions for those who harmed her. Sorting and signing legal documents, Lady Sapphire and those she chose to help watch over her interests, saw and agreed with the reasons given to restrict public access to some of what was hers. Left with no option, the female left in control of what was vast, set out to do what she could, to protect herself and all gained assets. *'Even if that meant upsetting others.'* Mangers of what were Sapphire businesses along with those employed to collect rents, were given a list of names of those who getting one thing wrong and stepping out of line would result in them being out. Sacked and, or evicted? Those Rosa knew to be guilty of harming her and suspected of causing her husband's death were to have their rents increased, their terms and conditions renewed and told that none would ever receive a pay rise. Able to leave if they wanted, any families abandoned by those Rosa saw to be unruly and cruel would be eligible to seek shelter and more of their own accord.

Witch

One sad time following another, calling the Sapphire staff together, all worried what their futures' held. *'Unhappy?'* The locals of Erebus and Déspoina weren't pleased to see the erection of gates and fences to prohibit them from the parts of Ebony Wood used to cut through from village to town. *'Privately owned.'* The spaces on the edge of the Wood designated as places to be shared, enjoyed, explored and used by those wanting to make the most of the great outdoors; were earmarked for improvement, but for anyone wanting to venture deeper into the trees, there was strictly no entry. *'Not wanting another goodbye,'* People panicked because no one liked change. *'Sorry,'* For those to have remained loyal, Rosa had a list of ideas she hoped each would agree to. For staff already living in outbuildings around the Sapphire estate, the way they lived wouldn't change unless they wanted it to and for those whose accommodation was inside the Manor, there would be cottages and other outbuildings provided for them to move into.

Offered rent free homes for life, homes to keep them and their families comfortable so long as they were maintained. Homes to be passed down through the generations, none could be sold, used for profit or sublet. Rosa wasn't surprised when those she employed said they couldn't live for free and do nothing. *'Jobs for all?'* Mr. Morris Minton was asked to continue what was his line of expertises, manager of the grounds around the manor house and employed to oversee those hired to keep areas including the village cemetery, market square and all recreation areas clean, neat and tidy. In charge of clearing, trimming and planting, the one Rosa saw to be an expert in his self taught field, agreed to accept what would be his and his sons' new roles. Instructed to take their pick of what properties were vacant, no employee took what was beyond his or her needs.

Grateful, appointing Mr. Arthur Ambers as manager and financial supervisor, from manor house butler, Ambers was put in-charge of collecting rents and overseeing hire costs with the help of those whose security roles would go on to include the protecting of Ebony Wood. Before moving out, Rosa wanted everyone connected to the Sapphire estate to be given the opportunity to move on in what she promised would continue to be life long employment if wanted. *'Kind, caring & generous?'* Those closest to Reece and Rosa; saw how they shared many a unique value. Left with no choice but to escape the place in-which she would continue to be targeted. Mrs. Sapphire did all she could for others, before disappearing into the night. Housemaids Juliet and Jemima Longly with their head cook mother June, were to take charge of what would be named Erebus House. Two cottages knocked into one and divided into a mix of one bed apartments and bedsits, furnished for sort term visitors and anyone abandoned by the household bread winner due to him or her being on Rosa's list of those she saw as harbouring great guilt. Manageress, the single mother of two who lost her husband to the fever when her girls were babes in arms felt like her dreams had come true.

Out of options, arrangements were made and contracts signed, with all further instruction coming from Mr. Sheldon and Mr. Holt, if and when needed. Six weeks on from the death of her husband, the Lady of the manor disappeared. Gone, leaving under the shadow of darkness, the one many saw to have been after her husbands' riches; left her luxurious lifestyle and newly acquired possessions, taking only what little she needed, having organised and made certain the finances of her dearly departed relatives were secure and the large Sapphire estate safe, the innkeeper's daughter handed her inherited obligations to those she trusted. *'Gone into hiding?'* Lady Rosa Ruby Sapphire, locked the door to the grand property which was her marital home before entering the surrounding trees. *'The first witch of Ebony Wood?'* A young and lonely female living in fear of her life.

5: Illusions

How could she move so fast? Had she moved? Where had she gone? In truth; in the bleak silent blackness of the night when wearing a long black hooded cloak, moving slowly, created an invisibility able to deceive the human eye. Moving when her pursuers moved and standing perfectly still when they stopped, the one they called a witch; made her way to the tree with the hollow trunk and slipped inside. *'Gone?'* The one believed to be a mistress of illusion was said to have become a shadow, able to dissolve into nothingness. Waiting until the coast was clear, for the one being hunted, that which she had stumbled across by accident became her go to place of safety.

With her hood up and her cloak pulled tight around her female form, she protected herself as best she was able from whatever inhabited the inside of the rotting tree. Be it beside below or above, a spider, a mouse, a bat or one of the thousands of other creepy crawlies whose natural home lay within live wood, Rosa couldn't allow what her being there disturbed to cause her to scream out, or squirm. *'Remain silent?'* Unable to move for fear of being discovered, she hoped those looking to find her would give up and return home soon. Aware of what was growing inside her and knowing she would soon struggle to fit inside what had proven to be the perfect hideout, the one living alone, wished she had been born a witch, because if she could, she would magic her husband back.

If truly capable of performing magic, casting spells and able to curse, the maturing female would do good. *'How could others get her so wrong?'* Why couldn't people see what was true and accept what was real? *'Able to take care of herself.'* Nothing more and nothing less, from her birth, Rosa had proven herself to be a female born with the instinct and ability to survive. Living within the trees of Ebony Wood, the constant intrusion of others wanting to seek her out and send her further away, meant Rosa's survival and ability to live her ongoing life in a way which was worth living, becoming more and more difficult.

Witch

Once the barn conversion was complete and their new living quarters made ready to move into Mr. Donald Dixon and his wife Daisy joined those leaving what was boarded and secured for its' own protection. Destined to remain undisturbed. *'Preserved in time.'* From the nursery to have never been used, to the refurbished and restocked library. Family portraits remained where each had been hung upon their completion and all beds occupying the ten bedrooms; lay made. *'Left how her husband found it.'* What could be covered to protect it from dust, stood waiting to be re-revealed, as those leaving hoped with all hope; the life to have prospered under its' vast roof, would one day return?

Ready, but nervous to be taking on new roles within the wider community. Dixon felt confident in becoming the Manor House caretaker and new stable manager. *'Loyal employees?'* All agreed to keep their employers confidence, aware there would be meetings to which each would be called and when necessary; decisions would be made. Work to oversee. *'A different way of living?'* With many in Erebus and Déspoina believing the innkeepers daughter didn't deserve what was bestow unto her, there were those to have gotten to know and so fought to keep her would-be attackers away. While some called for Lady Sapphire to be stripped of her inherited wealth and title, those whose wage continued to be paid, remained determined to protect what she left in their trust.

A simple woman seen to have seduced and married the Lord of the Manor. With the Manor House boarded up and its' loyal staff rehoused, locals worried about what would happen to all Rosa left behind. Why couldn't they leave her to live her life on her own? *'She could if she wanted.'* Rosa hadn't sought physical revenge or caused harm to those whose actions harmed her, playing a vital part in killing her husband. *'Not a witch?'* The Lady of Sapphire Manor left, not because she was a witch, because she was too afraid to stay. One year on from the night of her abduction, twelve months following her torture filled attack and six weeks on from the night Rosa disappeared from her home. Two months on from the death of her husband, that was when the actions of villagers and townsfolk was again seen to have upset the witch?

Rumbling clouds and a dark night sky illuminated by intense flashes of light, that which was released from what was rolling like waves, helped those fighting to save what was being ravaged by flames. *'A storm?'* Rain so heavy it soaked everything it touched. *'Floods?'* The brook began to bubble and rolling waters roared. *'Fierce?'* Walking over what was normally firm and steadfast; those moving quickly felt the earth beneath their feet turning soft and become slippery. Struggling to remain upright. *'Lost?'* As the flamed torches being carried extinguished one by one, those walking side by side began running together, rushing in different directions and drifting apart. In need of shelter. *'Was this the end?'* Some questioned what it was they were doing and many swore that should they survive, they would never do what they were doing again.

Perceiving the bad weather to be a warning, when the village square was struck by lightening, the tallest tree was reduced to a skeleton and the village clock stopped at the hour of 03.33 on the 31st day of October. *'Halloween?'* Some out in what was wild and uncontrollable said they would never go looking for the witch ever again. *'Lucky to be alive.'* Unable to make it to the shelter of their own homes, those to have spent the night said to be dedicated to all things dead seeking out the one they called evil, were horrified to discover the doors of the village church jammed shut. Hit by strong winds and ripped up by their roots, when trees began flying, all knew no one and nothing would make it through the night without sustaining damage and injury. A storm following which some would see their lives and livelihood changed forever. *'Never upset the witch.'* It had to stop and this; the second storm to be so strong it endangered lives and destroyed buildings, this was seen to be a final warning

Magical and mysterious, or coincidence? *'Gone?'* Some said at the very second the clock struck 03.33 on the chilled October morning, a scream like no other was heard to echo from out of the trees of Ebony Wood. A scream carried on the fierce winds of the storm, those close enough to see, swore it was the sound of a females scream and not the lightening to have struck and stopped the village clock. *'A scream many interpreted as the scream which signified the death of the first witch.'* A scream the likes of which only a mother would understand. With Lady Rosa perceived to be deceased, Ebony Wood was declared a place to be avoided. *'A long time dead.'* When alive, a witch is a threat, when a witch died of natural causes, her power was said to remain and lay in wait. *'Rosa would never be forgotten.'* Renamed by those said to have pursued her to her grave. The Witch of Ebony Wood, would forever live on through the generations; with many finding her story fascinating and her legend something to be forever wary of. *'Where was she?'* The truth which would come to light more than fifty years after the village square clock stood still, was a truth none was ready for.

Gone, dying alone in his luxury flat, some saw him as yet another victim of the one he went on to spend his life hunting down. Offering rewards for the capture of the woman he saw to have stolen what was rightfully his, the last known living member of the grand and respected Sapphire family, Mr. Roman Rich, never forgave the one he believed to have wronged him and those he loved. Tortured by what should be, Roman was the type to blame everyone but himself for the way his life turned out. Dressing in the finest clothes, what hung in his wardrobe was handmade and pieced together by the best tailors, using the finest fabrics and purest silk threads. Seen to be flamboyant, while many suspected Roman to be a man unable to come to terms with his masculinity, his strict and commanding business like manner; meant no one questioning the one born to be boss.

A seaman, unlike his younger brother Reece, Roman thrived when out on the ocean waves, commanding the cargo ships bearing his family name and ladened with whatever people paid him to transport, moving everything from exotic animals and animal furs, to the rarest and most expensive of jewels. *'No one chased up the pouch of missing gold coins or the single mislaid diamond.'* Some noticed, but no mere mortal questioned the boss. Roofless in business, no one said anything to the well educated male; happy to sit back and watch poorer people do what helped make him rich. *'A monster?'* He didn't flinch when those in his employment suffered for what he did wrong. *'When one man hung for stealing.'* The truth behind the innocent mans death was much more tragic than anyone could imagine.

Opposites, the Sapphire brothers were as different as stone and cotton wool, one being soft, approachable, sociable and there to help, the other was hard, cold and out to help no one but himself. The only attribute shared by Reece and Roman, was their flawless education and them being brought up to be gentlemen. Things Roman had long since stopped relying on. A seaman, not the Captain of the ship, Roman's role was more important and far more senior than the one responsible for commanding the crew and steering the rudder. Roman had his own private quarters and the power to hire and fire his Captains' at will.

Mr. Roman Rich Sapphire owned the ships on which he sailed. *'A seaman?'* The headstrong businessman never got his hands dirty, but could be seen watching those whose manual labour gave them reason to work without shirts. Down in the depths of the ships belly or up high in crows nest, it would appear the flamboyant bossman had a sixth sense when it came to seeking out semi naked males. Watching because he liked to watch, unsure why he felt tingled when around muscle bound sailors, the eldest Sapphire brother's first male on male encounter, was with his cabin boy Kyle.

An orphan in need of a place to belong, many who took to the seas to earn a living; had a sad, sometimes pain filled story to tell. Smiling on the outside, it was without doubt the younger males smile which first caught the attention of the man he was hired to serve.
"Kyle Sir," He replied when asked his name. "Here to cater for your every need." Had the much younger man known what he was saying, when saying he would do anything? From turning down his bed, to presenting his clothes, always eager to please and happy to oblige, Kyle assisted Roman when dressing and was happy to fill for him his nightly bath. Ten years his junior, when Kyle removed his shirt because he got it wet; the flesh he revealed was tight, smooth, unblemished and soft. When Kyle removed his shirt, Roman wanted him to remove more.
"Nice," Had he spoken out loud when entering his private quarters to find a half naked Kyle down on all fours scrubbing dry the floor. The one everyone looked

up to, couldn't believe he allowed his thought to escape through moist lips. "Good job," He stuttered in attempt to cover what his words meant. Smiling to himself as he continued what he was doing; Kyle knew, because when looking at Roman, Kyle felt the same. Making certain the door to his quarters was secure, Roman wanted to ask if he could touch? Instead thanking the cabin boy for having his bath ready.

"Will that be all Sir?" Unsure as to what would be the younger males reactions, Roman stood back and watched; as getting to his feet, Kyle stood much closer than was necessary. Was he able to sense how much the older male wanted him? "Sir?" He questioned. "You," Never before had either stood so close, close enough to feel the breath of the other crossing over their face. Reaching out and touching what was bare; Roman felt shocked when his advances were stopped, Kyle taking hold of the hand to have made contact with his naked chest. Eyes meeting eyes, neither wanted to stop what was getting started. Holding Roman's hand by the wrist, Kyle moved it from off his smooth hair free chest, down onto what was growing hard between his legs.

"Is this what you want?" Lips so close; them coming together in a kiss was inevitable. "Kiss me." Struggling to contain his own sexual excitement, while keeping one hand where Kyle placed it, Roman used his other to pull him in. Up close. Things were about to get personal? "I'm first." From lips kissing lips, Kyle gently encouraged his elder to go down, dropping onto his knees, the one use to being in-charge allowed another to show and advise him on what he should do. Removing his pants to show what he was holding, Roman licked his lips in anticipation of what he was about to taste.

That was how them becoming lovers began, secret meetings and sly glances, from acting like they barely knew one another and participating in the roles of master and servant, to discovering every intimate detail. When Kyle first took Roman's erect penis into his mouth; the elder male struggled not to explode. Told to calm down, relax and enjoy, the finger placed inside his anus whilst his erection was being sucked; proved almost too much for him to bare. From on top to below, from feeling afraid, to surrendering his passion, there were times Roman couldn't wait to allow his passion to let go. *'Sex?'* That which was good, wasn't all there was to what became their intense relationship.

Whenever they were alone, secure within his private quarters with Kyle, Roman explored and discovered what he did and didn't like in the bedroom. Sometimes having to silence their squeals of orgasmic pleasure with one another's hands, that which often started out as being loving and gentle, could turn rough and rampant in the blink of an eye. Roman liked men and Kyle proved to be one hell of a man. *'Lovers?'* Whenever words which described or revealed emotions came close to being spoken; Roman would do something cruel or unkind. *'Never equal.'* When the two being loving and showing one another they cared lingered for too long; Roman reminded Kyle of his place, often ordering him to leave and sometimes punishing him by removing his basic needs. **Passion filled orgasmic** connections, neither wanted to be the one who didn't; so both did, from his finger to his tongue, when Kyle replaced what was soft and gentle with what was hard and strong; Roman wanted to say stop, but he couldn't, not easy, the first time was difficult. Satisfying one another orally, each had masturbated for the other, over one another and each other; more times. From kissing to petting and on to discover what each could and would do. The first time Roman was the one underneath, was the time when he knew what it was he wanted and Roman wanted more.

When away at sea, the two keeping what they shared secret was easy, when navigating the oceans waves; many speculated about what the flamboyant bossman and his picture perfect cabin boy got up to behind closed doors? *'Nothing experienced men of the sea hadn't encountered before.'* Some saw Kyle as lucky, the underdog who got himself a rich man. *'Lovers?'* When Kyle spoke of them having a future, Roman became cruel. Slapped and forced to go down on him, there were times when what was pleasurable; caused Kyle to gag. Pushed down onto all fours, there were times when what Roman gave was too much, too hard, too fast, too deep and too rough. Gagged so he couldn't scream out, should his elder want to play rough, Kyle was told to be quiet. Seeing the pleasures they shared as being worth the pain, when accompanying the male for who he was a personal assistant; wherever he went, Kyle saw the comforts gained as being his payment for suffering the humiliation he was sometimes made to endure. *'Used & abused, or loved?'* Neither ever said what shone from out of their eyes and had become engraved in their hearts. *'First love, a strange romance?'* Men weren't meant to be with other men in the way Roman and Kyle were together, a man having a relationship with a man? When left to their own devices; what the two shared was a relationship which worked.

"Pansy!" Not the same as the others, a crew hired to man one of the cargo ships from London to Boston, was a crew made up of men heading home after war. *'Family & employment?'* For some, leaving England was to avoid doomed relationships, leave unwanted responsibilities and escape unwelcome communities. *'Escaping?'* Some left to flee prosecution, while others were simply returning home to those they missed. *'There was always the odd crew member who turned out to be a wanted man.'* Real men's men, outspoken and strong, when confined to the restrictions of a ship at sea, everything became everyones business.

"Puff." Kyle had heard it all before, but felt the ongoing hostility from the predominantly American crowd to be different. *'Too late to turn back.'* Roman said he would if he could, but it was against the law to push crew members overboard. *'Too many of them?'* There was always the odd one who disagreed and so attempted to scandalise the suspected all male affair. On this trip it seemed everyone had an opinion. *'Hard workers who played harder.'*

"Puffs and pansies." Ignoring the words of the Captain and the threat of not being paid, those to have taken work so to hitch a ride back to their homeland; saw the money they would lose, being a bonus they were willing to go without.

"Show us your cock and I'll buy you a frock." With no sign of the bullying and teasing coming to an end without intervention, Roman instructed Kyle to give him space.

Away from the protection of the bossman's private quarters; Kyle found himself spat at and urinated on should his work give him reason to be within range of those making no secret of the way each despised what was seen as not right. Shouted at and teased, waste meant to go overboard continuously found its way into the place allocated to Kyle to rest his weary head. *'Not so full of himself without his lovers protection,'* No one to turn to, in the absence of anywhere to bath and clean his clothes, it wasn't long before the young male described as being picture perfect, resembled a dirty and diseased ridden vagrant. Unkempt and made to stay out in the cold winds, burning sun and heavy rains, his health began to deteriorate. Without Roman, Kyle was deprived of his basic needs and began struggling to find fresh water and food. *'How long would it take Roman to prove his point?'* Lay smelling, shivering, wet and cold, Kyle feared it would take too long.

"Get away from me." The one who had once and for three years welcomed him with open arms; turned a struggling and suffering Kyle away like he was vermin. Laughing and joking, when sat alongside the Captain and others awarded roles entitling each to be upper class, Roman shook off Kyle's pleas for help, discarding his concerns. Roman sent Kyle back to be with those who threatened, physically bullied and continuously teased.

'Dead?' No one admitted to having any knowledge about what happened to the naked and battered body found dumped inside one of the lifeboats. Rumour was that each crew member had taken his turn with the male lay bleeding and bruised, but no true man was going to admit to having raped another. *'What had Roman done?'* Battered, bruised and bleeding, having given instruction for the body to be laid out and prepared for burial, the one to have rejected Kyle in his time of need, struggled to believe how thin and weak he'd gotten. *'Why hadn't he listened?'* Roman had intended to take his much loved cabin boy back under his wing and into his arms once the disruptive voyage was complete. Cleaned up and covered by a single white sheet, the body of a young Kyle Benson wouldn't be examined for evidence. *'Dead!'* The crews doctor said there was nothing anyone could do. *'Killed?'* Roman didn't want to think about what had been inflicted to cause a young, fit and healthy male to surrender to death. *'Murdered?'* Had those to inflict what they had; been aware what they were doing could kill? Yes, Kyle had been murdered. *'Death by mis-adventure?'* The Captain in-charge of the unruly crew declared the sudden death an unfortunate accident. *'Murder?'* Mr. Roman Rich Sapphire couldn't feel or be more guilty if he'd murdered Kyle himself.

An unfortunate accident, Captain Ward wanted to throw what he saw to be a terrible mistake overboard, willing to feed what remained of Kyle to the fishes. *'No family meant no one to miss him.'* No body meant no paperwork to fill in at the next port of call, Roman said he wanted the body bond and boxed, so Kyle could be returned to the country he came from. *'Lovers?'* Neither had said it, but both knew. If unable to carry out what were Roman's orders; Captain Ward was told he could look for another ship to sail when next they hit land.

Witch

Roofless and reckless, about to be caught with his pockets full of diamonds, Roman slipped what he'd taken into the pocket of the one to have replaced Kyle by his side. Not as loyal, not as handsome, sex with Peter French was nothing but sex and when the court found the younger male guilty of theft; sentencing him to death by hanging; sex with Peter would never happen again. *'Not following the arranged prison visit.'* Paid to turn a blind eye, prison guards took the money and left him to it. Thrilled by the thought of other prisoners watching as he took and encouraged his condemned lover to perform oral sex on him, Roman shown and felt no shame in becoming someone who cared about no one but himself. Unrecognisable in the dark, his facial features hidden beneath the large oversized hood of his heavy black cloak, having had sex in a prison cell with a man about to be hung for something he didn't do, the eldest Sapphire brother believed there was nothing he wouldn't and nothing he couldn't get away with. *'Except revealing his true sexuality.'* A man who believed he could do anything, couldn't believe it when told another two of his cargo ships had gone missing. *'Lost at sea.'* With others waiting in the wings to take over the journeys he could no longer accommodate, Roman was forced to conduct more and more of his business on dry land. Having lost his brother and told there was no more family wealth to come his way, his selling the ships he had for half their worth, left Roman counting his pennies while struggling to save the pounds. Able to live on the income generated from his warehouses, he should have been grateful for what his widowed sister-in-law provided. His rent and all domestic costs, weekly food packages and medical care when needed, watched because neighbours reported a single male not coping. Roman's thirst for revenge overshadowed what was being done to keep him safe and sane.

Moving from seaman to warehouse and storage manager, the man to have enjoyed life on the waves, struggled to stable what wobbled and felt unsteady when on dry land. Unable to flaunt his sexual preference when amongst those who were less open minded, his becoming more and more flamboyant with every birthday, from his late twenties into middle-age; saw the last Mr. Sapphire taking what he wanted and rarely giving anything in return. Keeping his vow never to fall in love again, his sexual encounters became more dangerous. *'Rent boys.'* The more thrilling meant more expensive, it didn't take much to get a man unhappy with his lot, to part with what was his dwindling fortune. Sex, drugs and gambling, with his businesses halved and his way of living subsidised by what he saw to be handouts.

Aware Rosa saw everything her husband Reece had been blind to, unaware of the fact it was those on his sister-in-laws payroll who sometimes saved him, coming to his aid when things on the streets got rough. Roman surmised, but never questioned the deep thinking females thoughts. *'Aware Rosa knew his truth.'* Living a life being paid for by others; Roman Rich Sapphire became a bitter man, fast becoming a shadow of the one he once was.

An addict, addicted to a life of drugs, gambling and illicit sex, perhaps it was a justifiable end for a man who lived his life believing he was above all others. Forty was seen by some to have been a good life, while others saw the discovery of the body of the third Mr. Sapphire to be sad. *'Too soon?'* Suicide, or death by misadventure, some said he was killed by a punter he couldn't pay. *'A crying shame.'* Arriving for burial, it was his wish to be lay to rest beside the only person he ever loved. The moving of the Sunday service to the Sapphires' private family chapel to coincide with the funeral; saw what would have been attended by none, observed by many.

Standing alongside those employed by what had become known as the Sapphire estate, most locals turned up to pay their respects to a man they barely knew. *'Sad for him?'* No one relished the thought of living and dying alone. Gone, with the last true member of the family lay to rest beside his lover, his mother, father, brother and unknown sibling, locals asked if things would change? *'Some said the witch had watched from the shadows.'* When burying the body of the one all saw to be the true last Lord Sapphire; those there to fill in his grave and erect the headstone baring his name, reported sighting a hooded figure standing in amongst the trees. *'The Sapphire's true bloodline was no more.'* Would she come out of hiding? Would her father return to take charge of what in the absence of any true family, could be transferred into the Tinker name? Was anyone brave enough to take on what was rumoured to be cursed? *'Sad?'* The lonesome burial of the least known family member was seen to be the end of a legacy, with even those who didn't see Rosa to be a witch, seeing a woman not capable of continuing the families good work alone. *'Women weren't designed for business.'* Witch or widow? No one trusted and so everyone worried about what would become of what was now owned and controlled solely by a woman.

When Grey
turns Black
its time
for a woman
to take control

*E*ntrusted with the daily running of the large estate; Dixon kept tight lipped when questioned about what would become of what appeared abandoned? When asked if he was in contact with Lady Sapphire, Dixon wasn't lying when he shook his head. Doing what they were paid to do, Dixon, his wife Daisy, Mr. Minton and Mr. Ambers continued to attend the regular meetings with financial advisor Mr. Sheldon and estate solicitor Mr. Holt. In receipt of account details and updates, those left to look after what needed taking care of, went from household staff to people of importance within what was their individual realm. Overseeing everything from the fencing off of Ebony Wood to the resurrection of Tinkers Tavern. *'Some changes would take years.'* With neither employee permitted to ask questions, all were required to do what was asked without judgement. Each instructed to attend Roman's funeral and told to host a wake within Tinkers Tavern, where the presence of Mr. Renfred Tinker sitting in a wheelchair shocked everyone.

'An aged man with a younger wife?' For those wanting to raise a glass to the established businessman to have passed, there was ale, wine and pies, savoury and sweet. A note Daisy saw as written by the hand of Lady Sapphire said all left over food was to be distributed to those in need. When those brought in, to cater, left, leaving everything behind, those to have sat and spent the time talking about what was to become of the Sapphire estate, shared the alcohol and set about taking the pies to the local families they saw as being appreciative of the gesture.

Not back to stay. *'Few wanted the tavern reopened.'* Locked up and abandoned for most of the time, a work in progress, many to attend the wake wondered what they were seeing when sighting what looked to be a wall dedicated to the Sapphire and Tinker families. *'A family tree?'* A place haunted by the lost souls of the past, opening the tavern for the day, was done in hope that

Witch

someone would see the potential. Renfred was there to answer the questions no one asked, because no one local wanted to take responsibility for the place ready to accommodate a community needing a place to meet, able to provide space, comfort and refreshment. A place able to welcome people wanting to rest and stay. All commented on how good the tavern was looking, different, no one living in the village or neighbouring town wanted to take on what they saw to be an ill fated business.

Safe, all employed by the one in control of the Sapphire estate were assured they would keep their well paid position and live in their allocated homes as agreed. *'Homes for life.'* Loyalty and hard work was rewarded with comfortable shelter and money enough to live a humbled but good life. Asked to meet with Mr. Sheldon following one of what would be many meetings. Mr. Dixon handed over monies earned from the stable business he and his wife established in Lady Sapphires name. Aware that locals disliked the one to have left, the couple wanting to show gratitude used their employers middle name of Ruby when naming what they called Ruby's Stabling, a business which would grow and see its' name adapting when becoming Ruby's Ridding School and Stables.

"The money is yours." The suited and tie wearing male said he would be happy to help the couple set up a new business account and sort how they went about paying taxes. Shocked, once he realised he was a man of means, Dixon agreed he and his wife were happy to continue running what was to be registered as their business. *'People with money.'* Those to have been employed by Lord Reece and his good Lady wife, were seen to be on the road to living easy. *'Protected by the witch.'* Unrest was enviable when others found life and them earning a living difficult. *'Gone?'* Those entrusted to look after what had been left behind, said they didn't know where Rosa was.

*D*isappearing into the night, when last Dixon laid eyes upon Lady Rosa, he saw fear and not evil in her tear filled eyes. *'Gone?'* Unable to stay, she left alone, vacating what was her luxoury filled home to go who knew where? With wealth enough to go wherever she wanted, Daisy refused to believe the Lady of the manor had left to live within the protecting shadows of Ebony Wood. Top hotels with clean marble floors and deep soft carpets, not a forest with its' leaf covered cold and hard ground. Bright shinning chandeliers, not darkness created by the thick heavy branches of a thousand trees. Why hideout in the cold, when one had funds enough to relax and recuperate in comfort? Believers said the first witch of Ebony Wood had no need for all things homely and nice. Returning to where she came from, the only thing everyone agreed on, was the fact Rosa, like all other members of the Sapphire family, was gone.

Leaving in the middle of the night, had her departure not disturbed the horses; Dixon would never have seen her go, carrying a small bag which appeared to be filled with nothing, dressed in long layered clothes beneath her full length, hooded cloak, Rosa looked good no matter what she was wearing. *'Startled?'* It was clear she hadn't expected anyone to be outside in the dead of night. *'The moon was full.'* If it wasn't for the natural illumination shinning down; he would never have seen her say the words goodbye and take care. *'Who was taking care of her now?'* She shouldn't have had to go, explaining why she couldn't stay. *'Not strong enough,'* The female left on her own, feared for her life. *'She wouldn't survive should those to have taken & tortured her once, decide to do it again.'* Goodbye and take care. Keeping to himself what he saw, it was when those given new homes within the village and town moved out of the staff quarters, locals realised Lady Sapphire was gone. *'In hiding?'* Some suspected the female left to fend for herself by her menfolk, was living within the boarded up house, with some accusing those securing the building of aiding the witch in her plight to avoid detection. *'The witch of Ebony Wood?'* How could any woman protect herself from what those out to get her, were able and willing to inflict? Some heard, some said they had seen, but no one ever found the one they would never stop looking for. *'Dead? If not yet, she would die one day.'* Everyone died eventually. Until her death, where could she be?

A place built for her by the man to become her husband, their special place to escape to, the chosen location wasn't meant to be easy to find. Their very own piece of paradise. While their fathers' enjoyed one another's company, exploring what there was to do within and on what was the Sapphires' extensive land, Reece and Rosa escaped into Ebony Wood to discover a place each said would be the place they would live, one day. A shed? When awarded the job of constructing what was to become a lovers hideaway, Mr. Gregory Ralph said he could do much better than what Reece and Rosa planned.

A man to have found his way in the expanding construction industry. Having met when attending the same private boys school, Reece calling upon the one he knew to be able to help; was because he didn't want anyone local knowing how to find what he wanted building. A lodge, discovering a water source nearby called for the construction of a well. *'Lovely,'* A place for them to be, a single storey dwelling. Solid and comfortable, built from the wood of local trees on a high rise base of unearthed rocks and stones from the banks of the brook. Rosa said she loved the way Mr. Ralph's creation blended into what caused it to be secluded. Having impressed those to employing and entrusting him with their very personal project, Gregory couldn't wait to show what he discovered and used as the true inspiration for what he said would be a building design he hoped to repeat.

Standing on underground caves, spaces to be used as cellars and extra rooms. Showing what lay beneath their new retreat, Gregory was excited to point out the potential for creating a larger property; should they want it. Reece and Rosa had gotten more than they needed, small and cosy, a private place, their very own space hidden from the hectic world and away from prying eyes. *'Plumbing was basic.'* To keep warm there was an inglenook fireplace containing a large indoor fire pit with seating to three sides, a fire over which one could cook. Basic, when first she left the large house, Rosa ran to the safety of what was the secret lodge within Ebony Wood. *'Not easy to find.'* Those to have created their special place, had done all they could to keep it and its' unique location secret. *'Only easy to get to if you knew the way.'* Only visible if you knew where to look. A pathway of red rose bushes planted in amongst others of varying colour to disguise their true intent. Arrows carved through a mix of full and broken hearts engraved into the thick bark of thirteen especially chosen trees, only the arrows through whole hearts pointed the way as what was there to give direction was also intended to distract. A secret map meant to mislead and prevent others finding those not wanting to be discovered. Discreet, where else could Rosa hide? *'A long time dead.'* Having disappeared into the night and believed to have found her solace within Ebony Wood, never again was more than a fleeting glance reported of the woman blamed for the demise of so many and loss of so much. *'A long time dead.'* Locals to search, believed the lone female had died of a broken heart brought on by untold loneliness and despair, some said she died of guilt and shame. Falling where she stood, the corpse of the witch was said to have lay decaying until it returned back into the earth from where she came, her demise setting her haunting spirit free to wander through the trees until the end of time. There were many who saw the witch of Ebony

Witch

Wood to mean the trees were haunted by the wandering spirit of an abandoned widow.

6: Go

When the body of Mr. Renfred Rocky Tinker was brought home to be laid to rest beside his parents, his son and first wife Ruby-Rose, returned home to lay within the walls of the village graveyard, many a local questioned his widow about the whereabouts of her stepdaughter. Living with her? *'Where was the witch?'* Happy to fulfil her husbands' dying wish. Mrs. Juliet Tinker felt herself being watched closely by those suspecting her of knowing more than she was willing to say. *'The next Lady of Sapphire Manor?'* Mr. Tinkers' widow assured all to ask; that she would be returning to take care of what was her and late husbands' home and fishing trip business. *'Had she met the witch?'* Surely a daughter would visit her father and introduce herself to her new stepmother. *'Had Rosa attended the wedding of Renfred & Juliet?'* Surely a father would want his only daughter by his side when celebrating such a happy day. *'Would the witch attend her fathers' funeral?'* Those with unanswered questions would love to see the wedding photographs Juliet said to be all she needed to remember the good man she felt proud to have known, lucky to love and proud to be loved by.

A couple to have found one another when each needed someone, happy to tell what had become of the man to have been innkeeper and played a vital role within a close village community. *'An accident,'* Many had seen how Renfred was to spend his final years confined to a wheelchair but none had asked why? Thrown overboard, *'Mermaid rumours abound.'* Juliet said the night trip to have almost cost him his life, was nothing more than an experiment gone wrong. *'Night fishing?'* Dropping his flamed torch onto the deck of the tour boat; Juliet explained how what caused panic and mayhem amongst those struggling to dampen the flames before they took

Witch

hold failed to notice Renfred no longer being there. Blaming what wasn't intentional; on his having seen a mermaid. Renfred being knocked overboard in what was the commotion, was because he was an ageing man becoming unsteady on his feet. *'Gone?'* Few heard the splash to indicate his having entered the water, with the flames of the fire extinguished, all onboard the fishing boat saw Renfred reappear on the other side of the boat, under for who knew how long? Unharmed except for the fact he could no longer walk, Renfred said he'd scarified his legs to the sea maiden so to save his life. *'An old romantic?'* Juliet said those living by the rolling waves of the ocean loved nothing more than a good story because all good stories helped, when it came to attracting those with money to spend. *'A chance of seeing a mermaid?'* The story being told turned what was dominated by wannabe and experienced fishermen into a pleasure cruse adapting to accommodate a mix of intrigued males, females and families. *'Never one to miss a given opportunity.'* Those to have known the innkeeper well, smiled when being reminded how relatable, friendly, generous and good story teller he was.

A stranger to what surrounded her, Juliet's requests were simple, a quiet and short service prior to the committal of the late Mr. Tinkers' body into the ground. Lay to rest beside the remains of his parents, within the same plot of land as his son and first wife. *'A selfless act?'* Juliet said the body of her second husband being buried in the churchyard of the village where he was born and raised was only right.

"A good man who once played a vital role in providing a much appreciated, some would say needed service here within our village." The male standing before the altar of the church of St Julian's hoped his words would remind those there to pay their respects; of what had been the good times. "A man who suffered great loss. Mr. Tinker brought up his only daughter Rosa alone, helping her to become a strong, independent woman. A pilar of the community, Renfred Tinker was a man who would help his neighbour and see every stranger as a potential friend." The man of the cloth didn't look old enough to remember the innkeeper to have left the place he loved; in fear of his life, truth was; like many of his generation, father Joel Connor had spent his childhood waiting outside Tinkers Tavern while his old man participated in drinking ale and playing cards. Ten years younger than the female accused of being a witch, Joel remembered the pretty young thing who always had a kind word, a jug of homemade lemonade and sometimes a piece of cake or a biscuit to share with him and those told not to go far. Allowing youngsters to shelter inside the stables should the weather turn bad, Rosa was always kind to those left by parents in need of alcohol infused refreshment. *'Caring & kind, A natural nurturer of the weak & vulnerable,'* Joel believed both Mr. and Miss Tinker should and could be proud of one another and the people they were. *'Good people.'*

Giving thanks, Juliet said she was grateful for all the kind words and pleased to see some; there to say farewell.

"Renfred will be smiling." She sighed.

"He was a good man." Joel assured the widow what he said was how he remembered the innkeeper and his only daughter. "I never agreed with what people did." He attempted to apologise for what he saw to be the sins of his elders. "I don't agree with what some think." Juliet told Joel he had no need or reason to apologise for the misunderstandings of others.

"Renfred never stopped loving this place." With those to have attended the short service and quick burial heading for their individual homes. Mrs. Tinker was in no rush to follow. *'Guilt, or curiosity?'* Being a wise woman of the world, Juliet knew those to have attended, had done so because they had questions. Smiling when asked about the existence of mermaids, Juliet told the man to have appointed himself as being there for those believing in and feeling in need of God; how everyone had a right to believe in something. *'Was fiction what made fact less scary?'* Some would say there was nothing scarier than a witch.

"There is a lot of this place to love." Joel agreed to understanding why someone born into a village like Déspoina would find it difficult to leave it all behind. Yes, he agreed how sometimes it was the belief and not what, a person believed in, which was able to provide what was needed by those in need. "Have you met his daughter?" Warned villagers and townsfolk would attempt to gain the information they sought, the female visiting out of necessity replied by saying she and Renfred had enjoyed a happy marriage.

"Too old to have a family of our own." She sighed as she looked down at the place marked with the names of Renfred's late wife and lost son; a headstone on which a fresh inscription told how her; husband had returned to those he should have never been without. Returned to a place Renfred called picturesque and peaceful. "He said this was the perfect location for the good lord to hide the gateway to heaven." She smiled. Admitting to believing that the gateway had to be somewhere? *'Why not there?'* Clean, tidy and picture perfect, the young man to have taken over the upkeep of the church and spiritual well-being of his congregation; agreed to being lucky to live and work within such beautiful surroundings.

"Would you like me to show you around." Joel offered when hearing how Renfred's widow wanted to see as much of what had been his home as she could before going back to continue her life by the sea.

Friendly and informative, having gained entry into the grounds surrounding the Sapphire manor because of who she was, expected and respected by those responsible for the security of the land and building owned by her step-daughter-in-law. Juliet was welcomed and advised to be careful when given keys permitting her entry into whichever building she wanted to see.

"Of course." Called to greet the first visitors in years, Dixon said father Connor was always welcome. Happy to show the two around the stables, chapel and private burial ground, Dixon said they should take care when inside the main house. Warned those responsible for taking care of the Sapphire estate may not have opened up the windows or curtains in a while, Dixon apologised for no one having seen fit to run around with a duster in years. Warned how some of what stood covered by sheets resembled figures, Juliet admitted to being curious, not frightened, not there with a view of taking up residence, when telling how Renfred spoke of the times he spent with his good friend Lord Raymond, Juliet said all she wanted, was to see what her mind had pictured.

"Nice to see." When asked if she was looking to find anything in particular, the stranger in town said she just wanted to feel close to her late husbands' memories one last time. *'Closer, she had visited her third port of call once before.'*

A chance few would ever get. Stood looking at the place her husband spoke of with more fondness than anywhere else, Juliet said she hoped the hostelry which remained boarded and locked for its' own protection, would find a new keeper soon. The grave yard, the manor house and Tinkers Tavern, Renfred asked that Juliet place pictures, a postcard and their story on what was the large feature wall displaying much more than the interwinding of two family trees. *'The mermaid tale?'* An intriguing account of what Renfred swore to be the true reason he spent his final years unable to walk, written in his own words by his own hand Joel said it was often the unbelievable which created what was believed most. One wedding picture, a simple black and white shot of the two on their quiet day, when comparing the face of her husband on the day they wed to his face shinning from the photograph of his first wedding day Juliet said their being a difference, was how it should be. "We never forget our first true love and nor should we." She smiled when placing photographs of Renfred with his mother and father and one of him with both his daughter Rosa and son Rock where each should be. *'Filling in the gaps?'* When Joel asked about her wedding, Juliet said they hadn't wanted a fuss. Second time round for both, the widow described her second marriage as being one of companionship. Two people being there for one another because neither wanted to continue living on their own.

"Not you?" Joel questioned her taking over what belonged to a family she was a part of. Shaking her head, the one insisting she was only looking, said she was happy with her lot, agreeing to it being a shame no one wanted to take on the vast establishment designed to bring people together. Sorry, with a business to run and a home she loved, Juliet admitted to being a busy lady. Sad, she failed to see what some admitted to being afraid of. *'Haunted?'* The oldest building in the village, when describing what they feared, those afraid; preferred the word cursed. "It's a fine building." Joel said locals were stubborn for boycotting the establishment which had once been the hub of the community.

"Sad," Juliet said she hoped the next generation would be more forgiving and open minded.

"Time will tell." Joel sighed. "You really don't mind your husband being buried alongside his first wife?" The maturing male asked the question he found himself asking ever since receiving the request to oversee what had been the last wish of Mr. Renfred Tinker.

"His first true love." Smiling, the female who was old enough to be his mother, perhaps his grandmother; corrected what she heard Joel say. "And their son," She reminded the one struggling to understand, how her late husband had much to be brought back for. "When I die, I will be buried alongside my first true love." Happy to explain what she and Renfred had understood since the first day they met, Juliet repeated how everyone only had one true love. "Many of us find friends and companions as we travel through life, but when a love is true, it's the only love one will ever have."

"Rosa and Reece," Joel sighed before revealing how he and others his age never believed what was rumour entangled in amongst myth and lies.

"Life goes on." Thanking him for his help and company, when back on the road by the graveyard and approached by her driver; ready to take her home, Juliet bid Joel goodbye. A hooded figure? Squinting his eyes as the sun blinded and took from him any clear vision, the one waving his visitor goodbye felt certain he saw someone? *'Who?'*

Stood looking down on the newly laid grave of Mr. Renfred Rocky Tinker, Father Joel Connor felt shocked to see a small posey of wild flowers alongside a card which said. *'Miss you Daddy.'* Had Juliet distracted him so Rosa could visit? If there, where had Lady Sapphire gone? If she was to show herself, in the same way she had always helped him; Joel felt sure he would do everything he could to assist her. *'Had he seen the witch?'* Years had come and gone, things and people had changed, with those to have been the next generation beginning to create a generation of their own, Joel Connor hadn't seen himself being a man of God, but enjoyed overseeing the day to day running of Déspoina's multi faith church. *'Had he seen the witch?'* If he was to mention what he thought to have been, people would ask if there was anyone with her, no longer wandering the trees on her own. People blamed the witch of Ebony Wood for being responsible for the many children to have gone missing since the day she disappeared?

Disappeared

It is believed two year old Emily Carter ventured into Ebony Wood, never to be seen again.

Witch

*N*oise, there was always noise, people everywhere and not enough space, so many voices; not even the loudest got to be heard. Lucky to have the small two bed cottage, unlucky, her parents' didn't know how to stop having more children than was comfortable. Eight into two didn't fit, not even with her mother and father using the downstairs parlour to sleep in. No sofa, dad had a comfy chair tucked into the corner beside the six seat dinning table. Six chairs meant some sitting on the floor or letting their meal go cold while waiting their turn. One double bed in each room meant everyone having to share, three girls, three boys and parents' all of who fought almost as much as each loved the other. Noise filled because everyone was shouting and no one listening. The eldest, how was she meant to develop and improve the basic skills said to be needed to improve ones life. Loving her family dearly, she believed her life could and should amount to more. Lucky to be provided with a place of education, Maria wasn't normally the type encouraged to learn how to read, write and understand numbers. Wanting to do well, when inside the classroom she was able to do her best, seen to be bright, her struggle was because she was unable to continue her learning at home. *'A girl?'* When home; her finding the space and having time for herself was impossible.

Impractical, her mother needed her to help with the house and the little ones, a daughters' duty, her father called her learning nonsense and a waste of her time when she was destined to be a wife and mother. Told to stop her dreaming and remember her place, Miss Maria Molloy was told to be content with being like everyone else. Destined to find herself a good man, set up home and have a family. Maria's only male friend was Bernard Berry, known to his family and friends as Blu, Maria being close to young master Berry meant her knowing he wasn't the type of boy who would grow up to marry a woman. A couple who were friends, children seen by their parents to be on the brink of becoming adults, the two were finding the world around them confusing. Misunderstood, neither wanted what was expected, Blu and Maria said them becoming man and wife could be a way for each to get what it was they truly wanted and the only way of them living a life worth living. Promising to be there to support one another, both were keen to learn more and achieve everything they could to create what each hoped for and wanted. A different future was what both Maria and Blu said they needed.

Talking about what the future held, each aimed to become what they wanted to be, Maria saw herself standing in the classroom and Blu wanted to enter the world of law so he could make a difference to what he saw as a cruel and unjust legal system. Ambitious, while others sat behind the small wooded desks contemplating their ability to go into service for the Lords and Ladies of the city, Maria and Blu saw themselves standing where those they looked up to; stood. Never before had the young been given so much opportunity; yet still their elders wanted them to follow what tradition said they should. *'Women became wives, men worked.'* Escaping what would be, wasn't going to be easy. Working hard to have her dream come true was a path cluttered with obstacles, but with Blu by her side to give encouragement and support Maria saw the two achieving much and upsetting no one. *'Their secret to keep.'* She wanted a career which would be hindered by her having children of her own and he needed a wife in name only.

People causing noise, loud, distracting and leaving no space to allow a person to think. Outside in the small rear garden of the family cottage; Maria was told to beat the carpet hanging over the washing line when what she wanted to do was to sit and read the next chapter of the book her teacher said she must study. A good girl, Blu was a good boy and together they would walk the outskirts of Ebony Wood until finding the ideal spot to sit and talk, sometimes laying on the ground to read beneath the warmth of the afternoon sun. Sharing and caring, each would be there for the other and when one spoke the other would listen.

Ridiculed for paying attention in the classroom, in the absence of the cotton mill to have been the largest employer in the area, Blu was told he should concentrate on understanding how to work the land. *'A farmhand?'* Blu had never liked getting his hands dirty and hated when having to assist with the annual picking and harvesting of local crops. Low paid hard work, Blu also hated the way his fathers' employment left him grumpy and tired while paying the minimum possible. A daily rate no matter how long the hours, missed days went unpaid and half days had to be made up with at least another half. Proud of his father, Blu wasn't built the same and Maria didn't ever want to be anything like the mother she admired for her patients and natural homemaking skills. A good partnership, different, neither Maria or Blu wanting the responsibility of a family would mean neither having anyone but him and herself to worry about. *'No one to concern them but themselves?'*

Intelligent and happy go luck, both teenagers saw how them getting through what was happening would lead to each achieving the future which when together; they were able to foresee. Beat the carpet, bath the baby and pick up the bread from the bakers. The quicker her chores were completed, the more time she would have with Blu. Saturday meant a morning of doing what needed to be done followed by an afternoon of walking, talking, reading and exploring what both wanted to be. A busy noise filled morning, barely time to catch her breath. Smiling, when others in the village square didn't smile back, Maria wondered what was happening? *'Did she have bubbles from the babies bath in her hair?'* Was there something on her face? Something in her teeth? Why were people looking at her like there was something she should know? Waiting in line for the bread, milk and eggs to have been preordered, Maria overheard her elders asking if they heard about what happened? *'A tragedy?'* Some said it was a crying shame, some said only the good die young and some said things were rarely as they seemed. Unable to hear the whispered details, Maria walked home aware someone had suffered a terrible misfortune, only when seeing Blu's mother leaving her house with her head bowed and tears in her eyes did she realise who?

An accident, a mishap caused via misadventure, the wrong place at the wrong time? *'Why was there no one to help him?'* Suicide? *'Why was he on his own?'* Was what happened his doing, or a cover for something done by somebody else? Everyone was sorry, all sympathised with the parents to have lost their only child, but no one asked why? Found hanging by clothes to have gotten caught on a tree branch and tighten around his fragile young neck as he struggled to break free, his feet were said to have been inches from reaching the ground. How? It was believed Blu had slipped when making his way down out of the branch filled tree, but no one questioned why he'd climbed up into the branches? Upset and angry, along with his life; Blu no longer being there saw all plans crumble.

Two deaths in the same day, one resulted in the burying of a body and the other left someone feeling lost, with nowhere to go. Why hadn't he come to her? Blu always came looking for his friend when in need of feeling safe. Who would she go to now? Upset turning to distress, running from the graveside into the woods; Maria was found kicking the tree said to have taken her friend, their future and her everything. Her teacher, not one of her parents, Mr. and Mrs. Molloy had other children in need of care. Mr. Robert Carter was the one to hear her sobbing when out walking his dog Sprog, the springer spaniel had led his owner to where Miss Molloy sat up against the cold dark tree, her knees raised and her head in her hands. Upset and angry, her teacher handed her his handkerchief and asked if she was hurt?

"Sorry," His loss of a pupil meant him knowing she had lost a good friend, telling her to dry her tears Mr. Carter gave the fifteen year old a hug.

Not her father, her parents said they were sorry, but they had more children than her and the way she was feeling to consider. Sorry for Mr. and Mrs. Berry, Micheal and Marsha told their eldest daughter she would get over losing her friend. Not her dad, in the arms of her teacher Maria felt safe, saved. He said he would help her feel better, encouraging the one he called his star student, to meet with him for extra tuition outside the classroom.

Aware of her shattered dream, the one responsible for her education, said he could help her achieve what she wanted. His undivided attention and extra learning, secret because her parents saw what she was working towards to be foolish. Sometimes at his house, sometimes in the classroom after school closed, some accused the two of exchanging glances not appropriate for a married man and the child he'd taken under his professional wing. Working, talking, laughing and sometimes crying because when aiming for what she wanted Maria remembered what she lost. When with Mr. Carter, Maria felt able to do anything, able to give courage her teacher helped a frightened maturing female to feel safe.

It was never meant to happen, it never crossed their minds and wasn't his intention. Brief, hands touching by accident, the two had long since stopped noticing how closely they sat when together. Not planned, Robert Carter loved his wife. When their eyes met, both saw what should never come to fruition. Not right, it should never have happened, but when it did, it happened again and again.

Pregnant? When Robert Carter asked his wife to speak with the young girl feeling sick, dizzy and faint Mr. Margaret Carter told her husband his fifteen year old student was expecting a child. Pregnant? *'No!'* Maria Molloy didn't want what she'd grown up seeing her mother having to do. Watching how the two exchanged knowing glances and aware of the amount of time they spent together, Margaret told her husband he should be ashamed and asked how he could be so stupid and thoughtless. *'An idiot,'* Telling others the baby had been fathered by Blu wouldn't work because her dear sweet friend had been too long dead. An abortion? The teacher said he would pay, but his wife refused to stand back and put someone through what could damage them for the rest of their life by leaving them eternally scared. When Maria became hysterical saying her parents could never know Mrs. Carter said she would think of something to keep what the three took to calling, their secret.

Mr. Carter continuing to help Maria with her learning was supervised by his ever watchful wife, keeping the teen healthy, hydrated and well fed. Being a professional seamstress meant Margaret adapting the youngster clothes to cover and disguise what grew. Tight corsets, wider strapped bras and panels added to new and her existing outfits, Margret did for Maria her washing.

"Your child is our child now." While the teenager struggled not to show what was growing, Mrs. Carter made a bump and loosened out her own dresses, telling friends and neighbours she was the one with child. Late in life, but not unusual, Mr. Carter hoped the private doctor paid to tell them his wife had been born minus a womb, wouldn't visit the village where others would see them starting the family he said they could never have.

Out with classmates, those Maria befriended were few, intelligent and asked to continue their studies beyond what was the norm, having shown academic promise. *'A glass of apple cider?'* They were laughing and joking around, doing what teenagers do. Chastised by the couple out walking their dog, when Margaret pulled Maria away from her friends and told her she should go home, those to ask if she was all right; were told she was being put in for a test she needed to revise for. Scolded for being a young girl out enjoying her youth, when the Carters said they would go to her parents', Maria said she was sorry and promised to do what she was told. Yes, she would be more careful and yes, she understood the trouble they would all be in if their secret was ever revealed.

Born in the middle of the night, Emily Carter was said to be the much loved daughter of Mr. Robert and Mrs. Margaret Carter, said to be? He was a teacher and she the local seamstress responsible for ballgowns and wedding dresses, hard workers. *'Older parents?'* They called their baby girl a blessing, but them being blessed hadn't come about the way it should. Leaving her cottage when the pain started, sneaking out, Maria hoped she would be back before needing to explain her absence. *'In labour.'* Barely able to walk, she staggered to the only destination she could. No one noticed what no one saw, the married couple ready to take what they wanted, told the one in more pain than she could ever imagine to bite down on a piece of wood, stop crying and push. A teacher not a doctor, a seamstress not a nurse, Mrs. Carter said she could stitch back together any and everything to tare apart. *'A baby having a baby,'* Ill prepared, Maria asked if the vast amount of blood she saw, was normal.

"Is everything all right?" When Maria asked about the baby she heard crying, she was told she should go home as soon as she was able to get up and walk.

"Goodbye," Having walked her as close to her home as he dare, Robert told Maria she could never come to his house again. Warned of how others wouldn't understand and told her parents would disown her because no man would ever want what was used, Mr. and Mrs.

Carter gave Emily's true mother money enough to go away, instructing her to leave, sooner rather than later?

Taken by the witch of Ebony Wood, the baby girl was last seen lay in her pram by the rear door of the Carter family home. A common practise said by doctors to aid sleep. Emily's mother said she did nothing wrong by leaving her child to sleep in the fresh air while she went about her daily chores.

The one they called the witch of Ebony Wood; was the only one to know the truth to have been woven from deceit, wrong doing and lies. Found wandering within the trees, someone too young to be a mother, used and abused by adults taking advantage of fear and naivety. *'Disappearing?'* There was no mention of the teenager who went out one Sunday morning never to return. No one mentioned it when Maria failed to turn up to school, no one said anything when it was her younger brother and second eldest sibling Michael Junior who turned up to collect what was picked up weekly from the bakers, butcher and grocery store.

One year on, the town of Erebus and village of Déspoina joined forces to search for missing baby Emily. Gone, the parents' of Miss Malloy failed to report her sudden disappearance because her being their eldest; meant her leaving home was one less mouth to feed. Maria being almost sixteen was seen as being her time to go find a life of her own. Leaving home alone, one year on from giving birth to a baby girl, Maria returned to take back what was hers. *'Why put two & two together when there was a witch to take the blame?'* Watching and listening for the baby girl to breath her first breath and cry her first cry, neither Mr. or Mrs. Carter knew whether or not the mother to have received no medical intervention had survived? Given money enough to leave town, neither adult calling him and herself the mother and father of baby Emily concerned themselves about where Maria would go, when both influential adults warned she was never to return. One year on from being forced to walk away frail, confused and bleeding. *'Expected to die.'* Stronger, having made a new life for herself in the city where she worked as a nanny, before meeting and marrying a man who said he understood her need to be reunited with the child taken from her aching arms. When able, Maria returned to take back what was hers. Stopping to leave a gift for Blu by what locals renamed the hanging tree, some blamed the doll placed high in the branches; for the death of many a child who attempted to climb what looked solid and strong; whilst proving to be slippery and sharp.

Babes in Ebony Woods

People in the village of Déspoina & town of Erebus report hearing the sound of children's laughter & babies crying within the trees of Ebony Wood.

Sensational stories, over the years there were many to have gone missing. Runaways, they would never admit to it, but there were parents to have purposely lost the children whose behaviour didn't comply, abandoning a child because they couldn't afford to keep. Unwanted pregnancies? Widows with children who saw themselves as doomed never to find employment, or a man willing to take on what came as a package. Emily Carter was reported to be the first, the youngest, she was far from the last child to disappear when living in or visiting Ebony Wood.

A vast lake of tears, some to go missing were found living and some were discovered to have passed. Some mysteries were solved, but reports recorded many a person to enter the dense shadow filled trees as destined to remain lost. *'Lost in the trees?'* Whatever the outcome, whatever the truth, the witch was the one everyone would continue to blame for any and everything. Whatever the truth, those missing and those to have died due to misadventure, were the only ones to know what had happened.

Blu had done nothing wrong, it wasn't him and it wasn't his fault he was a sensitive boy. *'Sorry,'* His mother told him to go, warning he should return when his angered father had calmed or retired to bed. Only doing what he thought needed to be done. The house being cold meant lighting the fire a necessity, how was he to know he shouldn't have used up all the wood without chopping more. Rain, how was he to know the weather would turn; making damp what needed to be dry so to keep a fire burning. *'Young?'* He was only trying to help. His father called him stupid while his teachers were forever assuring him he was academically gifted. *'A good boy?'* His well meaning mistake meant there being no hot water for his hardworking father to bathe in. A roar and large bright flames, the way he built the fire high and loaded it with logs saw what ignited quickly unable to smoulder for long. *'He was sorry.'* Running as fast as he could to avoid lashes from his fathers' thick leather belt, he worried what would happen when he returned home. Entering the trees, he believed he was being followed, climbing what was large with a mass of low and high branches, Blu didn't want to tire and get himself caught. Shivering, cold and wet, unaware of how long he stayed where he sat up high looking down upon what turned from solid earth to slippery mud. With what had been light and bright turning dark and black, Blu's discomfort had grown from mild to server. Wet and cold. *'A slip & a fall,'* When found, it was believed what had happened was intentional. Had he slipped while making his way down out of the branches? An accident? Had the one loved by his mother and misunderstood by his father;

meant his clothing to rise up, gathering around his neck and squeezing until he could no longer breath? Hung. Young, Master Berry, the boy everyone called Blu was fifteen years old when discovered hanging from what would become known as the hanging tree within Ebony Wood. *'The first, but not the last?'* Maria cried herself to sleep night after night, asking why her friend had left her and questioning whether or not his angered father had caught up with and harmed the son he struggled to accept because of his sexuality. Grabbing at and causing his jumper and shirt to move from tucked in, to up around his neck as Blu's attempt to remove what was being held onto, caused the one pulling him back to strangle him due to his greater strength. Had Mr. Berry lost control, had he not realised when his son stopped breathing and could it be that it was Blu's own father who hung his body where those to discover it wouldn't see what he didn't want them to see?

Unfortunate, careless, copycat tragedies, an easy way to misplace blame or plan suicides? Once the tree was seen to take a life; its' strong and firm branches began to take more. Children found hanging? Bodies discovered to have injuries beyond what was seen to be the redness of the neck; were suspected to have been put where they were found by parents' looking for a way out of difficult, unmanageable sometimes unaffordable responsibilities. No longer able to cope. *'Gone?'* Why was there no one to stop them? Why had no one been able to save them? A simpler question; was how had the young known the best way to attach the ropes and create the nooses used to end what should have continued for longer? Children should be encouraged to become adult, no one would blame the children, but few didn't blame the witch. *'A witch needed the blood of the young to keep herself youthful.'* Everyone loved a good story and in the absence of another explanation, all needed a reason. *'Do witches live forever?'* No one wanted the body of the one seen to be evil, lay to rest inside or anywhere near the village, but there were many wanting to know for sure; when the wicked widow of Lord Reece Ray Sapphire was dead. Afraid to upset the witch, the storms said to be the mystical females weapon of choice, was able to destroy much more than a field of wheat or towering tree. When it felt like one storm followed another, many wondered when what was seen to be them upsetting the witch, would end.

7: Shadows

One way in and one way out, paid handsomely to work under the cover of darkness, they numbered twenty-six, two for each. Told to do the job and get out quickly, people suspected, but not until the evidence was obvious; could anyone say for sure what it was they heard going bump in the night? Whispered voices, the creaking of large wooden cartwheels and the click, click rattle of metal lanterns swaying due to continuous movement and ongoing weather conditions. *'Someone moving something?'* Who and what? What from where and where did they go to? Reports and speculation ranged from the witch coming home, to Ebony Wood being sold to developers? Who?Difficult to see what was easily disguised by the vast mix of bushes and trees, shadows appearing here there and everywhere, strangers moving in and out without saying who they were or why they were there?

'Changing times.' Strangers residing inside the tavern, With no one willing to step into the shoes of the late innkeeper, listened to gossip from locals told how they saw the welcoming rooms within discontented bricks and mortar to be haunted. Cursed, the oldest building in the village was the only refurbished structure to be condemned. Not wanted by those who were once regular visitors, avoided by the next generation and the next because of what were terrifying stories. Tinkers Tavern was believed to be a building ravaged by spirits seeking revenge and there was many a local when running home with a tale to tell when those from out of town first arrived.

Busy, with so many strangers coming, men, a team of labourers there to carry out a task while making it appear like nothing was happening. Instructed to be polite, but not to give information to anyone, those living in the town and village didn't know what to think when they noticed people inside what remained locked and boarded. *'No local dare investigate too deeply into what was said to hold the distressed & wandering souls of the Tinker family.'* Things going bump in the night, strangers moving around after dark.

One coffin transported by two men, none to have taken the job, realised a rotting corpse would be so heavy. *'Bones turning to dust?'* Not being superstitions didn't mean any of the burly labourers were willing to open and look inside at what it was they were moving from one burial ground to another. *'Two families?'* The inscription on the headstones and name plates shown who was related to who while dates revealed which were the most recent to have been committed to the earth. *'Not right,'* Many believed there would be consequences for those disturbing what had been laid and should be left to rest. Told to do what needed doing as fast as they could.

Heavy, hard work, instructed to work in pairs under the shadow of darkness when moving, all men would dig up one body and refill one grave at a time. Transporting the coffin and its' contents into Ebony wood, each was told there would be someone waiting; to show them where to place what was being relocated. Not easy money, what was they were asked to do proved to be more difficult than perceived, when no longer able to manoeuvre the handcart over the rough, uneven maze of uneven pathways and intermittent trails hidden beneath the canopy of dark shadow filled trees, what each was moving, needed to be lifted up and carried on broad, strong shoulders. Heavy? Some saw the work needing more than two men to be completed. When carrying one coffin between two, those carrying, hoped the final destination wasn't far. Two men, one body, one way in and one way out. The plan was to move three coffins per night, with all being paid for their brawn, each was instructed that they would do what some called the treacherous journey only once. *'A secret location?'* Going somewhere once meant less chance of remembering the way. One way in and one way out, each was told they would spend a night in the wood before being sent directly back home.

Heavy, having to stop to rest, Mr. Billy Broughton and Mr. Jerry Milton agreed them being the third and final pair of the night meant them affording themselves the luxury of time. *'No money was worth incurring injury leading to one never being able to work again.'* Three per night, on night four, Billy and Jerry were the last, leaving one pair to make the journey alone on night five. One week, one more night would see everything being how it should be, by the weekend. A job well done, what most expected to be a walk in the park had for all been an eye opening experience.

"Do you think it's a body?" Both having heard others talking; questioned there being treasure, money or items worth selling inside what was used to house a person once dead. Speculation, what was a one way mission meant those they'd met and gotten to know when inside Tinkers Tavern hadn't returned to talk about how things were. "Do you believe in witches?" Unsure if it was nerves or exhaustion, Jerry asked Billy if he'd been drinking before they left? Free food and fast flowing wine, ales and spirits, being the pair to have drawn one the next to last straw meant both having more time to participant in what all agreed was easy to over indulge in. Mumbling and crackling on like a nervous school girl; Jerry asked Billy if he was all right. "I never realised it would be so dark." The one struggling to settle having agreed that they rest continued to look around. *'Told not to talk to anyone.'* Billy asked Jerry if he believed those to have done what they were doing before them had made it home?

"People in the country have nothing better to do than exaggerate simple stories and create gossip." Yes, Jerry had seen what was displayed on the wall, rumour and myth, not good with words, the elder of the two had understood some of what was said to be the beginning of the love story in-which the innkeepers daughter and the Lord of the manor became man and wife. Looking at the pictures more than the words, all being paid handsomely to move two families from where they were, so they could be together, had been instructed to study what was the mingling of the Sapphire and Tinker family trees. "A witch?" He shrugged his shoulders. "Who knows who or what lives out here." He sighed. "But yes," He insisted. "I do believe that the others will be on their way home." Not wanting to contemplate the alternative Jerry said he'd seen nothing which couldn't be explained. Shown the wall of historical facts before signing the agreement and swearing never to reveal the location of the burial ground in the Wood, Jerry worried that he'd missed the something, causing his companion concern. "I don't think there's anything to fear from an elderly grandma wanting her family around her." He said if the Lady of the manor was living, what they were doing would please, not anger the one others were guilty of hounding. "Wild animals?" Jerry revealed what worried him most.

"Lord Reece Ray Sapphire, we're carrying the Lord of the manor, the witches' husband." Billy said, jumping back when the swaying light from his lantern illuminated not only the name plate but also the fast moving, fur covered form of a large rat as it scurried over what the men placed onto the ground beside them.

"Wild life," Shivering and squirming, Jerry shone his lantern to see if there was anything else crawling around where their feet. "Wild animals are unpredictable and like it or not, we're in their world now." He said as he continued looking.

"What kind of animal is that?" Shocked. Billy having shone his light up and around caused his eyes to catch sight of a black figure crouching on the path they intended to take when ready to continue.

"Maybe that isn't the way." Jerry wished he hadn't looked at what his eyes were seeing. Dark? A man? Was it real? In attempt to calm one another, the stunned men said what wasn't moving; could be a statue? "I think we should go?" Assisting Billy in lifting the coffin and changing direction, *'A statue?'* If carved from wood, sculptured from stone or made of bronze, those leaving in haste; agreed what they'd seen appeared lifelike, but could be lifeless. Shocked, a shadow in the dark, both hoped them heading slightly off course to avoid what blocked their path wouldn't result in them becoming lost.

A large black bird? Sure they saw feathers, unsure if what each lay eyes upon was real, man, animal or beast? Neither city dwelling male could say for sure what had happened. *'A fright?'* Rushing, them going as fast as they wanted wouldn't happen when carrying a full adult size coffin. Walking away, were they being followed, nervous and struggling to watch their backs. Walking forward, at different points the two males lost their sure footing, struggling to keep going and questioning their going the right way? Both agreed they shouldn't panic, a statue, a fallen or sprouting tree, both saw it as possible they'd fallen victim to a trick of the dark, seeing something which wasn't what they saw it to be within what was minimal light. Moving, having walked around, both were relieved to reach the place marked with a cross on the map given to follow. What?

When reaching their destination, what flew overhead caused Jerry to duck and Billy to tell his companion to stop panicking. Reaching the burial ground and finding the open grave into which their coffin was to be placed. *'If not living?'* Who was the one they saw stepping out from the shadows, the one who brought calm, nodding a hood covered head. *'The witch?'* Disappearing, if no one and nothing other than wild animals lived within Ebony Wood, who and what had Billy and Jerry seen? Met by a man introducing himself as Hunter, Jerry and Billy agreed to being fine, happy to accept the offer of refreshment when entering the place in which they were invited to stay until morning. Warm and welcoming, each began to relax when sat around the fire set in the inglenook fireplace inside the wood and stone building.

"Did you see anything?" Gathered with those to have arrived before them, Billy and Jerry agreed to having seen nothing either; when made aware of how each burly male looked to Hunter, before shaking their head to the questioned none knew how to reply.

"How can you allow this?" When approached by those in the village to see what was happening and calling it wrong, Father Joel Connor said he had no choice. No name, whoever was doing what was being done had provided all legal documentation preventing anyone from preventing the removal of the Tinker and Sapphire family members. "They're gone." Watching the space to have housed the bodies of Mr. Renfred Tinker, his wife and their baby being filled in, and flattered, those wanting more information were told the semi circle benches engraved with the names of those to have been moved were being installed where grave stones once stood.

"A memorial of remembrance," Joel said what was, had been a long time coming, revealing how he saw the benches as a fitting representation of those who spent their lives bringing people together. Two semi circle benches creating a circle to represent life and encourage the living to take time to rest, two sets of seating which when stood face to face formed a circle to represent a family, a place to gather or sit alone to think about what is important, the dead reminding the living to think about life. Joel said what was being installed in place of what had been taken couldn't be more fitting and right, stating how there should be more benches, more trees and

Witch

places to encourage the living to spend time amongst their dead should they want to.

"Did you see anything?" When word got out about what was happening, those doing what they were hired to do, found themselves attracting attention.

"Who are you?" Asked where they were from and who they worked for? When going in or coming out of Tinkers Tavern, those moving members of both the Sapphire and Tinker family from their resting places, found questions from locals to be plentiful and at times overwhelming.

"You're all mad." Those seen to be selling their souls' were warned to take care and beware. Keeping themselves to themselves the men their to work remained polite whilst not doing much talking, seeing the local village and towns folk as the ones with a problem, most said they were glad their working contract wasn't for longer. *'People trapped in the past?'* Those from the city and larger towns said they couldn't wait to get back to true civilisation.

Work being work, the money offered was to good to turn down. *'Not what was expected?'* What invited strong hardworking men to be part of a team, was advertised in city newspapers and on flyers handed out wherever such manual labourers were seen to hangout. Strong men needed, tempting the tempted, what was printed hadn't explained everything? Taking on those he saw suitable, Hunter believed what he was doing was safe and the right thing to do. Paperwork signed, charges paid, the moving of bodies from one resting place to another needed to be done to stop the ongoing disturbances and constant disruption inflicted on the deceased relatives of the witch. *'Understanding?'* None was stopped from walking away when seeing themselves as being unable to do what would earn each a large pay packet. *'Two men per coffin, six men per night,'* Each man chosen would work digging up what needed transporting and spend one night moving one coffin from one burial site to another. Put up for the duration of their individual contract inside Tinkers Tavern, made comfortable, fed and given free-range of a limited bar, those chosen were told to pick themselves a partner

Stood waiting when Jerry and Billy arrived at the burial ground a little later than expected. Hunter said the large figure with black angel wings to fly overhead was nothing more menacing than a fast moving, low level black cloud. A deer, when they said they'd caught sight of a hooded figure standing within the trees, the organiser assured them he had also mistaken the outline of many a wild deer for the figure of a person; especially when being disguised by the trees and distorted by the light of the moon. Yes, those to have gotten lost and ventured down the wrong path felt sure they encountered something, but no, they hadn't laid eyes on the witch. When joining those to have transported the first and second coffin of the night and hearing how others saw nothing. Jerry and Billy blamed the darkness and their own imaginations, congratulated themselves for finishing the job.

No, none of the men to have entered Ebony Wood after dark and remained within the shadow of the trees until daylight had seen or heard anything to explain the existence of anyone or anything mysterious, because all had listen and agreed with Hunter; when he said there was nothing lurking in the dark which wouldn't be explained in the light. Installing new headstones, crosses and plagues over the graves he dug out by himself. *'The least he could do.'* Hunter told those to have bedded down for the night, they were free to go, directing them to the town of Erebus, the young male showing his gratitude for all the hard work, told those to have fulfilled their contract their belongings were waiting to be collected from Erebus House along with a ticket home.

Some from the village and all from the private burial ground within Sapphire Manor, moving the bodies from one resting, the second couldn't be more private. A small family cemetery created within a secure location which would keep them all safe. *'A family graveyard?'* Erecting statues and installing benches made from fallen trees, Hunter added what he saw as being needed in amongst those who should have shared much more than their last and final resting place.

Completing his mothers' vision, having heard what Jerry and Billy said about seeing something, with one last coffin to be transported Hunter hoped everything would be all right. Not willing to admit to having seen more than numerous shadows during his time in the Wood. *'Told he would be safe.'* Coming face to face with the coffin containing his father, Hunter swore his overseeing what his single parent wanted him to do, would be the last ever time he would enter the place of his birth.

*D*ark Angel? Hunter's search resulted in his finding nothing to indicate another name. Nowhere, no one had recorded the sex of the baby known to have been born on the same day, at the same time, to the same mother as the man who was his father. The sibling of Lord Reece Ray Sapphire, twins, when rearranging and relocating the bodies of his deceased family members; Hunter felt sad not to be able to add more detail to the last final resting place of the burial grounds' youngest occupant. *'Less than a day?'* Dark Angel was said not to have lived for one single second.

Why did such a small box need two, made of wood and the size of a shoe box, Mr. Keith Douglas and Mr. Lonny Bright found themselves taking a deep breath when faced with what they uncovered? A baby? While the simple name plate gave little to no information, the burly males with children of their own hadn't expected to be faced with the coffin of someone so young. *'Tiny?'* Both had seen Dark Angel to mean the black sheep of the family, the child of a forbidden lover, or someone to have lost his or her way. Disowned by the well to do Sapphire family, Dark Angel being permitted a final place to be laid to rest within the families fold, would be because they were blood. What could a baby have done to be buried beneath a name plate indicating something unwanted and unloved? Why hadn't parents' given their child a name? Remembering the notes on the mural wall, Lonny said he couldn't understand a father not wanting to know anything about his deceased child and when checking the dates inscribed on the tiniest of coffins, Keith said it had been a different time.

Lighter and easy to carry, not weightless, both men saw themselves able to get the job done quicker if they took turns to carry what needed to move from outside of to within Ebony Wood. Hand held lanterns, they had no need to use the offered handcart which would become useless before reaching the halfway point marked on their route. Wonderful, being from the city meant both Lonny and Keith seeing the land dominated by trees as fascinating and liberating. The fresh air of the countryside didn't always smell only of what was growing, not always sweet, when what was being used by surrounding farmers to fertilise their fields got transported by the breeze, the stench could become unpleasant. From a place overcrowded with people, what was produced by many a grazing farm animal, smelt ten times better than what was tipped out into the city streets. Dark, more use to smog and fog than clear night skies, Lonny said he never realised there was a time of night when eyes failed to be able to see through the blackness. Taking turns to carry what each saw to be their precious cargo, as one led the other through from where they began, to where they needed to be, neither paid any attention to what felt like being watched by a million eyes.

Owls, bats and foxes, both had to admit to never seeing any of the creatures said to inhabit what was encased by trees. *'Get the job done, get the money & go home.'* All to have agreed to do the work, agreed to wanting the exact same. *'Easy money.'* When together, the men from the city laughed about what they saw to be folklore and superstition. Thanking locals for their advise and countless warnings, those born and brought up in the city, prided themselves on being mens, men, strong and fearless. None was scared of the dark and some were heard to say he hoped the witch in the wood was sexy.

A knocking, dropping the box he carried, Keith said what was inside was tapping to get out.
"You fool." Lonny scolded his younger companion for being stupid. An automatic reaction, he hadn't meant to let the box go, but couldn't help feeling glad that he had. Sure he sensed something dark and heavy wrap itself around him; before whatever was inside the box moved, the tapping caused Keith to jump, his heart almost stopping as the box released itself from his opening hands.

"Don't tell me you didn't hear it." Having fallen and rolled forward, shinning light enough to see where, both men felt daunted to discover the path they were walking ran along and above a steep incline littered with tall grasses, tree clusters and bushes. "Be careful." When faced with what was steep, dark and obstacle filled, Keith suggested they wait till morning.

"We need to find it." The box moving fast meant neither seeing where it came to rest, a mystery. "I can't see it." Lonny insisted Keith help him look when continuing his search. This way and that, when wandering into what needed exploring, the incline wasn't as steep as the darkness indicated it to be. The box couldn't have reached the bottom without stopping. Surreal, both searching for what they lost, watched as feet disappeared into what had never been trodden upon before. "Wait." Believing he could hear something, Lonny told Keith to stand still. To his left, in front, to his right and behind him, moving the light of his lantern with his body, Lonny asked Keith if he could see anything? To his left, in front, to his right and behind, both sensed, both looked, but neither knew what it was they were looking to see. A child? Sure whatever was causing their senses to react was running around, mocking and making fun of their lack of knowing where they were, Keith told Lonny she was playing with them.

"She?" Lonny questioned who Keith had seen when the truth was he hadn't seen anyone. "She just wants to play." The younger male smiled when releasing words which to the one he was with made no sense.

"Who? Where?" Unable to see anything because all there was to see was the dark, Lonny asked Keith if he had found the box. "We won't." Keith said neither would find the box until her playtime was over. Seeing the man he barely knew to be someone losing his mind, Lonny moved what was thick and vast with his feet in his attempt to find what was lost. Not wanting to return home to his waiting family minus the promised money, Lonny told the one with him; to pull himself together and help get back what was gone. Moving like there was someone climbing within its' branches, when the tree by the side of them began to move, Keith told Lonny she would tire soon.

"Hope she doesn't fall." Watching the one watching what moved, Lonny's next step hit something hard, believing he'd found what he needed, when bending down to pick it up, Lonny called out and fell back. A sleeping badger, it was unclear which moved faster, only a baby, a youngster to have lost its' way and fallen asleep. "She's back." Standing over the one to have fallen, stood holding the tiny coffin in his hands; Keith laughed about having seen a grown man frightened by what he called a cute cub. When patting down what was the grave of Dark Angel, Keith told Hunter the nameplate should say Raven and Hunter asked where he'd heard that name?

"Sorry for your loss," Keith thanked the one paying his wage for allowing him to help.

Blamed for any and everything going wrong, many believed what they saw to be the repercussions for the sins of their elders as never coming to an end. A withering widow growing old alone within the shadows of the trees, when the bodies of the Sapphire and Tinker family lay within what was for each, his and her new resting place; many saw it to be because the witch was needed them close while preparing to die. *'Gone?'* Lord Reece Ray Sapphire, his parents' his brother and his brothers' friend Kyle Benson, Dark Angel, those to have lay within the grounds of Sapphire manor, lay close beside Rosa's parents, grandparents maternal and paternal and her twin brother Rock. *'Where was the witch?'* Fulfilling his promise, Hunter took one final look at what he created encased within a waist high dry stone wall, outside of which tall, thick trees stood to form a towering box, some branches overhung into where the graves he'd placed in small rows lay silent. Deceased family members, each body was lay under their own unique headstone adorned with something to represent the people they were and inscribed with the relevant information. Benches made from fallen trees positioned to look in at what was decorated with a mix of ornaments and statues made from wood, stone, mental and marble. In the absence of visitors bring fresh flowers Hunter had planted flowering bushes and evergreens in hope what was dark would always contain, brightness and colour.

8: Legend

Historical happenings dissolving into stories being told by grandparents and parents. *'Fear the witch.'* Words of warning handed down through the generations, all were told how locals laid blame with the one they saw to be bitter, twisted and out for revenge. *'A witch collecting children?'* Actual reasons for mysterious and unsolved happenings washed over the heads of those who would forever see Rosa Ruby Sapphire being the one to blame. *'Runaways, abductions, the lost, the frightened & the Suicidal?'* Legend said a witch needed young blood and no matter what occurred, the myth of the witch of Ebony Wood continued to flourish, turning what was the saddest of true love stories, into a tale of misguided misinterpretation destined to continue for all eternity. *'An old lady who never aged?'* Who else would want a village and town to suffer the loss which for some brought heartache and for all, created mysteries never to be solved.

Believing anyone to enter the wood, would disturb the witch, there were many who feared her return. *'Afraid of an old lady?'* Those giving the warnings where heard to say the age of a female, lost all meaning when she was a woman seeking revenge. *'A need to find her?'* The truth was; no one knew where Lady Sapphire had gone? With sightings since the night she left being nothing more than fleeting glances and a feeling of being watched. *'Old or deceased?'* From burning fire to flickering candles and illuminating lights, whenever they set out in search of what to many appeared mysterious, magical and strange, all agreed wherever the witch was and whatever she had become, she needed to be sought out and destroyed.

Feared without being seen, a story misunderstood, whilst happy to join in with what locals called the annual search for the witches hovel, few believed someone would willingly continue to live in isolation and even fewer could workout how anyone could live comfortably off the land, with nothing but what mother nature provided. *'A witch?'* Whatever Lady Sapphire was, the wife of the Lord of the manor was a woman of wealth. *'Alive?'* In a forever developing and evolving world, the town of Erebus and village of Déspoina moved forward, with searches for the one to have left, becoming more a celebrated tradition than a need, whilst others her age had long since past, not everyone wanted the witch gone.

Reports of encounters with a dark shadow, some to have become lost in Ebony Wood said they'd suffered a confused state of mind. *'Someone living in the Wood?'* Wary of change and rarely willing to accept progress, there were years when locals saw whomever inherited what made up the places in-which they lived; not doing anything to keep the separate areas from becoming an abandoned village and lost ghost town. Rumour becoming legend, as one year dissolved into two, before turning to three, four and five. Ten years passed and twenty years on saw times and what time brought with it moving fast. People living in areas whose remoteness meant being left behind. An ageing population, generations to follow were heard laughing at the reasons given for mass unemployment and poverty in what lay miles from any major city or thriving town.

Thirty years? *'Could a woman survive living alone at the age of fifty-seven?'* Where had she gone? Another thirty years would pass and many to know the story of the witch would pass with them. *'Suspicion & speculation?'* Whatever it was the locals grew up believing, none dared to say anything thought to upset the witch. No matter how open minded or sceptical, all living within the town and village around Ebony Wood, continued to fear the storm.

Progress, things continued to happen, because things always would. In a world where there will always be actions, reactions, events and happenings there are somethings for which the witch and her evil ways seemed the only explanation. Mr. Harold Sheldon and all to follow in his role, said they weren't at liberty to say; when asked if Rosa had vacated the area. *'Live or dead?'* Informing those who were employees about the things needing to be done. *'Gone?'* Her leaving or dying; didn't explain the reported sightings of a cloaked figure keeping watch from the trees. *'Still living?'*

Things which were changing sometimes changed fast. A cocktail bar visited by those traveling from city via what was the new railway. Once Erebus was linked to the outside world via train, locals of both the town and village saw the high class drinking establishments being introduced to attract passing trade, as over priced and too sophisticated. A rail link and new railway station, what seemed imposing brought jobs and visitors into places where everyone knew everyone. Changing too fast, *'Ghost stories to keep people out?'* All blamed what were inevitable accidents on the tracks on the witch being unhappy. Chased off, those to have died could say nothing, while the injured spoke of a cloaked shadow appearing and disappearing amongst the surrounding trees. Trains and a railway station, a ticket office, platform and space for luggage, new ways to travel were seen as progress, giving hope for a new world. All strangers continued to be told, to beware.

From horse drawn carts & carriages to cycles, motorcycles & motorcars, with the moving of time came the changing of everything. From dirt tracks to cobbles, for what was used most there would soon be a smooth, more durable

J Orton

finish as footpaths made way for pavements, roads became busier & transportation faster.

Landscapers, builders, designers and developers brought in to make changes seen to be more user friendly. Installing homes with what for the poorer had always been shared outdoors. Many panicked about such changes incurring a cost none could afford. Simple folk living easy lives, villagers getting by, suddenly found themselves being engulfed by spaces for recreation and the development of workplaces the likes of which none had imagined coming to fruition in their life time. *'Slow & steady.'* When things began changing; those responsible for much of what made up the small town and rural village made changes too. With the passing of time, that which was lived in, worked and looked after by one generation was handed down to another, another and the next. With time moving on, those living within and around the town of Erebus and the village of Déspoina began to change their opinions, outlook and views on what and what wasn't important. *'A growing realisation of what was & wasn't possible?'* With time going forward, the stories of the past, along with much of what many saw to be local history, began to fade into a mix of folklore and myth.

Unsure what was happening, uncertain what would be, those to have assembled as the new board overseeing the Sapphire Estate, said they were following instructions when introducing new and needed establishments. *'Nothing they could do.'* Told what would happen, the concerns of locals began to grow when noticing what had stood empty for years; being reopened. Strangers brought in to repair and transform the private chapel, barns, outbuildings and the stables belonging to the Sapphire manor.

A crematorium and large walled memorial garden, no matter ones age, people naturally feared what they didn't understand? *'Avoiding opposition.'* Locals weren't wanted to work on what was to include renovations to the large Sapphire manor house. Struggling to move with the times and go forward, what was being done was said to be needed. *'Old fashioned & set in their ways.'* For some it felt like the world and everything in it was moving too fast.

Twenty, thirty, fifty, sixty, eighty years went by in the blink of an eye.

Assured all changes were being undertaken with care and consideration, those now of age to partake in the consumption of alcohol welcomed the raising from the ashes of Tinkers Tavern. *'Tired of having to go into town.'* Villagers wanting, what was said to have been the hub of their community, welcomed the under new management, opening soon sign, while elders able to recall historical facts, worried about what would happen and who would be able to answer their questions? Who? In the absence of someone local; willing to take responsibility for the building seen to be the heart of all things to have gone wrong, everyone questioned who the new innkeeper/landlord would be? *'A brave man to take on what everyone saw to be haunted by the wandering spirits of the past.'*

Arriving in the early hours of the morning, the weary couple to have travelled by rail and road, saw what they found to be interesting. Discovering the place which was to be their home and livelihood boarded and locked for its' own protection, the young enthusiastic pair thought maybe they'd arrived at the wrong place? Shrouded behind large tarpaulin, people had wondered for years about what would happen to the oldest building in the village. Returned to its' former glory, fate and the actions of the masses had seen any plans for the structure; put on hold for what felt to be an indefinite time. *'A cocktail bar,'* In the absence of a traditional hostelry, the majority hoped what had spent years being occupied intermittently by visiting strangers, would be brought back to life in the shape of a place for locals to meet. *'A restaurant?'* When the under new management signs were erected, rumour and speculation was riff. Mr. and Mrs. Sapphire, *'Unexpected?'* Arriving unannounced *'Would they be accepted?'* Tired and a long way from home, sweeping in under the shadow of darkness, they unlocked the main door. *'How?'* Not surprised to find no one out in the village street in the earliest hours, those there to begin a new life, hoped there was a bed made up for them to sleep in. With what was brand new, in need of uncovering, the loving couple agreed whatever dust to have gathered could be removed in the morning. *'Home?'* The male entitled to be called the new Lord Sapphire, had no want or need to take up residence inside the large manor house. A descendant of the late Sapphire family, Hunter and his wife Lacey saw being landlord and landlady of Tinkers Tavern to be worthwhile.

A son? The arrival of Mr. Hunter Rock Sapphire and his wife Lacey Belle, answered what for years had remained a mystery. Answering a question asked over a thousand times, the witch had given birth to a son from who Hunter was a bloodline descendant. *'A new generation of the Sapphire family,'* Hunter and his wife smiled when reading the stories and seeing the few pictures, words and photographers said to personify the true and mysterious story reported to have been the life of the woman he called his great grandma. *'A Witch?'* Hunter laughed at what he saw to be a sensationalised tale. *'Genius,'* Having inherited what was family owned and taken the time to look into what was his ancestry, Hunter had discussed with his wife what he saw to be a business opportunity too good to miss. *'Easy money.'* Having examined the artefacts and recorded evidence, Lacey agreed to support her man; in wanting to be a more hands on land and property owner.

Witch

With the means to live wherever in the world they wanted, when last Hunter spoke to his great grandma, she gave her blessing and told him to do what he saw as being for the best, in the same breath as telling him to stay safe. *'The witch of Ebony Wood?'* A grandfather told his intrigued grandson of how his great grandma was far from evil. *'Interested in what was interesting.'* With personal beliefs, mindsets and perceptions forever changing, a young and enthusiastic Hunter Sapphire saw what was his families' history, to be something able to generate gains significant enough to help all living in the village of Déspoina to prosper.

Applauding those to have interpreted the facts, telling the life stories of those who were his blood relatives. *'A feature wall,'* Hunter being who he was and coming from where he did, saw what would become a tourist attraction as being unique. Stories he heard told by his elders mixed in amongst tales to have been greatly exaggerated. Hunter continued to collect reports which turned his great grandma Rosa into a local legend. *'Quaint,'* Told much, neither Hunter or his wife knew what to expect.

The large mural covering the largest blank wall inside Tinkers Tavern displayed two family trees becoming intertwined, to tell the story of the one locals chased out of town for being a witch. The Innkeepers daughter marrying the Lord of the Manor, was a love story of rags to riches many believed should never have been.

Copied from originals, the collected material included official documents & certificates alongside photographs, portraits, drawings, etching & sketches, scribbled notes & newspaper reports displaying what people thought, beside actual pages taken from the personal diaries of those who found themselves accused of doing wrong.

The Ships logs from what was the Sapphires' fine fleet of cargo ships, letters exchanged by the Sapphire brothers & their lovers. Somethings shocked, somethings were unbelievable & much for many in the modern day, was inconceivable. 'How much was true?' There were some local descendants who would swear it had all happened.

Ghosts, a witch & a mermaid? A mural documenting the life of a man & a woman from birth to death. All knew what happened to Lord Reece Ray Sapphire, but many continued to question the whereabouts of his wife? Where was the witch? 'Do witches live forever?'

Having travelled far, what they found upon closer inspection; saw both newcomers happy with the accommodation within what began and would continue life as a village tavern with added restaurant and guest rooms available for those wanting bed and breakfast. *'Excited.'* The happily married couple agreed history shouldn't be buried or allowed to disappear, along with those to have created it. *'Where was the witch?'* Honouring those who to him were family, Hunter wished he'd met the man to have fathered his great grandma and created the establishment rebuilt to include all original features; in his honour. Setting out on what he hoped to be a prosperous life journey, Hunter was quick to see the potential to create jobs to keep what was a growing interest in history and the one they called the first witch of Ebony Wood alive. Knowing what he knew, meant Hunter not being able to overlook the struggle which would be his getting locals to approve of his vision.

Introducing themselves, the couple in their mid twenties received looks which were filled with questions. *'Unexpected.'* There to help and happy to explain what was changing due to the world having moved on. An open day and invitation to all, those who came to partake in a free drink and sandwich, stayed to hear about what would be the shared town hall and registry office with tourist attracting museum, housed within the buildings known to be Sapphire Manor. *'Where had they come from?'* A young married couple. He said he descended from the late Lord Reece Sapphire and some portraits and photographs were seen to show the family resemblance.

The new landlord of Tinkers Tavern, Hunter appeared unaware of the reasons he and his good lady wife attracted the interest and intrigued of every local they met. Welcoming, Mr. and Mrs. Sapphire reopened doors to have remained closed for much too long. Happy and enthusiastic, those liking what they saw to be their workplace and new home, hoped villagers and townsfolk would give them a chance; by awarding them the time, all new establishments needed to become established and succeed.

Déspoina village and Erebus Town Hall would provide officials from both areas with a mix of conference rooms, offices to hold meetings and secure areas to store records. The large brick built barn closest to the road was earmarked to become a mini courtroom. *'Times were changing fast.'* Amenities destined to be moved out into the city, could be saved and introduced, should Hunter convince everyone how what he was doing would provide the much needed space when readapting his family owned buildings. *'Things would never be the same.'* Once the ball was rolling, those who saw what was being proposed, as keeping what they had, local, began asking for more. *'Happy to help.'* Those aware of what was needed were the ones responsible for the relocation of the vast stabling business left to Mr. and Mrs. Dixon and handed down to their niece before falling into the hands of the present manager Miss Samantha Jade.

New with much more land and space enough to build an indoor arena for those wanting to learn how to ride. Two stable blocks, each with twelve stalls, Samatha agreed she could fill what doubled her capacity. Three miles of bridle pathways would lead from the new location alongside and intertwining through some of the trees on the outskirts of Ebony Wood. Routes designed for walkers and riders only, would also lead from the new stables into both the village and town. How could Samantha refuse what would cost nothing, while providing the potential to earn much? The original stable block was to be removed so to expand what was the unpopular crematorium, allowing it to blend seamlessly with the Sapphire's family chapel and large walled memorial garden. Agreeing to clear trees so to link the village graveyard with what was new, allowed space enough for more graves if needed. *'Agreeing with what incurred guaranteed rental income?'* Giving people a choice, the village church, the Sapphire chapel and the town hall were all registered to hold weddings, christening and funerals. *'Shinny & new.'* All to be rebuilt and extended, was made to appear like it had always been there. Keeping the church of St Julian's as a multi faith establishment, those to have made and agreed the decisions, knew it would take a lot for everyone to see the changes made, as being for the best.

Having read all the paperwork; the well educated individual who was Hunter Rock Sapphire was aware of the fact the places in-which he had a valid interest needed to generate and stop haemorrhaging money. Seeking honest opinions about opening the main areas of the large manor house to visitors. *'A ploy to bring in tourists.'* Hunter pushed his idea for creating a village museum of local interest, insisting the huge attraction would provide those who enjoyed repeating their tales of old, with paid employment. *'The perfect tour guides.'* Charging those wanting to enter and see what remained of what was when, being paid by everyone intrigued about everything his great grandma left behind. The young man with the mind of a new style entrepreneur; felt sure they'd make money enough to cover both a moderate wage and basic running costs; whilst turning a profit. Told any entrance fee would be much too much, the handsome and distinguished young man proved he'd inherited his great, great grandfather's head for business as once started, visitors couldn't get enough of what at times were disturbing tales. The innkeepers daughter and Lord of the manor. *'Strange but true?'* Lacey said the interest was because everyone adored a good love story. *'A tale to capture the imagination?'* Many asked, but neither Hunter or his wife confirmed anything. *'Mysterious & scary?'* No one could say and Hunter never revealed whether or not his great grandma Rosa, Lady Sapphire, the innkeepers daughter and witch of Ebony Wood was alive or deceased?

Once people started coming, others with local businesses began to understand what could be gained by doing business with those outside. *'Some didn't want things spoiling.'* More people called for new picnic benches, water fountains and a need for public convenances, introducing what was needed to enhance the small clearings used as official picnicking areas, located at each of the four official entries into Ebony Wood, meant creating more places for visitors and locals to use. Places to sit and read, space to relax in and small clearings to be used for play. When asked, Hunter said he was continuing what other family members began. Having arrived and lived in the village for a number of months, Hunter and Lacey said they were doing what needed to be done.

'Supply & demand?' Providing everything from guided tours of the Sapphire manor, to ghost walks around the village and through selected parts of Ebony Wood. Any and everyone willing to pay, could see and be told everything known about the legendary Sapphire and Tinker families. *'Captivating,'* Once started, the tale of the Lord of the manor and the innkeepers daughter was a story people couldn't get enough of. *'From the witches first cry & the death of her mother in childbirth.'* Documented facts, took audiences through to how Rosa's twin brother Rock lost his life to the fever and her growing up loyal to her farther Renfred, before meeting and falling for the charms of the man who would be Lord. Wedding photographs turned into postcards, the twist in the rags to riches love story came when others blamed their own misfortunes on what was seen to be a mismatched marriage. The witch of Ebony Wood, saved by a freak storm, each and every storm to follow the one said to have saved Tinkers Tavern from fire and reunited the Lord with his Lady, was seen as a sign, someone or something had upset the Witch. *'Where was she?'*

Years had come and gone, people had lived and died with hundreds if not thousands of things changing. *'A Lord not wanting his manor?'* Hunter checked his inherited estate to discover most habitable properties were being occupied by paying tenants. *'Why change what was working?'* Able to live wherever they wanted, the new Lord and Lady Sapphire said they were happy to be in amongst what they saw to be a thriving village community. *'Newly weds.'* The in love couple had come in search of a new start and found it by stepping into the shoes of Hunters' great grandma and great, great grandfather. *'Coming full circle,'* Time had moved. *'Would he be accepted?'* Hunter Rock Sapphire and his beautiful wife Lacey Belle were energetic, ambitions and excited about what their new life held in store. Having sought legal advise, they arrived in the village in search of peace and tranquility. Having lived their lives within the hustle bustle and bright lights of the city, the two to have been through much, before finding happiness with one another, sought a settled life within the vast inherited estate. *'New comers?'* Each befriended the local's by assuring everyone they were there to help. *'Did they know what they were doing?'* Spreading the word, that which brought visitors, tourists and the curious, soon called for the introduction of the areas' first real hotel and more

Fast moving, willing to listen and wanting to learn, the young and enthusiastic couple to have swept in like a much needed breath of fresh air, found themselves being watched as much, if not more than they were being listened to. Aquatinting themselves with Tinkers Tavern and the surrounding areas, the new landlord and his lady insisted people call them by their christian names of Lacey and Hunter. *'Young?'* While there was no getting away from the fact dresses were getting shorter and for men, a more casual appearance becoming more accepted, there were many not amused by what they saw as being disrespectful and not right. *'Reconnecting a community.'* Hunter and Lacey prided themselves on the way each had been brought up to be open, honest and approachable. Landlord, land and property owner, the new Lord of Sapphire manor called what was his inherited position, outdated. Holding regular meetings and interacting with employees, tenants, neighbours and friends, neither would interfere in, or hinder what was the on going progress, expansion and development of the area. *'Unless they had to.'*

His family? Some questioned the actuality of Hunter being who he said he was? The current Lord Sapphire, where had he come from and what had taken him so long to step in and take back control of what was his? Why hadn't he come forward sooner? Where was his father, where was his grandfather and what had happened to his great grandma? Revealing how his absent family members were the ones responsible for breathing life back into much more than Tinkers Tavern. Speaking about, *'The son of the witch,'* He told how his grandfather Hunter Reece Junior, refused to visit, while he and his father Ray had taken a look around, visiting what earned for them their living; many more times than once. Hunter Rock Sapphire, the taverns' newest landlord told how his namesake and Rosa's son, took to using the initials RJ in place of his given name, when overhearing city businessmen making fun of him being too soft to be any kind of Hunter. *'Not able to face his fear?'* Because his grandfather couldn't, Hunter said he accompanied his father when making his way through town and village, where each saw the need for more than a few improvements. *'Investing in what was owned by the family?'* Where had locals seen the money coming from? *'Had no one noticed the things he & his family continued to do?'* Happy to tell those listening, about the one born within the trees. Hunter told how his grandfather Lord Hunter Reece Junior never wanted to return to live in the place where one parent had been killed and another not wanted. *'Lord Reece Ray Sapphire never knew he was going to be a father.'* Neither his son, grandson, or great grandson ever got the chance to meet the man Rosa said she would always love and never stop missing.

"My grandfather was the only son born to the women you call the witch of Ebony Wood, fathered by the man killed by those accusing him of marrying a witch." Placing a photograph of his late grandfather alongside the portrait of his parents' Lady Rosa and Lord Reece. Hunter said it was sad, what people would do when afraid of what they refused to understand. *'Stop the fear?'* Rosa told her son and those to come after that each should live the life they wanted, her sons' fear of returning to the place he was born originated from her fear of him not being accepted in the same way she was never permitted to be who she was. Driven out, Rosa advised her only boy to build up what upon her death would become his by making as much money as he was able. The one locals accused of being a witch, trusted her only child and those to come after, to do what was right. *'Where was she?'*

Calling it progress, from being used for storage, the old cotton mill was renamed Sapphire Towers before being divided into a mix of affordable housing and larger rental units. High rise, flats, tenements or apartments, each individual accommodation comprising of one and two bedrooms, stood within what was seven storey's at the highest points. What some called damp and dark, stood above a small parade of local businesses to include the butcher, baker, tailor and dressmaker. A cocktail bar, what many called unusual, had been the foresight of those living and brought up in the city. Hunter said his grandfather anticipated the arrival of the train which in turn would attract those wanting to escape the pressures of work and more hectic city life. Offices, shops and stores, the grandson of the one to have kept a thriving town alive; saw what was busiest as being the ideal location for the areas first hotel. Picnic areas and outdoor recreation spaces, not until the heavy machinery was brought in, did those Hunter and Lacey saw as being behind the times, see what was actually being done.

A hive of renovation saw the bringing back to life of places to have stood decaying for years, creating work for builders, plumbers and other local tradesmen, the repairs and rebuilding thrilled, exciting some, while scaring many.

"Grandad," Happy to reveal the identity of the one responsible for informing him about Tinkers Tavern and more, Hunter told those to ask; how his late grandfather had overseen what others saw to be needed and his great grandma said she wanted. Hunter Rock Sapphire? The man in his twenties, told how Lady Rosa had given birth to a son. *'Born within the trees of Ebony Wood in the early hours of thirty-first day of October:'* Confirming the fact his grandfather had been born during a storm, it could be that the time of birth was 03:33. *'Magical?'* Taking a photograph of the clock said to have stopped on the day his elder entered the world, Hunter agreed with those who saw what had happened, to be a strange and mysterious coincidence. *'Was the witch still in the woods?'* Approached by those proud to tell what were a hundred and more stories of strange, sometimes frightening occurrences, when asking why the clock had never been replaced or fixed? It was explained how the wrought iron railings surrounding the structure to have become frozen in time; wasn't purely to catch what might one day fall down. *'Domed.'* Elders said any and everyone to touch what had been stopped by the witch, had died soon after.

"No," Having met, spoken to and heard all about the woman he was related to, Hunter knew his great grandma could never be so cruel. *'Cursed?'* The stories told about the said same person, often sounded worlds apart. His great grandma had never forgotten the place she was born, the place where she worked to make ends meet and where she met the man of her dreams before giving birth to her only son. Aware of all to have happened, Hunter's grandfather and father had never wanted to look back. Having arrived to find those his wealth was both earned from and supported, Hunter saw a need to set up his own lettings and maintenance company, listening to everything he was told, Hunter felt surprised to see what was his family estate in such good shape. *'Maybe the witch continued to protect her own?'*

Settled and busier than either could ever imagine, time stood still for no one and them maturing meant Mr. and Mrs. Sapphire seeing the time as right for them to begin a longed for family of their own. Taking on more employees, a bar manager and waiting staff. The two living above what they turned into a thriving business; found little time for rest. A quaint and tranquil place where everyone knew everyone, where people helped one another and children played in safety. *'Most of the time?'* Having arrived under the shadow of darkness, there were still some to mistrust those seen to be out for themselves when making changes to what hadn't changed in for what for some was a lifetime. Arguments and disagreements, settling in to what was a well established community was never going to be easy and not without complications. *'Nothing to regret.'* Hunter and Lacey felt lucky, neither being able to prevent their smiles when those they upset, reported the changes having improved what was their life and livelihood. *'A good man.'* Hunter vowed to never make changes without the change creating opportunity.

Months turning into years of hard work, when his wife said it was time, Hunter set about making sure those he hired were trustworthy enough to be left in charge and able enough to cover his and his wife's duties during what could be their lengthy absence. Home and settled, those from the city; never wanted to go back to what each called the fast living in amongst the smog and smoke. Needing somewhere they could live without it being the same building to house their work. *'A Tavern was no place for a baby.'* A summerhouse? Visiting the place said to have been Rosa's temporary residence, Hunter agreed, when Lacey said they could use what was peace filled to get away. Weekends and holidays, his grandfather had been the Hunter to oversee the instillation of the private burial ground. Able to recall how as a child he found visiting his great grandma's cottage in the trees exciting. Older, Hunter didn't feel any wiser when having to admit to his paying little attention to the place locals and the mural wall, called the witch's hovel. *'A hideaway?'*

"Wow!" Where others saw nothing more than a rotting shack, the one to have assisted with the completion of the first hotel and more, saw potential. Setting out in his task to create a warm and cosy, comfortable retreat for him and his wife, in the same way his great grandfather Reece had, Hunter aimed to make a place with space to relax for himself, his wife and their future family. *'He knew the truth.'* Seeing the true story of the shack in Ebony Wood to be love filled and romantic, Hunter felt honoured to be back in a place which to his eldest elder had meant so much. Building onto what for years had been nothing more than a wood and stone shack hidden within the fine forestry of Ebony Wood, Hunter and his wife set about creating what would be their place, a new house, the two wanted to build a home from within what all knew was there somewhere, but few would ever see. *'Romantic?'* Lacey saw the secret maze and carefully placed directions, to be romantic and clever.

Built originally by the bestfriend of his late great grandfather, what resembled a grand garden shed, had for a short time been the place where Lord Reece and his wife would escape to. *'Their love nest.'* It never ceased to surprise the young and intelligent man; how so very many things had been misinterpreted and overlooked, when those looking for the truth, didn't really want to find it. *'A hideaway?'* The building to have stood empty for years, was a place of peace and tranquility.

Red was the colour of the home grown rose; meaning the red rose bushes planted to lead one home made perfect sense. Red was thought to be the colour of ones heart and the hearts carved into the chosen thirteen trees with arrows showing both, the way and misdirection; was seen by those knowing about them as ingenious, smart and romantic. A unique way to mark a secret pathway, signpost which were almost impossible to notice. Once uncovered, Hunter and Lacey found what was installed to mark the way, easy and fun to follow.

Basic, the place Rosa escaped to, when being hunted by those accusing her of evil doing. *'A witch?'* The old lady Hunter recalled, couldn't be more gentle and kind. His great grandmother, a woman like any other. Wanting to remain as close as she could to the body of her dearly departed husband, Lady Rosa Ruby Reece Sapphire blamed grief for her reluctance to leave the area. *'A born survivor?'* Mr. Renfred Rock Tinker told the one who was his only daughter; she could do anything she wanted and Rosa had done everything she could.

Living within Ebony Wood for as long as she could, the lone female had remained where she was, up until the day her son was born. Concerned for the safety of the one her becoming a mother made her responsible for, Rosa ran first to her father, experiencing a taste of life living by the sea. Helping out with what was her father's second business, it wasn't long before the strong, independent female sought the help only Mr. Sheldon could provide. A need to live somewhere where she wouldn't stand out saw Rosa moving to a large home situated behind what were described as being, the back streets of the big city.

9: Hidden

A large victorian house turned into a warm and cosy family home. Hunter knew because he was Rosa's great grandson, she never remarried because her love for Lord Reece Ray Sapphire never died. Aware of all the facts, Hunter saw what other's surmised and invented, twisting so to create their interpretation of Lady Rosa's truth. When asked why she never returned? The young man brought up to be a fine gentleman, knew it would be wrong to betray a trust. A good woman, through those appointed to look after the Sapphire estate, Rosa spent her life much closer to what she called her village home than anyone would ever know. *'Her true home.'* What many called the witches hovel, Hunter and his family saw to be grannies' cute country cottage. *'Was Rosa alive?'*

A large multi roomed victorian townhouse, Hunters grandfather spoke fondly of his full time nanny, Miss Maria. The one who would look after him when Lady Rosa travelled for what she called family business, was young, kind and caring. RJ said Maria leaving to become a teacher after marrying a man called James, had made him sad, not only because Maria was like a second mother, but because her leaving meant him losing his friend, Emily. RJ understood his mother wanting to remain close to where the bodies of those she loved were buried. *'A hut in the forest?'* None had visited often, but Hunter remembered visiting his great grandmother's small, secret, secluded property more than once and how one of those times led to him seeing Emily.

Older but not as old as Rosa, washing what looked to be her blood stained hands in the bowl of water by the window as they entered. Hunter would never forget the look to receive a nod, Injured? the woman his grandfather embraced when greeting seemed hurt. Hurried away, Hunter was taken by his mother, who said they should go outside to see the deer and rabbits. Cleaned packed and leaving, Hunter remembered noticing how Emily looked just like Rosa when dressed in her long black cloak with large hood. Two years of age, there were some things you never forget no matter when it was you see them. Emily apologised for still being where she was. *'Sorry,'* Hunter recalled how those around him saw Emily apologising for much more than her not having the accommodation ready in time for their arrival?

Asking what Emily had done? When reading through what was archived within the local library of Erebus town with the intention of discovering more information for his wall, Hunter came across a story the date of which; he calculated to be the time he and Emily met. Heart attacks, Mr. Carter was said to have been out walking in Ebony Wood and his wife home alone when both died. Same day, same cause, it was reported both looked petrified when found by police called by neighbours who discovered the bodies of the married couple in separate locations.

Reading, Hunter found himself questioning what Emily had done? Why? Lacey convinced her intrigued husband there was enough mystery hidden within what was his own family, without his looking for more. Not a witches hovel, Hunter said he remembered his great grandmother's woodland residence as being much more than what others were calling it. *'Her get away, not her home.'*

Lady Rosa Ruby Sapphire continued to use her full wedded title; when mixing with the elite of the city, a young woman with the means to do whatever she wanted and be wherever she wanted to go. A woman with few friends, a single mother to her beautiful boy, her large home saw a continuous flow of people passing through. Staff, children young and younger, some single females appeared lost and frightened.' *The witch in Ebony Wood was responsible for those seeking refuged within the shadow of the trees.'* Not in the way others saw, perceived or thought. Happy to help, when in the city, Rosa became the person to go to, for the upperclass requiring hardworking, loyal, trustworthy and polite staff, changing names and finding their place to be. Parents wanting children and families needing staff, having served others since the day she was born, Lady Sapphire made a name for herself, helping all in need of what was her expert help. *'Doing what made sense.'* Rosa spent her time saving, not taking the lives of those she found wandering in the woods.

Witch

*P*eace, prosperity and harmony, Erebus town grew fast, transforming itself into a place where adults worked, families shopped and those brought up in the cities; visited in search of space and more affordable living. *'Second homes for the rich.'* Local townsfolk liked how money generated by those who left their second houses empty for most of the time; kept them in work and their rents low. Separated by Ebony Wood, Erebus towns' nearest neighbour shared facilities to include a school, sports grounds, the town hall, village chapel, a court room, crematorium and memorial garden.

Quaint and tranquil, the village of **Déspoina** was said by some to present itself to be paradise, while hiding within its' stunning beauty the true gates of hell. A village to have recorded its' history, incorrectly. Déspoina was a place where everyone knew their neighbour, where people helped one another and where children played in safety. *'What could go wrong?'* Having established important roles within the joint communities and brought back Tinkers Tavern, those responsible for the flocking of visitors from far and wide; felt in need of a break. *'Time to look after themselves.'* Good people, *'Why did everything go wrong?'* How could people who had never known or laid eyes upon the woman they called The Witch of Ebony Wood, blame historical myth for everything? *'Was the witch to blame?'* When using what became their second home within Ebony Wood more regularly, some said the witch wouldn't like it.

Part time, with her husband busier than ever; running between businesses and overseeing rent collections, Hunter assisted with solving disputes and supervising new ventures, while trying to find time to interview all prospective employees. Part time, his wife insisted she cut her working hour, understanding, Lacey said she wanted the two to think seriously about slowing down and starting the family both talked about wanting. When pregnant, she planned to stop work, asking her husband to sort things so he could be by her side more than he was behind a desk, conference table or the taverns' long busy bar.

Having the means, didn't equal having the ability to hand responsibilities over to others. Thriving on what had become his new role within a community he was growing to love, when his wife asked what she asked, Hunter promised he would try. Part time, he agreed, when they began their family, he would reduce the hours spent away from home.

The old shack made into a new home within Ebony Wood, quaint and picturesque but not fitted with any modern day convinces. An outside water closet and running water, what Lacey wanted installed prior to parenthood, proved difficult. No way of installing electricity, the ground over which power cables would need to run was vast and the environment too harsh. *'Not possible?'* Those told money was no object; were force to declare defeat and admit taking money would be under false pretences. *'Not up to the job?'* There was no machinery tough enough to do what the young couple wanted.

A tin bath and large pans to boil water; using either the inglenook fireplace or newly installed wood burning stove. A hut with a seat to sit on and a deep hole in the ground, the choice was to bury and move the structure along, or install a receptacle which could be emptied when full. Laying pipes to be used for sewage from the fresh water well, would risk contaminating what proved to be pure enough to drink. Sure it would be possible one day, those giving their honest opinions and expert advise said it was best all collected waste be disposed of safely. *'Composed?'* When looking to the surrounding space filled with trees, those doing the talking, pointed out the many local uses for natural fertiliser. *'Sorry they weren't more helpful.'* Those who were asked, struggled to solve what Lacey saw to be the only problem faced when creating more substantial accommodation within Ebony Wood. Oil or fire? The choice for light and fuel seemed obvious in a place where wood to burn was plentiful. Agreeing to go with what was suggested, Hunter and his wife looked forward to seeing what would be the minimal, but appreciated improvements being made to the two intended to make their family home.

A baby crying? Walking onto what was the Juliet balcony outside her bedroom in the loft space of Tinkers Tavern, having woken to a sound she failed to recognise, Lacey looked both up and down, to see if there was anyone there. A busy night, no one remained on the village streets in the early hours. Peace filled, the female who saw no sense in waking her husband, believed she'd heard a cat? *'A drunk, on his way home?'* The landlady proud of her role, also prided herself for her people skills and awareness which often allowed her to persuade people to switch to none alcoholic beverages, or leave the licensed premises before reaching the stage where each would need assistance, or struggle to find their way home. *'No one?'* Her searching eyes saw no one and nothing until, there it was again, who would leave a baby crying?

Separated by too far a distance to be hearing the sound inside a neighbouring property, the one standing outside by herself, wondered if someone had abandoned their child? Weeping? Was there a toddler to have become lost? A sleepwalker? Glancing back to the street having looked to the stars, Lacey saw children, one, two, three, four, five. What were they doing and where were they going? All walking forward, each would pass by what were the gates to the horseshoe driveway; allowing carriages to drive in, drop off and drive out with ease as it scooped by the main front doors of the tavern. *'Why were there so many children outside?'*

Watching, Lacey saw those walking slow and in silence being followed by what she could only describe as a growing ground cloud. Thick, dark and rolling, *'What was it?'* As whatever it was, grew in size and began to move faster, her attempt to shout out a warning and tell the children to run, was lost within a sudden gust of wind. *'Silence?'* What was happening? Seeing what she believed to be five youngsters in danger of becoming smothered and lost within what was a thick and dark

Witch

menacing ground mist, the concerned female turned to enter her bedroom, her intention being to make her way down and out into the street, wanting to redirect those unable to hear her calls. **Slammed shut!** Shut out!

What was happening? Prevented from entering her room, Lacey looked for a way down, the Juliet balcony protruding out from the loft of the building in-which she lived and worked, meant her being three storey's high, too high to jump, there was nothing to use to climb down.
"No!" With what was following; beginning to engulf those she felt an urge to save, when turning back to try the closed door, Lacey was shocked to step into the large, solid chest of a male. Letting out a short sharp scream, only when recognising the voice telling her she was safe, did she realise, Hunter had stepped out to see where his absent wife had got to. "We need to save them." Asking who? When both looked down out onto the passing road, they saw no one and nothing.

Silence and the darkness of the early hours of a new day. Returning with her to her bed, Hunter convinced his confused, upset wife, she was dreaming. *'A bad dream?'* Lacey agreed to being over tired and Hunter saw a need to strengthen the locks on the patio doors if his wife was going to go sleepwalking. Restless and confused, the resettling couple agreed to disagree about ones mind playing tricks, especially in the dark when one was over tired.

Continuing to work beside those learning how to tend to the needs of the locals acquainting themselves with Tinkers Tavern, Lacey agreed, when Hunter said what she called her strange encounter, didn't need to be shared. *'Sad?'* The female informing new employees on the stories and facts related to the mural displayed for visitors to examine and discuss; agreed that maybe it was her having added the news cuttings and stories related to lost and missing children; which triggered what Hunter called her strange dream.

"Can I help you?" It was early and they weren't quite ready, but if the front door was unlocked, they were open and there was an unwritten rule which said anyone entering Tinkers Tavern would never be turned away. *'An older lady?'* With those there to prove their worth and hospitality expertise joining the chef in the kitchen, Lacey asked her first customer of the day, what she could get for her? Refreshment or food? In the absence of a reply; the landlady use to dealing with most things believed maybe the one wrapped in a cape and wearing her hood up to shadow her face, could be hard of hearing. "What can I get for you this fine day?" She rephrased her inquiry with a smile as she approached the booth table *'She hadn't seen her enter.'* Lacey had no idea as to how long the lone female had been sitting where she sat up against the wall, her fragile looking form hunched up into the corner, her hood covering her head, bowed over the table at which she sat. "Good morning miss," Lacey wondered if the one she was talking to, had fallen asleep? "What can I fetch for you?" Watching as the one before her twitched and turned to face her, Lacey stepped back, sure she had seen the stranger somewhere before, the younger female recaptured her breath and replaced her welcoming smile.

"Things are not always as they seem." Words Lacey didn't fully understand due to them being words she didn't expect, not the answer to her question. "Water." With a nod the landlady agreed to fetch what was requested.

Stepping into the kitchen to ask Hunter to join her inside the bar area, when they returned, they discovered the older lady was gone.

"Shall I unlock the front door?" The last to enter when arriving for work, Jerald Miller said he was certain he relocked the door behind himself. Checking the door

Witch

together, all three found evidence proving Jerald to have secured the internal bolts. How had the one Lacey spoke to get inside? How had she left? *'Where was she?'* A search of the property found nothing and no one who shouldn't be, inside. Both Lacey and Hunter agreeing when told they were in need of some time away from their work to relax and be together.

10: Broken

The day being hot and sunny meant flowers needed water. *'Fine?'* With her husband visiting his regular haunt. *'Overseeing Hunters' Estates & Lettings,'* Lacey tended to the vegetable and herb garden before venturing over and into the plot of land surrounded by a low dry stone wall, hidden beneath and standing within tall dark trees. *'A private graveyard?'*

Having stumbled across the place where his mother buried her husbands' wedding ring beneath a simple wooden cross engraved with his details and a poem, the loving and sensitive son of Rosa and Reece Sapphire had made arrangements for the bodies belonging to relatives of both the Tinker and Sapphire families to be relocated. *'Difficult & expensive,'* Knowing no local would want to dirty his hands, outsiders were hired to carry the deceased from where they lay to where he saw Rosa wanting them to be. *'Not wanting to upset the witch.'* Aware no one would accept his mother being lay to rest beside either his father, or her family within the village, the one wanting nothing to do with those responsible for him being born within the trees of Ebony Wood, sorted the paperwork to lead to all future generations being offered a private plot within what he created. *'Was the witch dead?'*

Hunter assured his wife, his grandfather had known what he was doing. *'Putting his family back together.'* Reuniting his father with his wedding ring by embedding the gold band within the stone cross shaped headstone erected to mark his new place of rest and adorned with the wooden cross baring the poem composed by Rosa. The first in the family to be given the name Hunter saw to it; no one told anyone the exact location of what locals called the witches hovel. Their future family home, having began spending the weekends within the trees, Lacey convinced her hard working husband they should stay where both felt rested from Friday to Monday. *'Where was the witch?'* Lacey looked, but she hadn't come across a grave containing the one named Lady Rosa Ruby Tinker Sapphire. Together forever, Hunter said maybe his great grandmother was buried in the same plot as her husband. *'Reunited?'* Lacey's loyal husband agreed to sorting a second headstone should what he suspected be proven. A safe place. *'Happy.'* Buried for a second time; beneath a mix of engraved headstones, statues, wood crosses and nameplates; those loved and treasured by Lady Rosa, lay together in a place hidden within and protected by Ebony Wood.

'Quaint,' A space others imagined to be spooky and surreal, was a place Lacey liked to sit, relaxing, a space to sit and daydream, somewhere to sit and read one of her growing collection of novels. *'Peace filled & tranquil.'* On a hot sun filled day, the plants planted to bring life to a place dedicated to the dead, needed watering. Happy, Lacey saw herself having everything she ever wanted, a loving husband and comfortable home. A profitable workplace, when within Ebony Wood, at the place others thought to be nothing more than a shack, Lacey and Hunter felt they were truly home. *'At peace,'* The place they called their woodland retreat, was a space where the two could be themselves.

Having cleared weeds and given the area a sprinkling of water, the smiling female sat back on the bench engraved with the names of her late mother and father-in-law. Alone, sitting back with her fingers crossed, she patted her stomach. *'Hopeful?'* The contented wife hoped what she suspected was true. *'The icing on a wondrous cake.'* Hot, the sun was blistering and its' brightness blinding as she looked up from the book, sure she heard someone and certain she could see the outline of another standing beneath one of the tall shadowing trees in the furthest corner from where she sat. Startled, she stood, stunned, was there someone there?

"Hello." Shocked and struggling to see through the bright rays of the high set sun. "Is there someone there?" Unusual, there was nothing stopping visitors dropping by. "Can I help you?" Shielding her eyes, she couldn't make out what was blurred, one two, three, maybe more, unsure if she should welcome, or ask them to leave, the female home alone, saw three children. Two boys and a girl, turning to place her book on the bench, when she looked back to greet them, they were gone?

"Hello?" Had she imagined them? Walking over to the tree and looking over the wall, she saw and no one. Silence? Certain she saw something, Lacey listened but could hear nothing. Where had they gone? Maybe they were shy? *'A game of hide & seek?'* If growing up with a place like Ebony Wood on her doorstep; the one from the city would have made the most of the vast space and wonderment too. *'Childs play?'* Returning to the bench and her book, Lacey smiled to herself, sure the youngsters knew the woodland better than she did.

A day drenched in sunlight, a book telling the tale of a woman in search of her Mr. Right, Lacey felt fortunate to have found Hunter. Warm and comfortable, absorbed by the story. Mrs. Sapphire jumped when something caught her eye for a second time. One of the children was back, able to see more clearly, Lacey asked the child if she was all right?

"Have you lost your friends?" Watching as the young female child bent over the grave marked with a raven belonging to the one named Dark Angel, Lacey asked if she could help? "Hello." Standing and walking forward, the older female stepped back in shock when the one she was approaching turned around. How could a child have no face? What? Who? Lacey remembered feeling faint, but couldn't recall her eyes having closed. *'A female child with no face.'* Opening her eyes to find herself sitting on the bench having dropped the book she was reading from her hand. Had she fallen asleep, was she dreaming? Blaming the intensity of the heat, too hot to remain outdoors Lacey prepared to go inside, hot and bothered, there was no escaping the fact that the vast brightness of the day was beginning to subside. Feeling her whole self jerk with fright, eyes lay upon the three children she felt sure were there earlier. Standing before her, standing within arms length, how had they gotten so close without her seeing?

"Can I help you?" Able to see the forms of not one but three children, all had their back to her. "Are you okay?" She asked. "What are you doing here?" She wanted to know? "Who are you?" She questioned, but received no reply.

Lacey didn't mind children playing, but she would rather they didn't trample over what was a place of rest.

"Are you lost?" Silent, as she stood, each standing before her moved slowly; while appearing to close in fast. Smiling, the one who longed to be a mother, liked that those she saw to be local youngsters; saw fit to pay her and her second home a visit. "Can I get you a drink?" She remained polite, her smile turning to a look of concern as those moving slowly, suddenly moved fast. "What do you want?" From thinking she knew what was happening, to worrying about what they were going to do? "Where are your parents?" Not wanting them to trample what she and husband kept neat, clean and tidy, the one beginning to feel disorientated, asked those wandering through the small burial ground, to stop. "Stop!" In front, to the right, to the left and behind *'What were they doing?'* Moving this way and going that way, "Stop!" She called. Reaching out to touch the one closest to her. "No!" Stopping the young girl she touched caused Lacey to step back and stumbled. "No!" How could a child have no face? "No!" Had she fallen into an open grave? Why did she feel like she was falling? Unsure what it was she was experiencing. *'Where was she?'*

Walking forward, the one acclimatising herself to what felt surreal, failed to recognise her changed surroundings?

Encased by a much different environment than the one she was use to, the one born and brought up in the city believed she must be dreaming. Walking forward, her having fallen asleep was the only explanation for the fact day was now night. Aware she wasn't alone, those who she struggled to see, could be heard giggling as each ran from tree to tree, their identity hidden by the dark. *'Why was it night?'* Where had the day gone? Walking forward, her foot became entangled with a protruding tree root, causing her to trip and fall. *'Where was she?'* Looking at what stood before her, her eyes came to rest on the tallest and most branch filled tree she had ever seen. *'Where was she?'* The female wished she wasn't on her own and wanted those she could sense to go away.

Rubbing her ankle and feeling the urge to look up, Lacey hoped she wouldn't see anything. Met with a sight she would never forget. A large branch filled tree, hanging from three of the branches, three babies. *'No!'* Aware she could do nothing, she realised those to have been hung by the tying of ropes around their young and fragile necks were gone.

"No!" Unable to say what overshadowed her, the lone female believed she fainted due to the heat, passed out due to a lack of water. Back in the Sapphires' burial ground; watching her hands disappear into a deep pool of dirt, her attempt to push herself up; only caused her hand to sink deeper into what turned from black mud into red blood. Unsure what actually occurred and not sure if there had ever been anyone else with her, the cry she let out when noticing her blood stained skirt brought her returning husband to her side.

"What happened?" Her hands were clean, but her skirt was bloodstained. *'A miscarriage,'* The doctor said he was sorry for their loss. Sorry they couldn't say whether the baby was male or female? A baby was a baby. Mr. and Mrs. Sapphire lost their first child.

Heat stroke? When revealing the events of the day, the doctor agreed heat stroke could be a possible cause, yes she could have fainted and yes it was possible she had fallen into a sudden deep sleep and experienced a nightmare. A sudden plummet in bloods sugar levels, or dehydration? Possibilities were countless. Physical or environmental? Something caused what was growing inside Mrs. Lacey Sapphire to leave where he or she was growing, too soon.

"Sorry," Everyone was sorry. *'A miscarriage followed by a still birth & one who took a single breath.'* Lacey knew there would be three and following the loss of the one she cradled in her arms, she asked Hunter to help find the place she believed shown what was the horror of her future. Locals blamed the curse of the witch. How could those without medical knowledge know the cause of what professionals called unfortunate? *'The Witch?'* Some saw what was happening to Lacey as occurring because the witch was returning and wanted her hovel back. *'Taking what she needed to remain youthful.'* Those to have relaxed when Hunter introduced more picnic and recreation areas for them to enjoy, again warned and prohibited youngsters from entering Ebony Wood.

Forbidden to play in amongst the trees for fear they would fall victim to what was perceived to be making a return. *'Rosa wouldn't do that.'* While believers in the witch speculated about Rosa being alive and needing young souls to survive, Lacey and her husband put faith in the medical doctors and trained nurses who were sorry to have to inform them there would never be any children. *'The curse?'*

Attending a short, meaning filled service held within the village church of St Julian's, Mrs. Lacey Belle Sapphire ignored the gossip and insisted the tiny body of the daughter she and her husband named Bluebell Star, be buried alongside the remains of her siblings in the private tree encased burial ground. One single solitary breath. *'So close.'* The loving couple would forever be a million miles from becoming parents. Having miscarried her first child too early to know whether the baby would have developed into a girl or a boy? *'No face,'* Lacey's body rejected her son Ray at twenty-seven weeks and delivered her daughter two weeks after what had been her given due date. *'Too late.'* A difficult birth, Bluebell Star was perfect on the outside, but nothing inside was where it was meant to be. No beating heart, the single breath Lacey was sure she heard; could have been the sound of something else, no loud cry. *'Her parents' were the ones shedding tears.'* Sorry, having lay the remains of their children to rest in amongst the bodies and ashes of other family members, Lacey and Hunter wanted the spiritual souls of their offspring to be with those who would have treasured them if all survived for longer. *'Laid to sleep in eternal slumber.'* Not wanting his grieving wife to suffer more than she was suffering, Hunter agreed with whatever she wanted, hiding his own grief he continued to look after his wife. *'Wandering souls allowed to walk within the confines of the private burial ground & roam free in amongst over a thousand trees forever.'*

Seeking out and discovering the tree Lacey named the tree of fate. The hanging tree. Upset, the mother who should be holding her babies, insisted her husband set out to destroy what she saw to be the true evil within Ebony Wood. *'They couldn't.'* <u>The hanging tree.</u> Church records discovered within the history books; found in the archives of St Julian's described what stood within Ebony Wood as being a tree with more branches than any other, large, strong and easy to climb. A natural frame all children would find easy to get onto and a structure enabling each climber to get up high. The hanging tree? When discovering how some to explore what was inviting had fallen to their death, Hunter and his wife felt horrified to learn how others had been left with life changing injuries. Hung, What was recorded as the first hanging was followed by a list of seen to be intentional and accidental happenings.

Shocked, Lacey reading what was found only went to strengthen her need to see the tree destroyed. *'A tree?'* Much too big, much too strong and much too old, a task no one seemed willing to do. Using any and everything they could, those to try, only succeeded in turning what was leaf filled and thriving; into a smouldering black skeleton. *'Not dead? Not dying?'* Failing to rid the Wood of what was found responsible for taking the lives of children and more, Mr. and Mrs. Sapphire found many wanting to assist, when it was decided to created what they saw to be every child's dream, out of what brought every parents nightmare.

Unable to be removed, the tree would be changed in a way which would protect what was unsafe from being touched. Wrapping what turned black; within a soft, tight netted fabric containing chips of coloured glass so it sparkled when hit by the natural lights of the sun and the moon. Protecting the skeleton trunk and branches meant preventing access to even the lowest parts. No more being climbed, no way of anyone falling from what was transformed from looking large, mean and evil into the centre piece of an enchanting forest of fairies. A place to explore and play, creating a small woodland maze littered with colourful sculptures, toys and dolls encircled by a tall gated fence, so it could be locked at night. The Enchanted Fairy Forest was developed in the hope that no one else would be harmed or killed.

Not dead, what wouldn't fall or crumble; was given a new and very different lease of life. *'Till death do them part.'* Lord Hunter Rock Sapphire and his wife Lacey

Belle oversaw many changes done with the intention of allowing people back into parts of Ebony Wood. *'Everything dies in the absence of being filled with life.'* Good people, young people, when the happily married couple were discovered dead in the bed they shared inside Tinkers Tavern, no one could take in what was another family tragedy for the Sapphire's.

Arriving in the village of Déspoina to begin a new life and bring back what locals believed was lost forever. *'Too young?'* Many found themselves left questioning how they'd escape the curse of the witch; when her own family failed to. *'Had the witch taken the young couple to be with their children?'* Death is said by some to be the only sure way of ending ones' misery, could it be; Rosa hadn't wanted to see her great grandson suffer anymore? Or had the witch removed those she saw as standing in the way of what would be her, return.

Discovered by staff, use to being greeted by the two who despite their inner pain and known heartbreak never failed to welcome others with a smile. No one could believe they were gone? Young and healthy, passing together, the sudden deaths of Lord Hunter and his dear, sweet wife Lacey, for some, was suspicious. Too young for it to be natural causes. *'Suicide?'* The residents of village and town were use to scandal while continuing to dislike and worry about change. *'Settled & happy for seven years.'*

Time seemed to move faster; when the world refused to stop developing. When Lacey and her husband were discovered dead, some said they would never step inside Tinkers Tavern again. Frightened by ghosts, some saw their souls to have been ravished by wandering spirits. *'The curse?'* Those put in charge of the Sapphire estate; saw it as making financial sense to place an employee into the role of landlord and keep the tavern open.

Keep things ticking over until the next to inherit was found. *'Who?'* Was there anyone? Hunter never having spoken about his own story; meant no one knowing how, like his great grandparents' Reece and Rosa, he too had been born a twin and his twin was his sister Raven.

Added to the wall the night before he passed, those to discover what seemed to be the landlords final message, admitted to not knowing where they would begin to look? What would happen to such riches when there was no family to take control? Those to have attended the funerals of Mr. Hunter Rock and Mrs. Lacey Belle knew nothing about whether his sister was near or distant? Alive or dead? None to have attended the service held inside the Sapphire chapel, followed when the bodies of the happily married couple were taken to be laid to rest within Ebony Wood.

Some had wanted to use the crematorium, some saw burning the bodies as the only way to destroy the cursed bloodline. Believing it to be the work of the witch. *'Who?'* Those to ask about the next owners of what was now the Sapphires' extended estate, were told planned works would continue until someone was found to stop them, or the money ran out. Not wanting more to change, having seen what change brought the villagers and townsfolk to attend the multi faith church; gathered and came together wanting to discover what they could and should do about those who if found, would be yet another generations? Having welcomed what Hunter and his wife introduce to create new jobs and bring investment, many feared the next generation would take the reins and go a step too far. *'Who & from where?'* Lady Rosa and Lord Reece Sapphire were parents to Hunter Reece Junior and his son Ray fathered Hunter and his twin sister Raven, Hunter and his wife having died without an heir, left only Raven, but no one knew who, or where the last Sapphire family member would be found?

Stood looking at what was the mural showing how two families had intertwined together, the one brought in to oversee the running of Tinkers Tavern, said the only thing he could see was a story, telling how one tragic event led to the next before running into another. *'The witch must be dead.'* The dark ages were over and it was time for man and business to prosper, a new and exciting era where banks listened to the money making ideas of everyday people, allowing all who wanted; to take control of his or her own financial destiny. Having a regular income meant the opportunity to own ones home and for anyone willing to break from the norm, life was good. No longer were cars, homes and ambition reserved for the privileged. *'Some still believed in witches.'* Many remaining wary of the curse put on Ebony Wood. Young and ambitious, Mr. Dwight Forest agreed to everyone enjoying a good mystery.

Enthusiastic Mr. Forest was the son of a city landlord who brought with him his fathers' wealth of knowledge and backing, alongside a billion of his own fresh ideas. *'Folklore & legend?'* When discovering why no one employed to work in the thriving tavern wanted the well paid position with food and accommodation included, Dwight continued to collect what he saw to have turned the fine establishment into a comfortable place for locals to meet and a popular space of interest attracting tourists from near and far. *'Interesting?'* True historical fact spiced up with the rantings of days gone by. Manager not owner, Dwight saw no reason not to tell those to ask, he was there looking after what had been put into trust until the next eligible owner was found. *'If no one?'* Dwight said his experience had taught him never to look beyond what one was able to see, when it came to what would and what wouldn't be? A manager happy to go wherever he was put, the young man with a welcoming smile and a gift for talking, said he didn't know how long he would be around.

Witch

*I*nteresting, transformed from dreary and uninviting, it was time for Ebony Wood to be given a new lease of life. Too much land not to be put to good use, when more areas were cleared for the installation of themed play areas alongside updated public conveniences, many were impressed by the way what had been uniquely designed, blended into what had always been. Excited and intrigued, youngsters were told to be careful and stay together when insisting they be allowed to discover the challenging spider web climbing frame in **Creepers Corner** and attempt to become champion at chess and other oversized games in **The Giants' Lair.** Falling in love with the magical wonderment of the sparkling **Enchanted Fairy Forest Maze** where a canopy of fairy lights encased the magical world of the fairy in amongst scatterings of tiny doorways carved into trees and strategically placed ornaments, some fairies moved, suspended on invisible lines and for those who found the centre of the magical environments, a fallen, hallowed-out tree created the ultimate fairy playhouse, complete with fairy furniture and dolls.

For those able to recall the stories related to **The Hanging Tree,** no amount of sparkle and fairy lights could make what towered like the large black skeleton of an evil giant, look bright and inviting. **The Dungeon and Dragon Maze** was a tree top adventure of suspended wooden bridges, rope swings and scrabble nets above underground passageways, following which led the brave and the fearless to the dragon of slides. Impressively designed, communal areas were kept to the edge of the Wood, making each unique space easily accessible by foot or car. Free to locals, visitors were asked to leave a donation in honesty boxes set within the areas where safety and the wellbeing of those to use what was provided, was shown in the child friendly matting and the way the mazes could be locked at night. *'Who would be park keeper?'*

Embracing some of the regeneration more than others, the people of Erebus town and Déspoina village flocked to seek employment in the large shopping complex named Rosa's Retail shopping mall and put down their names to occupy stalls in the refurbished Village Square and Market Hall. Times had changed and Dwight told all willing to listen, it was time people embraced and stopped fearing the tales aquatinted with the families whose stories; brought people in to where none wanted to lose what they had. Time to stop worrying about the buildings and places seen to be haunted by the ghosts of days gone by, time to start looking forward and learning how to provide what people were willing to pay for in the present and the future.

"Obsessing with what is dead is what causes places to die." Dwight said he had seen it before and didn't want the place he saw as having potential, becoming a ghost town. Stubborn and set in their ways, hanging like a stubborn cobweb, or dark rain filled cloud, that which was history continued to rule how some chose to live their lives. *'Happy & content?'* No local would willingly disturb what lay dormant for years. *'Afraid & frightened?'* Scared of bringing back what their ancestors said was bad luck, while it was probable the witch had died, the threat of what a witch could do, would forever hover over where she had been given power enough to become Lady.

A witch given power, was a witch all should fear, unruly, What a witch should never have, was all the things Rosa was presented with, when becoming the Lady of the Sapphire Manor. A woman of means, a female with what was needed to put her head above the heads of many men. The money didn't matter, Rosa's feared power was in her words and the fact she gained the ability to go wherever she wanted, do what she wished and condemn those she saw in need of condemning.

Witch

*B*lackness illuminated by flaming torches, over the centuries naked flames were replaced by hand held lanterns as curious individuals formed small groups happy to gather and display their narrow mindedness for others to see. From heat filled flames dancing in the cooling, moving night air, to the flickering shimmer of lanterns, some powered by candles and some by oil, the changing times saw the arrival of searching spot lights and directional beams, as many continued in their attempt to seek out those said to be monstrous masters of illusion. *'Something hiding in the Wood?'* When asked, those to question the existence of witches and witchcraft accused witch hunters of being delusional. From flames to hand held lanterns and pocket size torches projecting light through the stubborn darkness enhanced by the vast amount of shadowing trees. From the curious to the determined, from the sightseer to the fanatical, what had only happened occasionally, began happening all the time, as many sought, but few found actual proof to authenticate Lady Sapphire as having had any of the attributes said to be possessed by a true witch?

Hand held lanterns with flames protected from the chilling night breeze. What they carried and the way they were dressed; were the only visible indications of the passing of time. *'Another generation?'* Was the witch dead, or continuing to live within Ebony Wood? Had Rosa died of old age, perished through loneliness or was the one said never to age, the real reason no other felt alone when wandering between the trees. *'Not a bad person?'* Most saw it being an impossibly that any one, male or female could and so would live for the amount of time Rosa was said to have lived for. An old wicked witch, all to read the wall inside Tinkers Tavern and visit what was the Sapphire manor house museum accused the story being told of being a mythical fantasy. An urban myth and on going legend, everyone liked a good story.

Flustered and barely able to catch their breath, the boys who ventured into the trees while waiting for their fathers to partake in a little lite afternoon refreshment, returned to Tinkers Tavern in a state which could only be described as server shock. Arriving in a state of almost exhaustion and stating claim to having stumbled upon the grave of the female said to be the local witch. What started as two adventures friends seeking something to do? Resulted in the curious coming together to search out the truth. *'Frightened boys with a story to tell?'* When darkness replaced the light, covering the tree filled wood like a blanket, keeping it warm and hiding all but the outlines of what stood strong tall and proud. *'No one willingly entered what turned from white to black.'* Told about what had been uncovered, many saw themselves as having no choice but to seek the truth and see with their own eyes. *'Two frightened boys.'* Like someone had flicked a switch, darkness engulfed the wooded area with a density to caused those to have entered, to believe their eyes had been welded shut. *'What were they doing?'* Those to have taken it upon themselves to search, wanted to find the truth, while failing to remember how truth always comes at a cost. Tomorrow, or the next day or the next, intrigue wasn't able to replace what was an in-bread fear of things to go bump in the trees.

Ignoring the warnings not to meddle in what he didn't know. Mr. Dwight Foster was seen to revel in what elders warned should be left alone. *'Let the witch rest.'* None wanted their changing fortune to be taken away. *'Not again?'* The newcomer found it amusing how all long term residents found it easier to believe in a curse and the existence of a witch than believing in the truth of a raising economy. While others carried what illuminated the dark and trod carefully, Mr. Foster carried his camera everywhere he went. His intention was to add as many factual artefacts as he could to what his patrons came to see. Them telling him he shouldn't, didn't mean they could leave him to who knew what fate when he failed to return before nightfall.

Heading out in search of the truth and another story to tell, the one appointed manager, continued in his plight to keep the villages' only public house from ever turning to ashes again. *'His excuse, others wanted his truth?'* Accompanied by those employed to oversee the upkeep of the communal areas dotted within the boundaries of Ebony Wood, twenty-seven year old Dwight explored what many a local avoided. Going their separate ways in attempt to see what the boys reported seeing, before they lost daylight what they went in search of was proving impossible to find. A figment of their young and over active imaginations, the boys apologised for venturing further than any official signposts permitted.

A wooden cross inscribed with the name and registered date of birth, below the recorded date of death. Lady Rosa Ruby Tinker Sapphire *'The witch was dead. Gone?'* Adorned with wild bluebells, the discovery of a burial ground hidden within the trees, was confirmation of what some called myth; containing actual fact. A grave, buried? But how? *'How could a person bury ones self after death?'* Some said she crawled into the ground to die, while others suspected her being murdered and buried by someone with who she lost a fight. *'Gone?'* Mysterious, magical and strange, from the beginning to what was seen to be the end, the tales of the witch to have lived within Ebony Wood, continued to be told.

'A decoy?' Those to see the photograph of the grave, saw its' existence as untrue. Planted to be found, so all would stop looking. A secluded location far from the edge and well hidden by shadowing trees, no pathway or road, it was thought the wood and stone structure described as being no larger than the average garden shed; had been home to Rosa since the night she left the grand Sapphire

Manor House. Some said the witch in the wood, and others called her a Lady. *'Could she be gone?'*

The peasant who married a Lord? While many disagreed about her title, everyone agreed about wanting to know who she lived with inside her hovel? *'The witch was dead, long live the witch tales.'* Stumbled upon by two mischievous boys, none visited the simply marked grave, because no one was willing to exhume the body of the female perceived to be lay beneath what was marked with a cross. *'How?'* There was no one who didn't question the way in which Rosa lost her life. *'Who?'* Someone was responsible for laying her body to rest, someone had buried and marked the final resting place of the witch with a wooden cross etched with plan and basic information. Her great grandson Hunter? When tracing from the top to the bottom of the entangled family tree, most everyone saw the only family member to have returned to the area as being the one responsible for covering the body of the witch when also covering up the facts about the life she led.

A second witch? Had Rosa given birth to twins? If a subsequent child was a daughter, would she inherited what were seen to be her mothers' wicked traits? Could it be the witch of Ebony Wood had lay herself in the ground? *'Aware of her own pending doom.'* Could Rosa have been the one to erect her own memorial; before laying down to die and dissolving back into the earth from where all life came. Maybe the cross had been placed in the ground as a deterrent. *'A warning not to touch.'* A reminder of the curse many believed to be living under since the fire, meant to destroy a witches reputation, had taken from her, her one true love. *'Magic or mysterious, tragic or romantic?'* Was it not said that true witches could never walk over a cross? Masters of illusion. *'A decoy?'* It was believed by some, the grave had been placed where it was, by the female herself, in attempt to put an end to the continuing witch hunts. The discovery of details indicated that the commoner to have married a Lord, had died sixty-six years after leaving civilisation. *'Untrue?'* Photographic evidence or not, what was shown to the villagers and townsfolk, didn't fit with what their ancestors had been told.

Those to believe in the existence of what was mysterious and magical, were accused of suffering delusions. When unable to find evidence of life and not willing to uncover proof of death, believers warned those who referred to the stories of Rosa, as legend and myth, to be careful, stating that when making reference to a true witch, no one could afford to be flippant or foolish.

'Dead or Alive? The witch would always be listening. Living or Deceased? Many saw the spirit of someone to have inherited powers capable of evil, as being a spirit to be avoided & a force to be feared.'

*D*ark, fast moving shadows, a chill which pierced ones very core and the sound of laughter carried by the wind. *'A witch?'* What began as fact, was quickly turning to fiction, with stories, rumours and old-wives-tales about Lady Sapphire; referring to her as being a ghost. A wandering spirit, a lost and lonely female who had seen everyone and everything she loved taken from her, before disappearing and becoming lost within the tall and dark shadowing trees of Ebony Wood. *'A ghost?'* A witch, a wandering spirt and lost lonely soul. Uncertain of what had become of the Lady of the manor following the demise of her husband, the local people of Déspoina village and Erebus town stopped looking and began avoiding the space all saw as being inhabited by a being no longer of their world. Having discovered the burial sight of the woman they called The Witch of Ebony Wood. Ebony Wood would again become a place people were warned never to enter after dark. *'A place best left unexplored.'*

What did he think he was doing? Walking as fast as his feet would carry him, Dwight struggled to reach what he needed to find. A maze created by nature, a space where every entrance, the centre and every exit was continuously changing because that which caused it to change was alive. Like people, trees and plants are born, sometimes becoming out of control as they grow; each able to spread in its' individual search to discover its' rightful place before establishing its' preferred lifeline and eventually beginning to wilt and die. Like people, tress and plants live and grow, able to move before ageing and preparing to die, each spending a different amount of time above the earth before returning back into the ground from where they came. Encased within a structure created by mother nature herself, there were some areas too dense for a male of his build to get through. *'Where was he?'* Unsure he was going in the right direction, the man wanting to be first to photograph what he saw to be his prize, hoped the daylight would last long enough for him to see and get what he wanted.

Having entered together and walked side by side, only Dwight got to see the grave. Startling those out searching to find him, the newest landlord of Tinkers Tavern was found when making his way back home. *'What happened?'* He wasn't sure.

"Who buried her?" The photograph of the witches final resting place brought with it yet another mystery to be solved. When examined closely, the photograph of the witches grave was seen to be overshadowed by what looked to be a figure shrouded by a long hooded cloak. *'Dusk?'* The one to have taken the photograph of the wooden cross etched with a burnt script, blamed the time of day and poor light for what some said was someone standing over the leaf and bluebell covered grave. *'Why had so many leafs fallen in the summertime?'* Dwight swore he saw no one, because no one would believe what he'd seen.

Alone, or surrounded by the children she'd taken because they were no longer wanted. If the witch had a family and had been surrounded by so many, someone would have seen. Whatever she had done and wherever she had been, it was over. The grave marked the end of a woman to have escaped civilisation and led a life to have created a story filled with mystery. How had a single woman survived for so long?

"Did you see her?" Older and wiser, those to have met her great grandson, knew from the look in the younger males eyes, he'd encountered something. "Ebony Wood is no place for sightseeing." Most shook their heads.

"No," Dwight agreed.

"Her grave?" Those questioning the one they saw to be hiding much, examined the content of the photograph taken at dusk.

"Do you believe a person is able to bury them self, or did she lay in the ground and wait to die?"

"No," Dwight couldn't see how anyone would know the exact day they would breath their last breath. Concluding that the witch must have had someone with her, everyone wondered who? Not her husband or father, not her son, grand or great grandson.

"A long black hooded cloak, jet black hair and blood red lips. I've seen her too." His grandfather had been the youngest to assist with moving the bodies from the grounds of the Sapphire Manor house and village graveyard, into the plot dedicated to the dead hidden within Ebony Wood.

Having fallen for the charm of the countryside, Mr. Keith Douglas moved into the village and married the one he called his local lass. "I saw her and I've felt what you're feeling." The male born to live in the town of Erebus due to his fathers' inability to settle in the village, admitted to him, his dad and his grandfather understanding when asking Dwight what she'd done? Dwight wanted to say nothing, but the truth was, he didn't know. *'A brief encounter?'* Dwight wasn't sure what happened when agreeing to tell what he could recall.

Unable to allow someone else to be the first, he walked on ahead, taking what he saw to be the way into the trees when those with him agree to them being able to cover more ground if they separated. Heading deeper into the wood at his first opportunity Dwight had become lost in the maze created by what only nature provided. Taking seconds, confusion led to his becoming disorientated when finding himself alone, engulfed by trees Dwight realised he should have taken a whistle, food, water and a blanket incase of having to spend the night beneath the stars. *'Replicated a thousand times.'* Everything, everywhere looked the same, left, right and forward, before he thought to look back, the lone male found himself surrounded by nothing he recognised. Trees and bushes, the uneven earth beneath his feet provided no clear pathways. *'Where?'* The businessman born and brought up in a large town before moving around from city to city, saw rumour and myth as nothing more than another money making opportunity. Alone, why was he feeling nervous and unsure. *'Who was that?'* A shadow, the snapping of a twig he hadn't stepped upon and the rustling of leafs in the distance. *'Was someone following him?'* When alone within the trees, Dwight agreed to having experienced the sensation of being watched. *'Eyes in the trees.'* Like when people said walls have ears, locals were convinced the thick dense woodland separating town and village was a place where the trees had eyes. How else did the witch keep watch over everyone and everything. *'How could a woman alone, survive surrounded by nothing but greenery?'*

Seeing something shinning through the branches, the dry stone wall having fallen down, meant him almost tripping on what needed stepping over because he couldn't see what was hidden beneath his feet. A single wooden cross and hand tied posey of heather in amongst a bed of wild bluebells. Dwight looked for what else was around, but couldn't see anything.

"Sorry," Why apologise? *'Sorry for being where he shouldn't be.'* When his sight moved from his feet and he looked up across the mound of earth towards the wooden cross, Dwight lost his balance and fell back. Feeling foolish, his loss of control meant him having to pull himself up from off his hands and knees. His eyes meeting a pair of feet protected by black lace boots and a body covered by a long dark hooded cloak. *'Yes, he saw her.'* Dwight agreed her hair was the colour of a ravens wing and her lips as red as freshly split blood. Nodding, he agreed to having encountered the witch of Ebony Wood. Not old? *'Not dead?'*

"She stepped forward and I stepped nowhere." Having gotten to his feet, he found himself unable to run. *'Trapped.'* "She stepped forward and I."

"You experienced sensations like nothing experienced before." Both men nodded in agreement. Sexual and sensual, neither could say exactly what happened, but both agreed everything had. *'Taken?'* Neither ever wanted to experience what they had, ever again, because ever since coming across the woman in the woods both men had struggled to live with the uncertainty of guilt. Wondering if he should leave his family, when the one to have approached said how he felt, Dwight found himself admitting to not knowing if the female had given him permission to do what he believed he'd done.

Placing the photograph taken of the said witches grave at what he saw to be the end of the mural. Mr. Dwight Forest believed he'd discovered the ideal conclusion to the many stories of the witch of Ebony Wood. *'The witch was dead.'* From her traumatic birth to the cross which represented her final resting place. Stepping back to admire what he'd done, Dwight believed the journey of the Sapphire and Tinker family was over, while at the same time feeling, his and the journey of others, had only just begun.

11: Two

*W*ithout the medical advances of the future, no mother knew if she would give birth to a boy or a girl, one, two, or more? Reece would never know, because no one knew the gender of the one his father called Dark Angel. Rosa's twin brother was Rock Red Tinker and when Hunter was born, he was born on the same day, to the same mother as his twin sister Raven Rose. Twins, unusual, what some saw to be good fortune, others believed to be bad luck. The same, many believed when having two, the two would be complete opposites of one another. One good and one bad, mischievous and deceptive, when babies; twins can look as cute as two buttons, but it was said double the love would bring double the trouble. In some areas and at some times, twins were seen to be abandoned more than single birth babies. Twins left more fathers minus their wife because the traumatic birth of two, proved more difficult to survive. Parents unable to cope due to the lack of money, or space, young single mothers not being given any other choice, for some, two was quite often, two, too many.

Happy and overjoyed, them living in the city meant there being a hospital to go to. Not the easiest of births, RJ and wife Heather congratulated their son Ray and wife Liberty on having succeeded where other generations of the Sapphire family failed. *'Twin grandchildren?'* A double christening, Ray and Liberty agreed when them asking the eldest member of their family for middle names resulted in their son being named Hunter Rock and their daughter Raven Rose. Not many could boast about becoming a great grandmother, Rosa believed her continuing to live was so she got to lay eyes on the one she said would return to continue what his great grandfather, her husband had begun. *'Prove her innocence.'* When of an age to speak, both Hunter and Raven assured their eldest relative, no one believed any woman to be a witch, not anymore.

Another generation and new way of life, unsure if it was because people were discontent or just the worlds' way? Rosa struggled to understand why mother nature was handing everything she governed over, to man. Strange, there were things being invented and used not even witchcraft could be used to explain. Another generation, the old getting older and the young having vision far beyond what many saw as being achievable in ones lifetime. Men and women, boys and girls, the one thing which never seemed to change, was the way some appeared to fall for the wrong one.

Having listened and learned the harsh lesson of Rosa's and Reece's tragic love story, none would stand in the way of what was said to be true, but she was young. When meeting Kieran Knight, Raven Rose Sapphire was still a child, fourteen was no age to know ones own mind and all her parents asked, was that she wait and give it time. None related to Raven ever told her no, but when under the impression her elders would stop her seeing the boy she loved because he was two years older and from the inner, not outer part of the city, the two made their plan and ran. *'Gone?'*

Those with money enough to offer a reward, found themselves and their desperation taken advantage of, the policed saw the money to be dropped off in the local park, as being requested by the missing couple themselves. *'Runaways would need money to live.'* Instructed to stop all requests for information and advised not to offer rewards, those suffering the pain of having a missing teen, were told to leave the searching to the authorities. Raven had to be somewhere. *'All wished they had the foresight of a witch.'* From the age of fifteen to his death, Hunter never knew where his twin sister was.

Alive or dead? The story was told in copies of the news articles to report her missing, alongside the heartfelt letters her mother wrote and went on to place like posters, putting them up where and whenever she could, Mrs. Liberty Sapphire walked the city streets, continuing through all neighbouring towns so to leave messages for her missing child. *'Gone?'* The one born on the same day as her bother was the apple of her fathers' eye. A princess, a female child born to into a family enabling her to have any and everything her heart desired, loved. *'Cherished & adored.'* Intelligent, unlike her brother; Raven's ambition didn't lay in wanting to work hard to achieve what others saw to be the ideal family life. *'Beautiful & smart.'* Raven never brought trouble to her door, because when she was fifteen years of age, Raven walked out of her family home and never returned. A maturing young lady with money enough to do whatever she wanted.

Raven fell in love with Kieran Knight, older, Master Knight was someone wanting to spend her money on things he shouldn't. *'Forbidden love.'* Lost souls meeting and causing one another more pain than others would or could ever understand. *'Not the right type.'* Her parents asked she wait, but to their daughter time was a luxuory she couldn't and so wouldn't waste. Living to die? Living the high life, moving from one hotel room to another, they sometimes slept in the car purchased with money each knew they would have to use well. In love and loving the freedom of being wherever they wanted to be, together, sleeping under the stars on the beach and joining others who chose to squat inside buildings they said shouldn't be left to stand lonely.

'Ray & Hunter searched their family owned land.' Making their way through the town of Erebus and village of Desponia it seemed Ray and his son Hunter were

always one step behind when told the boarded up Tinkers Tavern was again clear of those to have inhabited the property illegally. Accused of being ghosts, the father and son were directed to the vacant stall within the grandest of grand stable blocks where them speaking to the manager meant them learning how she threatened to call the police on those she found using her stable as a temporary home. Discovering the person in-charge of the local church to be unaccommodating and unable to find what Hunter remembered being her great grandmother's cute cottage in the woods. *'On the move,'* While supplying all the information he could, RJ said he was sorry he couldn't bring himself to again be in amongst those responsible for his growing up without his father. *'Always one step behind.'* Other than discovering all the places and spaces they owned Hunter and his distressed father found nothing and when Raven proved to be nowhere, all her family could do was to hope she would be nowhere, alive and well.

One year turned to two. *'Money enough to do whatever she wanted.'* When receiving a reply to one of her letters; Liberty sent whatever her daughter wanted, to the addresses given. When an attempt to bring Raven home almost ended with her being killed by the train she ran in front of to get away. Her parents said it was time to stand back, an allowance, sending details of how there was money being sent into a post office account for her to collect, all agreed to allow Raven to be wherever she wanted to be, because they believed them staying away was what would keep her safe.

No fixed abode, a car and money enough to buy more drugs than food. Raven finding Kieran in the bed of another, with a friend, brought arguments which led to them not being careful when making up. *'When Raven gave birth to Lloyd, his father Kieran was by her side.'* Married, those to witness the joining together of the two who said they could never be apart; were strangers brought in off the street and given money in return for the needed signatures. The long white cotton dress had been let out and the large bouquet matching the flowers in her hair hid what was about to make the two, three. Married? When everything the two had done was discovered, it appeared they did everything a young and in love couple should, leaving everyone including the authorities to question why, they saw fit to do everything in the blink of an eye?

Man and wife, Mr. and Mrs. Knight documented and registered what the law of the land said they must. Being married and having a baby meant them becoming a family, but when leaving the hospital, Mr. and Mrs. Kieran Knight left new born Lloyd Sapphire Knight, on his own. *'No time?'* Raven and the boy she said she loved, did everything together, with everything they did being done too soon. *'Too fast to live & too young to die.'* How had no one noticed them go? When discovering what they did? Investigators couldn't say whether or not there was a child within what had fallen from a great height before bursting into flames and exploding on impact. *'Boyfriend & girlfriend.'* Having met in the classroom and fallen in love in the school yard, they married in what was the quickest of ceremonies, before taking themselves into the nearest hospital where both said hello to their baby boy and then left.

Leaving Lloyd where they believed he would be found, the baby wrapped in a blanket with a photograph of his parents on their wedding day and a note asking he be send to his uncle Hunter Rock Sapphire along with an address, wasn't discovered by the authorities. Not found by someone wanting to do what they knew would be the right thing. What happened meant no one, but the one to have found and taken him; knowing for sure that Lloyd Sapphire Knight was alive? Alive and kicking, alive and screaming, alive and breathing, eating and sleeping within the gentle embrace of his new parents' arms.

Another mother without a child, she knew who he belonged to, because she was there when he was born. *'As close to him as his true mother?'* Taking what she found, leaving with what no one else had seen, not right? It wasn't right for a defenceless newborn to be left to the elements. *'Anything could have happened?'* Lots of things almost occurred, a fox sniffing what was unfamiliar took the bottle of milk almost knocking the basket off and down the steps on which it sat. Rain? If the sudden and heavy downpour had lasted for longer and the baby tucked in tight not been lay on his side, he might have swallowed the falling water too quickly and drowned. A baby shouldn't be given to people he didn't know. *'What if his uncle didn't want him?'* Keeping one eye on the health of the baby she saw to be a gift when discovering him on the steps of the hospital she was leaving having finished her night shift, nurse Mrs. Mavis Scott and her builder husband Trevor; read every newspaper reporting the sad story thought to have been a suicide pact, or terrible accident. *'Difficult to identify burned bodies.'* Discovered on the rocky beach at the bottom of a cliff, the remains found within the burned shell of their car; took time to identify.

'Time had always been the enemy.' Him having avoided falling into the hands of the authorities; was why Lloyd Knight Scott grew up not knowing who he was. Dying, some said her grandfather and parents' along with her twin brother died young, because it's difficult to gain age when suffering a broken heart. The existence of official documents and the large estate needing an heir, was why the case of the missing Lloyd Sapphire Knight was re-opened.

Allusive, having removed the Sapphire and kept Knight as a middle name when adding the family name Scott. Those to have taken Lloyd into their home and held him within their heart for what remained of their lifetime;

saw what they did as respectful and right. Nurtured and loved, adored and treasured. Brought up as their own, Lloyd would never have had any idea of his true identity had others not come looking to find him.

Lloyd Sapphire Knight would never have been found if those he called mum and dad hadn't kept what was his given Christian name. Born to a young couple unable to keep him. *'Forbidden lovers?'* Lost souls meeting and causing one another more pain than happiness. *'Not right,'* When Raven gave birth to Lloyd, Kieran told her it was time for them to leave. *'No time,'* Investigators discovered how Miss Sapphire and Master Knight lived a whole lifetime in the blink of an eye, becoming parents one day, after agreeing to become man and wife, on the third day they died. Rebellious, young and foolish, *'Husband, wife suicide.'* It was discovered how Raven and Kieran had become addicted to much more than one another. For Mr. and Mrs. Kieran Knight time had always been the enemy. Dying before the body of their daughter was identified, Ravens' parents never heard about what happened and her grieving brother Hunter felt guilty for not trying harder to find the sister he lost.

12: Arrival

From flamed torches and flickering candles inside protective lanterns to hand held torches and directional beams, that which was dark needed artificial light to enable sight when the moon shone and the sun went down. From dancing flames to directional beams, the type of light being used was what indicated the way in which time, the world and everyone had moved on. Searching for somewhere minus its' postal address, walking for what felt like hours, with torches in hand and all items needed to keep them hydrated and warm packed into the assortment of bags each carried. Where? The delving spotlights uncovered much before illuminating what they were looking for. *'Dark?'* Those use to city living, street lights and keeping up with what was on trend, wanted to wait until morning, minus the money for a hotel room, their vehicles being full to bursting, meant them having to find what they were looking for. *'Where to sleep?'* Parking his transit van and what had been the late Mr. Scotts, family saloon car in what looked to be a safe place by a sign directing them to **Hunters picnic huts, the** father of two told his family everything would be fine. *'Wrong?'*

When setting out on foot, the time said 16:00, how had midnight come and gone so fast? From wonderment to fear, Lilly loved the maze of different pathways leading from picnic area to adventure filled attraction, hating when the canopy formed by so many trees restricted her sight. *'Far from everything?'* Ebony Wood: The place name was the only address; giving little away while describing exactly what it was. *'A dark forest of trees.'* A woodland dividing a village and town, a place inside which; finding anything seemed impossible.

Witch

"Sorry Sir," The males locking what during the day was open to all; told those requesting directions, they didn't know how to find the accommodation said to be situated within what was growing dark and becoming more dense by the step. "We've never seen a house in these woods." Neither was lying, but both were hiding what each knew to be true. *'The witches hovel?'* When Lloyd said he was looking for what belonged to the Sapphire estate, those denying all knowledge of what he was talking about, were quick to realise they knew much more than he did. *'A new bossman?'* When daylight turned to dusk before dissolving into the deep darkness of night, the Scott family found themselves jumping at their own shadows and imagining what wasn't there. *'Where were they?'*

The back of beyond, in the middle of everywhere, they could be anywhere? The truth being that they were lost. Lost and wearing what wasn't appropriate, heels sinking into the soft earth, tired feet tripping over protruding roots and everything becoming caught on any and everything because what each wore was much too thin to keep them warm. Arms scratched by sharp branches.

"No," Martha told her daughter she shouldn't remove her shoes.

"Don't think they do fashion in the countryside sis." Walking together for hours meant bickering was bound to start sooner or later. "This is like the beginning of one of those haunted house films." Once all daylight faded; the younger members of the Scott family saw nothing good in what looked wrong and caused them to shiver.

The wrong shoes and inadequate coat, her having no gloves to cover her manicured finger nails was just another of the many things Lilly saw to complain about. *'Uncomfortable?'* The young female told her family she didn't like what her father said was them getting back to nature and her brother agreed, before reminding all, how his sister didn't do natural. *'Only fourteen, Miss Lilly*

RoseMay Scott was rarely seen without as much make-up as she could get away with.' Long false eyelashes and big hair, Miss Scott was a girl making the most of being girlie. *'Beehives, mini skirts & heeled knee high boots, she'd wear stilettos if she thought she would get away with it.'* Advised to rethink her fashion preference and ditch what was in her bursting wardrobe the one for who fashion had been her way into the hippiest group on the school yard saw her having to rethink her priorities.

"Cold," The dropping temperature was the one and only complaint made by the mother struggling to remain positive. An owl, numerous bats of various sizes and what felt like a thousand sets of eyes. Lloyd said it would do him and his family good not to relay on all the things they took for granted. Startled by something reaching out and touching her on her shoulder, Lilly told her father she saw street lighting to be a necessity, not a luxoury.

"What was that!" What Lilly described feeling, no one had seen? *'Too dark to see any & everything lay outside of the directional beams of the hand held torches.'* "I felt a hand on my shoulder." The youngest female insisted someone was following, telling those with her how someone had reached out in attempt to grab her?

"It was probably a tree branch." Her mother assured her she was fine. *'Twigs not fingers?'*

"It's why trees without leafs are called skeletons." Louis explained how branches looked like arms and twigs the fingers. Pushing him ahead, Lilly thanked her sniggering brother for turning every tree and bush into a potential monster.

"They're only trees." Lloyd told his children to stop their squabbling a leaf falling before Lilly's face and causing her to scream.

"I can't do this." Rushing forward and holding onto her brothers' coat Lilly hid behind his stronger male form in hope of gaining warmth and protection from what was her growing discomfort, fear and pain.

'Creepy?' How could anyone live within a place so inaccessible? Walking more slowly, slowing down because they were tired and being more observant because it was dark, Louis felt sure they'd walked in a circle to get to what stood within a billion trees.

"Is that it?" Disappointed, confused, tired and shocked. *'Their inheritance?'* The family from the city were told they'd inherited a family estate, unsure what to expect, neither expected what their searching eyes saw. Believing they were in line to take possession of a house they could turn into a comfortable family home, each struggled to hide the disappointment of finding what looked to be a wooden shack. *'It couldn't be could it?'* A wooden hovel surrounded by trees, not in the back of beyond, but far beyond what either imagined.

"Didn't you ask to see pictures?" The father of the family of four said there wasn't any documented information available for him to look at. *'A shed in the trees?'* Upon arriving at their destination, Lilly said she couldn't see what they'd found, being worth anything and her brother agreed.

A shed in the woods, a shack in the trees, all looked, but each failed to see another building in amongst what was seen to be their destination. *'How would they live in a shed?'* A shelter to have stood abandoned for years.

"A shed?" His offspring questioned how what stood before them, could be described as being a family estate? "It's a shed." The fourteen year old twosome said they couldn't live in what should be used for storage.

"A lodge," Seeing her husbands' smile dissolve and his bright hope filled eyes dim, Martha attempted to sound positive by telling her children not to be so judgmental.

"We've inherited a shed in the trees. There isn't even a road to drive in on." While being aware of what many would see as being inconvenient, Lloyd and Martha saw what was to be their new home as different. *'Unusual?'* Interesting and challenging, what lay before them would mean adapting to another way of life. *'Not what they expected.'* Perhaps they shouldn't have allowed their imagination to rule what was probability and common sense. What was one to think when the inheritance form said family estate? How were they to know what they would find was a single storey property made of wood on a stone base set in amongst a billion trees? *'Sorry,'* All felt sorry for him and herself, before feeling stupid for having misinterpreted what each read and Lloyd had attempted to take in. *'A family estate?'* Lawyers speak for a collective amount, surely his family would forgive what his being a builder; caused him to misread? *'His being a builder meant he could put things right.'* A Summerhouse? Shed, shack or lodge? What stood before them was a detached property and a lot of land. *'He could, he would build them an estate.'*

Property developers? It wouldn't be the first time others had attempted to take what had been left by the Sapphire family. *'Too much to lose.'* Those who lived and worked in the village of Déspoina and town of Erebus could ill afford losing what had been relied upon for generations, none would willing hand everything over to those ready and willing to destroy everything in the name of progress.

"You left them out there?" Legend and myth had long since become something kept alive for visiting tourists and fantasists, no longer believing, didn't mean those to have grown up in a place filled with stories about the witch of Ebony Wood were willing to enter what was said to be spirt filled after dark. *'Haunted?'* Even the realists took the views of the pessimistic when it came to not wanting to upset the witch. *'Not again?'* Fiction born of fact, there was no getting away from what was proven and no one wanted the horrors of the past to return.

"You didn't warn them?" Those to have bumped into the strangers in Ebony Wood reminded those asking their questions that their job was land maintenance and security, not tour guide, or estate agent.

"Shouldn't we go find them?" All concerned for the well being of the family searching for the house few had ever seen, agreed what would be, would be. *'The witch will decide.'* Drinking inside Tinkers Tavern, those who met at the end of each week to feedback on how things were. Agreed there was no need to jump ship until the ship started rocking. *'What would be, would be?'* All locals would be wary of those who quite clearly didn't come from the village, or neighbouring town.

Shocked, stunned, mesmerised and knocked for six. Surely there had to be a mistake? Momentarily speechless, each knew all would have much to say.

"Maybe it's the lodge for the big house." Shinning his torch in hope of finding a path which would lead them to somewhere more inviting; the younger male repeated his words of disbelief. "This can't be it?" Louis muttered. His young eyes straining through the dark as he felt sure he saw something moving? *'What was that?'* Was there someone out there? Sure he saw a hooded figure dashing from behind one tree and then another, the tired teen guessed the dark must be playing tricks. *'The dark was the true master of illusion.'*

"Here will be fine for tonight." Martha reminded her children of the fact they each had blankets and water. "We'll fetch everything else we need from the car in the morning." She forced a smile.

"Did we bring a bulldozer?" Lilly failed to share their mothers' optimism as her concerned brother rejoined them. "It's dirty and damp." The youngest female complained. "Where's the toilet?" Looking beyond his daughter to what surrounded them, Lloyd told her to pick a tree?

"Yuk!" Lilly complained loudly. "I hate sheds."

"Right now this is shelter." Martha sent a look to her children which said they shouldn't be so ungrateful, each looking to see the disappointment on their fathers face.

"Sorry," Louis apologised, nudging his sister. "I'm sure it will look better in daylight." All agreed there wasn't much hope of them finding the way back to the road in the middle of the night.

"It can't look any worse." Lilly's whisper disguised the fact she was holding her breath and keeping her fingers crossed in hope the key wouldn't fit the lock.

Hearing a rustling in the trees, Louis looked around himself before rushing to stay close to his parents who at that moment were walking up the steps leading to the only door into the small building. *'Was someone watching?'*

"What's up with you?" Lilly asked. Feeling the sudden urgency in her brothers' action as he sped by and she followed. Having found what they were looking for, all secretly wondered and worried about what would find them? The first night in what all believed would be a place where they could begin a new and much better life than the one they left behind.

Unlocking what was the only building for miles, Lloyd and his family had to come to terms with the fact, this was it. *'A shed in the trees?'* Louis asked his father if his biological family were a family of elves? *'Lloyd hadn't known his true family.'* His biological parents having abandoned him, meant any true relatives never knowing he existed. Why had he thought what was left for him to inherit, would have meaning? How could he be so foolish as to think a pair of runaway teenagers would have something of value to leave?

"Some estate?" The disappointed male sighed. His son pointing out that at least it hadn't been occupied by squatters, fingers crossed. "Or worse?" His young mind continued to question what he thought he saw outside? Searching for a distraction as all headed inside. *'Ghosts or wild animals?'* Could there be something worse than what was conjured up inside a teenagers' imagination?'

"Like they'd be able to find it." Being girlie didn't stop Lilly being brutal with words, especially when believing her opinion should count. "Hope you didn't hand back the keys for the flat." She muttered as all entered what was now their only place to be.

"Lodge, estate, or shed? This is home." Lloyd wanted to tell his daughter to stop being so down on the place, but if honest, he was thinking the exact same. *'What had he done?'*

Dark, dense and filled with shadowing trees for as far as the eye could see, anyone and everything could be lurking in the Wood, anyone could be waiting, ready to do who knew what? A billion bodies and a million eyes, Ebony Wood was a place able to keep much more than its' secrets safe, sound and out of sight. A feeling of being watched and a chill which caused a shiver. Quivering and shaking, a deer caught in the headlights was never as frightened as a deer trapped by what circled its' fragile form within the trees. Wise old owls and big black crows, ravens and bats, foxes, badgers and the scattering of a thousand mice, spiders, frogs and wart covered toads, moving branches and growing tree trunks, there was nothing which didn't live within the trees and everything to live within Ebony Wood was aware of the fact the next minute could bring death. Living, breathing, moving, hunting and hiding, staying alive within what was natures garden meant knowing how to survive. Anyone wanting to live in amongst what was natural, would mean them having to learn how to live within what was mother natures harsh land whilst abiding by what were her strict, unforgiving rules. Survival of the fittest, natures way meant a death being necessary so to preserve what is life.

"A shed," Lloyd felt if he heard the four letter word again he would flip, he understood and he was sorry, but there was nothing he could do. Unlocking what crept open to reveal a large single room with bare wood floor and walls. *'A box?'* He hoped his family couldn't read his thoughts. *'What had he done?'* No electricity, each placed his and her torch so to best see what was the large room they entered with caution. Lloyd spotting and saying he could get a fire started within the large inglenook fireplace. *'A nice feature.'* Martha said they should check what was behind the four doors and find somewhere to sleep. Making fires and any exploring could wait until morning.

Four empty rooms of the exact same size, double bedrooms, maybe? Same wooden floor and wood walls, all agreed what they found was as blank as any blank canvas could be. Feeling tired, all agreed each would be able to think more clearly after getting some sleep. *'A room each?'* Something the twins said they wanted wasn't something either was looking forward to having; when told to take their sleeping bag and chose a room.

"Maybe we should stay together." Louis hadn't meant to sound as anxious as his words revealed. "Mice?" He said there was bound to be something to have made its home in what stood empty for who knew how long?

"I'm not changing my clothes. I'm sleeping in everything." Lilly said she would stay in the main room with her brother, seeing the built in seating within the inglenook as being off the floor and suggesting they could sleep one either side of the fire pit big enough to take the largest of cooking pots. Using bags for pillows, the brother and sister agreed to being fine when their parents left to settle inside one of the rooms.

"I saw something." Louis waited for his parents to close the door before switching on his torch and telling Lilly he was sure he saw someone outside.

"I don't want to know." Lilly told him they were locked in and she needed to sleep. Tired, what was an uneasy sleep didn't come easy for the youngsters putting on a brave face while being fearful of the dark. Much too old to sleep with the light on, coming from the city meant Miss and Master Scott never before having encountered what each was calling the black dark. *'No artificial light,'* For those born and brought up in a place where all things natural felt unreal, a place where what was real had long since been replaced with what was manmade, nature was something the Scott's only ever saw in pictures and read about in books. *'Where were they?'* When waking the next morning, the question was, where was she?

Waking to find their daughter gone, Lloyd and Martha asked Louis where his sister was? He didn't know. She couldn't have gone far, but one didn't have to go far to become lost within what looked the same at every turn. Which way? Lost and out on her own. *'Who could they turn to for help?'*

"Lilly!" Not impressed to be woken from what had turned out to be his comfort filled slumber, Louis saw his spending his first morning away from the city out searching to find his sister as something he didn't want to have to get use to. "Maybe she went back to the car for her make-up bag, you know she can't start the day minus her foundation fix." No sibling ever willingly shown concern for another meaning no one being surprised when Louis attempted to make what had happened, sound like something not to worry about.

"Would you know your way back to the car?" His father asked and his mother said if they planned on staying, they would have to make the route from the property to the road, more visible, once they figured it out. *'Easier said than done?'* Mother nature was known to retaliate when what she created was disturbed.

"We should have thought to mark it last night." She scolded herself and her family for not thinking, as all realised they would also become lost if straying too far. *'Maybe they already were?'* How could anyone find the way, when every tree looked the same as every other tree? *'Where were they?'*

"We should split up." Louis said they needed to cover more ground, but his parents didn't agree.

"No," Martha shook her head. "Having one missing child is more than enough for one day, what if someones taken her?" She asked.

"They'd soon bring her back." Continuing in his attempt to ease the growing tension. Louis reminded his anxious parents' how even they struggled to put up with his sisters' wining once she got started.

"Lilly!" All called.

"What we need is a map." Lloyd said. No roads, no electricity and no way of knowing where in the Woods they were.

"Why would she leave?" Before going to sleep; the family agreed to explore their new environment together in daylight. "Where is she? Where are we?" Martha told her husband and son how what she thought would be a dream, was fast turning into a nightmare?

"Lilly!" All called.

"Lilly!" Those searching hoped the breeze they could feel; would carry their voices to the one they were looking to find and bring her back.

Witch

A darkness the like of which she had never encountered before, a stillness sending shivers to the base of ones spine. A body, nobody should feel how she was feeling. *'Fear.'* Coming from where she came from meant believing she was strong. *'Gangs.'* Streetwise, she knew to never allow herself to be venerable. *'Drunks, Flashers, Gangs & Groomers?'* In a place with so many hidden dangers, her parents' hadn't hidden what she should be aware and stay clear of. Maturing, Lilly's mother, father and her teachers were forever reminding her and others how what was dangerous and threatening in the city, could hide in clear sight. Someone disguised with a hood and those sitting behind the wheel of a slow moving car, when on the busy and fast moving streets of the city, all learned to protect themselves from what was out there. *'Pickpockets & Chancers?'*

Lost within a billion trees; with no knowledge of what surrounded her and nothing but her own instinct to rely on, Lilly didn't know what it was she was looking for? *'Where was she?'* How could darkness be so black it felt as though ones eyes were closed? *'What was she doing?'* How could one be sure they were alone, if they couldn't see what was around them? She thought she was sleeping. *'Cold?'* When she complained; her brother gave her his jacket, lay one either side of what if lit would keep them warmer than toast. Uneasy about sleeping in the shed hidden by trees on her own, she would never admit to agreeing to be in the same room as her brother because she was anxious. *'Locked.'* Lloyd assured all that he had checked and double checked there being no one and nothing inside with them, before turning the key and locking the only door. Safe. *'Where was she?'*

A darkness the like of which she had never encountered, could she be dreaming? One minute she was walking in amongst the trees with her brother and parents, the next she was on her own. *'Where was she?'* Ebony Wood, a place framed by picnic areas and dotted with attractions designed to be visited and enjoyed by the general public. Lilly imagined a large national park. Safe, her parents' said a village and small town would be safer and more friendly. Walking through the trees, Lilly didn't feel like she was amongst friends. Not safe, a million bodies and a thousand eyes. Lloyd told his daughter what she was sensing was the wildlife. The figure standing before her didn't look like any animal she'd ever heard of or seen. *'Who was she?'* Wrapped in a long black cloak, her head covered by its' oversized hood. *'What was she doing standing alone in the dark?'* Alone and feeling lost, Lilly followed, but she didn't know who she was following, unable to know why? Lilly knew not to take the lead ahead of the stranger.

Startled by a strange sound, in the absence of any curtains, shutters or a blind, the outside darkness appeared black. *'Was the outside coming in?'* Rolling like smoke through what she saw to be ill fitting window panes. How could what contained no light, seem brighter than what was coming in. Dark, what lay outside the glass resembled a blackboard and what suddenly appeared up against it, looked to be a single finger with long pointed finger nail, scrapping and making the mark of a lightening strike on what turned from black to white. Who? What was there? Why had she stood? Why hadn't she felt frightened? Why had she left the rest of her family sleeping and why had she stepped out when the door burst open?

Not afraid, the female who was a stranger to her surroundings; felt her every emotion subside when finding herself stood looking down on what was fast running water. *'How had she got there?'* One minute she stepped outside the door of the shed in the woods the next she was engulfed by trees and then she was stood looking into a river. *'Where was she?'* From darkness to a bright white light, Lilly gasped at the wonderment lay before her. *'Beautiful?'* From feeling like she was walking with her eyes shut, she saw a sight to cause her eyes to open wide. From standing and looking down; the lost female found herself standing on what felt like a pebbled beach overlooking a lake. Able to see the land and tall trees on the other side, the stretch of water which veered both to the left and the right was vast. *'Breathtaking,'* Feeling her body shudder when realising there was another standing by her side. *'Who was she & what did she want?'* Knowing without seeing, Lilly believed she was in the company of another female, an older, wiser female, a female whose features remained covered by what she wore to cover her head, neither spoke because both knew what each should do. *'Enter the water.'*

"Lilly!" He called. "Lilly!" He continued to shout when running full speed towards her. "Lilly what do you think you're doing?" Stretching out and pulling her back from the waters edge, joined by their parents, all believed Lilly was sleepwalking.

"Your first job is to secure the door and windows." Lloyd agreed he could and would do whatever was needed to keep their daughter from wandering out on her own again.

"Where did she go?" Having seen only Lilly, those to have found her, said she must have been dreaming when she asked about the woman to have been by her side?

"Now all we have to do is find our way back." Telling them she knew the way, Lilly shrugged when asked how? Perhaps she'd created a map in her mind while wandering through the trees in her sleep. However Lilly had discovered her way in and around Ebony Wood, her family were glad she had, especially when later that day, she was able to show them a much quicker way from the road to the property they intended to make their new home. *'The shed in the trees.'*

"You memorised the way?" Louis question his sisters' new found ability to navigate her way as they walked ahead of the elders discussing how to best create a path.

"I guess." Lilly nodded.

"Were you going to jump in?" When out of earshot Louis needed to know why his sister was going to throw herself into the river?

"Not alone," The young female shook her head.

"There wasn't anyone else."

"She was by my side." Lilly disagreed with being alone when Louis found her.

"You must have been dreaming." Aware of how rarely he won an argument, her brother said what had happened was probably nothing to worry about. *'A reaction to being in a new place?'* The twins agreed to look out for one another like they always did. Lilly agreeing to share what she learned about Ebony Wood by helping Louis with what she told him would have to be his improved sense of direction.

Moving into what had been left in the last will and testament of an unknown uncle. Mr. Lloyd Knight Scott and his loved ones were curious.*' Together,'* Having moved the mattresses brought with them from the van into the room each chose to be their individual bedroom, a second night in the shed in the Wood, saw each awake to a bright but confusing morning. Looking around what would be their new family home, those hoping to have found something better, wondered what they were going to do with what they had? Having discovered new pathways and cut-throughs missed in the dark, each realised what had taken hours to discover on the first day, could be reached in a matter of minutes. *'Curious?'* Arriving under the shadow of darkness, the family of four hadn't expected anything like what they found. A cottage, the village location indicated something small and run down. Prepared to work, Lloyd hadn't imagined what was being called an estate, being made up in the main of trees. *'A forest?'*

Witch

Arriving unannounced, Lloyd mistook those standing at the front door of their high rise flat as being people they weren't. Bad news? His wife Martha and him taking over what had been his council run family home; wasn't proving to be as easy as they thought. Struggling to pay mounding bills while meeting outstanding funeral costs and trying to catch up with months of arrears. His parents had been good people and them falling ill, meant both losing what had always been wages amounting to just enough to get by. Friendly, streetwise, city savvy and approachable Mr. Scott found himself sought out, tracked down and accosted by two officials he perceived as wanting something from him. *'Suffering enough?'* Having lost the people he called mum and dad, Lloyd hadn't wanted to reply the letters sent by those he found himself coming face to face with when returning from a rare family night out at the annual fair. Having written and called him at work in attempt to make an appointment, afraid he and his family were about to be told they were in more financial trouble, Lloyd was stunned to discover he could be the last in line and sole beneficiary of the Sapphire family estate.

'Who?' There were more checks to be done, but once all the sought information was gained and all other interest registered, Lloyd would be invited to claim his inheritance. *'Too good to be true?'* With processes and procedure to be completed, the father of two was assured there was property included, when told he was entitled to the estate. A builder tired of having to take orders from his ungrateful chain-smoking boss, a father living in constant fear for the safety of his children and a husband wanting to provide a more comfortable life for his hard working wife. *'Wrong to dream?'* Martha aired her concerns, but agreed them living in a place with no rent to pay, would be a luxury they could ill afford to turn down. *'Their own place?'* A couple being worn down by trying to do the best they could, there was no doubting Lloyd and Martha were and always had been good to-

gether and together the two believed they could face and succeed whatever came their way. *'A change in location & lifestyle?'* The misfits who fit together had met at school, friends to have fallen for one another's defensive charms; Martha and Lloyd had quickly become what they called one another's everything.

Shocked, his unexpected visitors had forced something Lloyd believed he would have a lifetime to do. Not a task anyone looks forward to, Lloyd had to look through what were his deceased parents private papers. Checking through both personal and official paperwork kept in keepsake boxes by Mr. Trevor and Mrs. Mavis Scott, the one brought up as their only son; found what confirmed Mavis being a registered nurse and Trevor a qualified builder. Professional people, Mavis was the carer who found herself having to be cared for when her memory started to fail her. Was memory loss the reason she never told him? A wonderful woman, when Lloyd and Trevor began to struggle, Martha stepped in to help. Together since the first day they met and there for one another no matter what. Moving in with the father and son to be on hand to support them, Martha had gone on to change her place of employment from stacking shelves in the local supermarket, to support worker at the nearest care home, becoming Lloyds' wife while her mother-in-law still knew who she was. When helping her husband to find what they found, Martha said she was sorry.

'My name is Lloyd Sapphire Knight. Please be gentle with me & take me to my uncle Hunter Rock Sapphire.'

The address was for a large house in the city, a property sold by his uncle when his grandparents passed. A memory box, Lloyd couldn't understand why those he loved and respected hadn't told him what a hand written note explained. *'His genuine birth certificate.'* The letter said they kept his given name out of respect for the young couple Mavis would thank everyday for having gifted him to her and her loyal, loving, hardworking husband. Nurse Mavis Scott had been there at his birth, the first to hold him, the one to have fed and settled him on the night before the early morning when her leaving her nightshift led her to find him on the hospital steps. *'Waiting for her, not abandoned?'* The words written were typical of the way Mavis always saw the good in everyone and everything. *'Not who he thought he was?'*

A photograph of his biological parents on their wedding day. When checking dates, Lloyd questioned why Raven and Kieran had committed to one another the day before he was born? Why become a family and leave their only child behind? *'An accident?'* Newspaper cuttings reported both what could have happened alongside what authorities investigating the tragedy believed to have occurred. *'Suicide.'* Martha said she was glad his parents hadn't taken him with them. Explaining everything in the letters they left; Mavis and Trevor apologised to the one they would forever call their son, for doing what they saw to be the right thing. Wanted, treasured, adored and loved, both said they were proud of the man Lloyd had become. No regrets, Mavis said finding him, convinced her she should be a mother and Trevor told how he visited the city address to discover the building had been sold to people who didn't know his uncle or where he was. Fate, how could Lloyd argue or be upset about what just was? Thrown from the falling car out onto the beach and swept away by the sea. Some reports saw there being a possibility the young couples' new born baby was with them when the car went over the cliff. *'Not who he thought he was?'*

Martha didn't know where her true family were because, she was the one who walked away. Tired of being sent out to walk the street whenever one of her many uncles didn't want her around. A child only wanted, when her mother had nothing and no one else. Martha wandered into the local police station to tell the officer on the desk she didn't know who, or where she was. A mother who never owned up to having lost her child. Martha Green named herself when aged ten years, quickly forgetting, because she stopped using her given birth name. Growing up in care, Lloyd's wife called him lucky and knowing her past, he knew she was right. Not who he thought he was? Given the key to what officials were calling his. Lloyd realised what he inherited, wasn't what he thought it would be either.

Having arrived unannounced, the last surviving relatives of Lord Hunter Rock Sapphire and his twin sister Raven Rose were immediately seen by those unaware of who they were as being different. Odd, secretive and mysterious, almost everyone saw the Scott family as being people with something to hide. A family? *'Them not sharing the Sapphire name meant people seeing them to be outsiders?'* A family? From where? Hunter had added his twin sisters' details to the wall, but them having lost one another at the age of fifteen, saw his hurt as the reason he failed to disclose or discuss their truth. Hunter couldn't mention what he didn't know and he didn't know his runaway sister and her older lover had gotten married and had a child.

The last will and testament of Hunter Rock Sapphire left whatever was his, to his only sister. *'Lloyd being Ravens' biological son, meant he received everything.'* A nephew he never knew and family member no Sapphire ever met. *'Flesh & blood.'* His true families' estate, Lilly and Louis refused to promise they wouldn't sell what had been gifted under the heading inheritance. *'Lucky to give it away?'* When laying eyes on a building the like of which neither had expected to see, the teens had at first been confused. Looking better in the light, not quite a garden shed, the younger members in the Scott family struggled to see what their parents' called their new home as being a lodge. A raised stone base with built in

Witch

steps leading up to what formed five rooms under a sloping roof, a structure built from wooden planks which in places were cladded by full and half logs. When sat thinking about what was, the disappointed twins concluded what they inherited amounting to nothing more than a whole heap of trees.

Once their presence became public knowledge, the Scott family failed to understand why they were seen as the type of people to be avoided. *'From the city?'*
"Of course we're odd, we gave up bricks and mortar to live in a shed disguised by trees." Lilly RoseMay agreed she and her family must come across to others as being crazy. "We inherited the Sapphire family estate and our surname is Scott." The intelligent teen pointed out what she saw others questioning. Arriving unannounced, having moved from a place where each had been born, to be somewhere none had ever heard of. Lloyd and his family were strangers and strangers should never be trusted. *'Squatters?'* The more suspicious saw them as being a family placed in witness protection. Relocated, some suspected one, or more new arrival to be an ex-criminal living under a new identity. Whoever, from wherever, many said they didn't want their type, moving in. Home, the truth was that Lloyd and those he brought with him, had nowhere else to go.

Deep within land eclipsed by tree saturated with shrubs and littered with both clear pathways and concealed trails, secluded, but never isolated, hidden but not in hiding, living how nature intended, the Scott family from the city needed to learn how to survive off what was provided naturally within and across the vast and varied acreage which official papers said they owned. *'What choice did they have?'* Not sold, not a cooperative, the Scott's had no idea about what was the extent of their fortune?

"A Shed?" First impressions weren't good, but the family had made their decision and for Lloyd, his wife

Martha and children Louis and Lilly there was no going back. *'Running away?'*

"I can make it better." The head of the household assured his doubting offspring, him being a builder by trade meant him seeing what they had, to be a true gift. Certain planning permission wouldn't be restricted should they decide to build above or below what was already there, Lloyd assured those he loved and wanted to protect what they had could be turned into a dream home.

"Without money?" All questioned how he would achieve what seemed an impossible task. *'Disappointed.'*

13: New

*W*hen leaving the city, Mr. and Mrs. Scott, left what was their paid employment. *'What had they done?'* Crazy, able to agree, Lilly and Louis saw how their new way of living could be more peace filled, but struggled to understand how what had been given to their father, could be described as a family estate. A single storey wooden lodge engulfed by trees, even the most imaginative of house sellers would have their work cut out coming up with a way of making what the Scott's inherited attractive. *'Better on the inside?'* Inside was one large square room with four smaller rooms, each able to accommodate a double bed.

"A holiday chalet," Louis announced while his sister called the wooden shake a shed. Discovering an outside water closet? Lilly said they couldn't stay. Spacious, whilst each family member would have their own bedroom, all wondered where and how they would wash. *'A large shed?'* There was nothing anyone could say to change the mind of a teen once it was made up. *'Dirty.'* Once what looked to be the years of accumulated dust was cleared, what the Scott family found; felt empty and cold.

Having run away from a life filled with constant struggles, Lloyd assured his concerned wife everything would workout. With no rent to pay, the male who prided himself on his skill as a builder, promised he would take whatever work was on offer to pay their way. Aware his offspring would never accept them having to use a tin bath, the proud father promised his first wage packet would be spent on installing a shower. Yes, for every problem Lloyd said he'd find a solution. What he couldn't fix, he would make new and what they needed, he promised to find.

Overshadowed, dark and smelly, having found and figured out how the outside toilet functioned, or rather how it didn't, Lilly told her father he had to sort something fast. *'Chemicals?'* When finding something else they needed; all realised what they didn't have, was money.

"Is this place better than being in the city?" Hearing what his family were saying and understanding how each had a point, Lloyd asked they give what was their new situation a chance. *'Time?'* Kept busy with what didn't need cash, the builder with no paid work, set about repairing and preparing what he could.

Turning over the soil within the high walled veg, fruit and herb garden, Lloyd came running when he heard his wife scream, startled by what she found within what from the outside looked like a box created by the precise positioning of sixty-six trees. Trees forming an archway over a broken gate and standing strong on the outside of a dry stone wall which in places only stood to waist height.

"A graveyard?" What Martha saw as spooky, weird and not right, Lloyd said was practical. *'Money saving?'* A private burial ground housing the remains of his bloodline ancestors, walking around what they explored together, Martha insisted everything be tidier, organised and secured, In need of mending, starting with the broken gate and what in places was the falling wall. Finding what they found, to be both sad and disturbing, Martha said she didn't want wandering spirts making their way out, over and into the house. *'The shack?'*

"Uncle Hunter?" Lloyd looked down on what was one of the most recent graves, a grave occupied by the man his biological mother wanted him to live with.

"And his wife," Martha read what was inscribed on the headstone to the left of what her husband was reading. "They died together." She gasped. Sad and tragic, when realising how young the couple had been; Martha agreed she and her family should see themselves as fortunate.

A burial ground filled with many who were too young to die. Questioning what was the countryside and outdoor living, asking if living in amongst the trees, was healthier than living in the city? Lilly wasn't the first to notice the fact her fathers' relatives led much shorter lives than she, or any of her generation expected.
"My grandparents?" Walking amongst headstones, plaques, statues and memorial benches telling of those whose bodies were buried and ashes scattered within what sat within his land, Lloyd agreed to it feeling strange to be in amongst those he should have known. "Mavis and Trevor should be here." Being in possession of the ashes of those to have brought him up as their son, Lloyd said his mum and dad belonged with his family.
"I think they'd like that." Louis agreed when Lloyd said they should scatter the ashes of those he'd loved, in amongst those all felt sure would have loved him.

People separated in life, reunited in death. Agreeing to help, all saw the installation of another memorial bench with a plaque dedicated to those Lloyd called mum and dad, was both a great idea and fitting tribute.
"Of course not." Martha said she didn't mind; so long as all remained within the trees and wall designed to keep them confined. Asking her husband to make the wall higher. "I want a lock on that gate." While aware what they had on their doorstep; blended seamlessly into what were their new surroundings while being a place none had to enter, the nervousness in Martha's voice was heard to reveal what she tried to disguise. *'A fear of the unknown?'* Appreciative of her support, the man of the house agreed to being willing to learn new skills when taking on the tasks being set.

Dry stone wall rebuilding, weeding and landscaping, marking out new garden areas to fit around what was already there. When permitted to take as much land as one wanted; so to create ones own outdoor space; all found it difficult to say when enough was enough. Chopping down long grass, upon discovering a swing attached to a tree; Lilly said she was a little old, but agreed when cleared and cleaned, what blended into its' surroundings, should stay.

"I hate this place." When daylight faded and he was unable to continue working outside, Lloyd sat drawing up plans to transform the five rooms into a much grander family home. *'His project.'* Enthusiastic, when Lilly said she hated where they were because it lacked a proper bathroom, her father worried what little money they had, would run out too quickly.

Having seen the opportunity and taken it, upon arriving at what their children called a shed. Mr. and Mrs. Scott worried the decision they made, was reckless. No paid employment, the local school agreed to having space for the twins, but how would they live without money for food? *'Homely?'* When clean and cleared, the inherited structure appeared stable and sound, no electricity meant not being able to use many of the items each relied upon. No music system, even if they could afford to replace the batteries for the radio normally listened to whilst having breakfast together, them being in amongst so many trees, made picking up any kind of signal impossible. *'Other things to do?'* Neither adult had ever operated a cooker to run on logs, or relied upon lights powered by oil. Basic, when the weather cooled, what used fire to work, would need to be kept burning so to provide heat. Fresh running water direct from their own personal well. When Lloyd said he could and would modernise what was their new living accommodation, his wife supported him in front of the children, while asking how and with what, when the two were alone.

No income and no other place to be, no friends to turn to, each was the others only family. *'What to do?'*

Witch

Without words, when their children complained, both adults questioned what it was they'd done? *'No going back,'* What had they expected? Something sounding too good to be true, very often turned out to be just that. *'Stupid?'* They should have known they weren't the type whose luck would change. Happy, loving and loyal, not the kind of people who won big, or inherited a fortune. *'Why had they ran?'* While being over a billion percent certain the man she felt proud to call her husband would keep to his word and create something out of what was nothing. Martha had to ask how? With no income, what little money they had, would vanish fast once the food was gone. *'His vision?'* Plans to transform what locals called the Sapphires hideaway when being polite and the witches abandoned hovel behind the backs of those there declaring their right to ownership. *'The new owners of the Sapphire estate?'* The new unknowing, disappointed residents of Ebony Wood, wondered how they'd create a new life out of nothing?

Situated between a prosperous town and quaint village, Lloyd believed their new home would provide them with everything they needed. *'Grow their own food.'* They still needed to buy seeds. *'Sell veg & herbs at market.'* Such things had to grow first and growing things took time they might not have. Ideas of how they could survive within what Louis called the wilderness, were plentiful, but all knew them putting what they thought, into practice wouldn't, because it couldn't happen overnight, not easy. *'A new struggle?'* Coming from a place where space had been minimal and paying the mounding bills something they would never get on top of, Lloyd and Martha couldn't believe they'd escaped what felt to be a doomed fate, only to be faced with what each saw to be more problematic.

Determined to do what they could and wanting what was new to succeed. *'Let down.'* Having spent their life living in a high rise tower block maintained poorly by the local council, Louis and Lilly couldn't believe the freedom which came with space. Roaming through what each said would be wonderful; if being experienced on a day trip. Racing around like children; when they believed no one was watching, what was free felt exciting, exploring what was Ebony Wood, when taking a break from assisting their parents with the cleaning, clearing and adapting of what was basic. Unable to see the hidden potential in anything, those accustomed to keeping themselves and what was their business to themselves; saw others not wanting to mix, easier to accept than the lack of electricity, cold water and what on the first time it rained, turned out to be a leaking roof. No friends; seemed little price to pay for everything they believed they'd gain. *'Surviving with nothing?'* A strange place to live, turned out to be a nice place to be and great place to visit.

Together, alone in a place where mother nature was quick to take back and recover everything manmade, including the pathways weaving through and between areas cleared for public use. **Hunters Picnic Huts,** six wooden tables with benches beneath canopies made of straw. **Reece's & Roman's Rest** A recreation area with a field of soft green grass boarded by more wooden picnic benches to provide places where visitors could rest and relax or play ball games. Family fun areas placed beside the four main entries into Ebony wood. **Rock's Picnic Patch** was closest to where the local stream ran in through the trees containing a stone filled stretch of shallow water and a bridge, more picnic tables, the only area visible from the village, Rock's Picnic Patch, sat across the road from the market square.

Walking around and standing back, Louis and Lilly observed how others backed away, seeing the two as strange. Looking and listening, the newcomers were informed that they could segregate what was their personal dwelling, but couldn't restrict public access through, or to the recreation areas situated within the privately owned Wood. *'Hidden but never in hiding?'* Within days, Lloyd and his loyal family were struggling to take on the challenge of living how nature intended and going without all the things taken for granted when living in the city?

"A Wood?" While exploring and saying somethings were nice, the younger family members were far from impressed with what was inconvenient. Agreeing any where was better than the cold, damp, unfriendly high rise, neither teen liked how it felt, when them being within the tree, felt scary.

"A Forest?" Louis told his sister those they left behind would be impressed by the fact they were land owners. *'It could work.'* Like their parents, Lilly and Louis agreed to give what was proving difficult, a chance.

"It could be fun." The youngest male of the family disagreed when his sister said they were too old to enjoy the attractions which the many printed signs said were free to all locals. *'Honesty boxes?'* When told about what his children had seen; Lloyd agreed they should look into what happened to any money collected within what belonged to them? Maintenance and repairs, when checking things out, Mr. Scott wondered who was responsible for paying the wage of those he saw tending to what was open to all. The Enchanted fairy forest, Giants liar and Creepers Corner, when looking at what was there for the amusement of others, the confused family questioned whether or not someone would owe them for using their land.

Doing what they could, arranging their mattresses and making their own beds. Carrying the old armchair to have belonged to his father, his' favourite and something Lloyd said he could never be without, When placing what was old but comfortable within the large open room, Martha said she wished she'd thought to bring the sofa too. Shoes coats and all the things they saw as being personal items. Louis questioned why his sister insisted on having her vinyl collection and record player when she wouldn't get to use them anytime soon. *'No electric?'* Lloyd said he would try, but them being connected to power lines was low on his growing list of priorities. Glad he brought his tools, the leaking roof was patched quickly. Pleased to have packed cleaning products, her sweeping brush, bucket and mop, Martha cleaned any and everywhere she could, turning sheets into curtains, Lloyd chopped into a fallen tree, to make shelves for his wife to store her pots and pans.

Cleaner and more homely, each did what they could to adapt and make the most of what they had. Clean clothes, discovering a launderette in the village, Martha had her husband agree to there being some, things she wasn't able to do without enough hot water. An on-going expense, Mrs. Scott applying for and being given the part time position of laundry assistant went some way to them having a regular household income. *'Cash in hand.'* What was minimum, was better than nothing and three days a week meant what Martha earned would put a little food on the table, no one relished the thought of having to handle what others made unclean and Lloyd hated his wife having to walk through the trees on her own. *'Realistic,'* When becoming parents' both said they would always do whatever needed to be done for themselves and their family. Unable to install a road and not permitted to run any direct path from their new property to either the village or town, Lloyd assured Martha he would find work enough to support what would be their new life. *'A brighter future?'*

Handing in his notice to quit his job and waiting until he received money owned. Mr. Scott told his family to gather up their belongings and take whatever would fit inside the family estate and his transit van. Leaving the city in the middle of the night, savings amounted to little more than enough to purchase the fuel needed to get them from where they were to where they needed to go.

Witch

'If their clapped out car made the distance?' With food enough to last them the week. *'A moonlight flit,'* His hope was to find new employment and have money in the bank before those he owned; caught up with him for missed rent, unpaid utility bills and an unsecured private, heavy, interest increasing loan taken out to cover his mother and fathers' funerals. *'A better life?'*

"We don't need money." While his wife and children worried, once he got started, Lloyd saw only the potential of what was theirs. A good father and qualified builder, he would build a Palace for his Queen which was strong enough to be seen as a castle able to protect and keep safe his growing Prince and Princess. Whilst the future promised much, Martha was worried about now. *'What would happen next?'* With space enough to build up, down, out and all around, he had the knowhow and capability, but Lloyd lacked the needed materials and money. *'Good thing he thought to keep his tools & a few which weren't his.'* Using what he had, the man of the house set about fixing what he could. *'No more leaking roof,'* Moving inside, the one brought up within the building trade, envisaged a place with four, maybe five bedrooms. Smiling when he thought about what he saw being made of wood and slate, the ideal materials for a fully fitted kitchen to blend seamlessly and look magnificent set around space enough for his family and houseguests to lounge and dine. A separate sitting room would be where they would gather to sit, play board and card games or watch a film on tv. *'A television?'* The family didn't have funds enough to purchase an aerial, let alone a working tv set. *'No electricity?'* What they needed was a generator. Burning logs inside both the inglenook fireplace and Rayburn cooker kept them warm, but boiling water for the tin bath they placed inside the fifth room and doing everything by torch and candlelight once the sun went down would soon loose its' rustic romance. *'Turning a shed into a dream home?'* For every problem something was needed and what was needed cost money. *'Money they didn't have.'*

The Scott family had never had money. In one hand and out the other, losing his wife Mavis allowed Trevors cancer to bite hard and take him too, two deaths within the same fortnight meant two funerals needing to be paid for. Everyone was sorry while no one saw what amplified Lloyd's actual pain. Wishing Trevor was there to help him build what he and his family dreamt of living in. Everyone deserved the right to dream, his dreaming meant the mother of the family having to remind Lloyd about being practical. *'A job meant being paid?'* There was more than enough to do to keep them busy in and outside their gained property but them being minus funds meant no one would eat.

Master of all he surveyed, receiving head shakes and not handshakes; between job hunting and handing out his hand written CV, Lloyd kept himself busy. Mr. Scott finding himself unemployable, wasn't something he anticipated. Over qualified and not needed. The role of school caretaker was given to someone local and there being no building or maintenance contracts to be had anywhere, Lloyd having looked everywhere led to finding nothing. Highly skilled and more than willing, the workman wanting work, was left waiting to hear from those in need of an odd job man. *'Checking where to purchase materials.'* Helpful, Lloyd found himself advising and instructing those asking about how to do simple repairs by themselves. *'Good people,'* Those to encounter and talk to the new residents of Ebony Wood; failed to find fault but continue to be wary and worry about their intent.

Master in his new home, with time on his hands, Lloyd set about extending the external wrap around wood veranda so it could be duplicated with a first floor balcony when he eventually built up to create the ideal place to stand and survey his tree covered kingdom. Optimistic, having uncovered a series of caves in the basement where tunnel like corridors led into spaces ripe for creating an organised maze of unique rooms, Lloyd's inner caveman foresaw countless possibilities to include a wine cella? Even if neither he or his wife knew very much about wine, fine, or otherwise. A private bar? His wife said it would be more practical to use the vast space for storage, should the family ever own anything they needed to store? A workshop? The fully trained; experienced builder could and would turn his talented hands to anything, but had to admit his personal skill was in mending and expanding what was already there, never having had the opportunity to be creative Martha agreed when Lloyd said what he didn't lack was vision.

A games room, a friendly social person, Mr. Scott could see himself hosting card games and men only nights in his very own man cave. His being new meant him not having any friends yet. A mini cinema? Should they ever install a generator? For someone with so little, Lloyd had never been afraid to dream big, his never having been a smoker didn't stop him liking the idea of a bookshelf encased room housing coordinating hardback books around large green or red leather armchairs smelling of important cigars. What man didn't want his own crystal decanter and whiskey glass? *'A true old style gentleman.'* With no paid work, Lloyd had more than enough to keep him from being idle while still finding plenty of time to dream. What city dwelling male hadn't dreamt of being an estate owning country gent?

A new place and new home, while the adults needed new jobs, Lilly and Louis had to go to a new school. Making do, Martha found being able to wash and dry what she needed for free; so long as there was a machine not being used during her shift, to be a bonus while the use of the iron and press was priceless. A man of his word, a property and land owner. *'A stranger in town?'* Master in his own home, when everyone else pointed out the negatives, Lloyd found what was positive. Space and situation. *'No mortgage.'* Discovering stones enough to reinforce the foundation of what he foresaw becoming his fortress, Lloyd fixed and made higher what was the dry stone wall encasing the small yet busy private burial ground. *'Kept busy.'* Doing all he could to improve their shed in the trees, Lloyd collected whatever materials his vast land provided in attempt to improve what he knew he could make better. *'A wheelbarrow & some discarded pipe.'* Whilst not being or providing the riches they'd hoped, Ebony Wood proved fruitful in giving what was useful. Repairs and prep work, what his wife called time consuming, Lloyd knew to be necessary for his vision to become a reality.

"It's free." His time, the rocks he collected, wood supplied by fallen trees and whatever others saw fit to discard within enough trees to hide it. "It will be amazing." He promised he wasn't ignoring what was important. A wheelbarrow and different lengths of pipe. Called upon to do simple plumbing jobs and hired to replace a large kitchen. Lloyd returning with some of the items he removed from the homes of others, wasn't as bad as his family saw it to be. *'Making old new?'* Unwanted appliances and secondhand fitments, *'Beggars?'* Lloyd told his children they would never live on handout, but called his accepting what he was given; different.

"Tomorrow," Returning home tired from their first day of school, the twin brother and sister asked their father to be kind. *'Normally happy to help.'* Louis and Lilly had hoped their parents wouldn't rush to find them a new place of education. Surely they could have waited to see if they were staying? Their mother suggested they put what they'd inherited up for sale and their father asked his inpatient wife to wait. The Law on the other hand wouldn't be so lenient if it was discovered responsible parents were keeping their offspring from what was compulsory.

Witch

"Tomorrow," Questioning her son when hearing the same word leaving his mouth for a second day. "Tomorrow, I promise." Louis used the excuse over again while never one to hold back, Lilly informed their parent it had been a hard day, adding the fact them not sleeping on what was uncomfortable and cold didn't help. *'It will get better.'* When seeing her children upset, Martha told her husband things needed to improve fast.

Quaint, the picturesque village of Déspoina felt like it had been painted, not created. *'Unreal?'* An oasis within a desert of five hundred shades of green. With row after row of cottages dotted in amongst larger semi and detached period properties, nothing looked out of place. Clean and fresh, open and inviting. The couple use to the sights, sounds and smells of the city; found the cobbled market square framed by perfectly designed and immaculately kept mini gardens with small patches of lawned and raised flowerbeds containing integrated wood and stone seating beautiful. *'Breathtaking?'* Encased by a vast and varied array of small family run retail businesses. *'Comfortable?'* Use to the smells of the streets, Lloyd and Martha savoured the armours of the fresh grass and growing blossom. *'Impressed.'* The exploring newcomers saw where to gain whatever it was they needed. *'The butcher & the baker,'* Martha admired the hand crafted candles and trinkets alongside what was advertised to be local glass and pottery. *'The cobbler & Key maker,'* Knitwear which had never been anywhere near a machine was joined by fabrics waiting to be turned into individually fashioned designs. *'The fish monger & green grocer,'* While Martha's attention remained focused on the practical, Lloyd was drawn to the antique furnishing, the carpenter and the stone mason. *'Strange?'* A sign inviting people to design their own coffin was seen as being a service which took the pressure off the bereaved, while making certain the deceased got what they wanted. Holistic therapies and counselling sessions, Mr. and Mrs. Scott joked about making notes of the time for the advertised group sessions, just in case?

Old fashioned, small cafes and uncluttered coffee shops, inside some of the hospitality units, customers were given the chance to browse the works of local artists hung on the wall while others encouraged people to stay and read whatever from the small library of newspapers, magazines and books. When making enquiries about the

Witch

things they couldn't see, the new arrivals were directed into the neighbouring town and nearest shopping mall. Happy to promote what stood on the other side of Ebony Wood, Lloyd and Martha were told the town of Erebus sold almost everything the village didn't have space for. *'New beds.'* They couldn't afford what they were looking to find, but they needed to know how much they were looking at having to save.

Quaint, different, more open, more old fashioned, compact but not closed in. All which the newcomers saw as being traditional was what their judgmental offspring would call outdated. *'Tea & coffee shop,'* A sweet and ice cream shop, the parents of two had to read what described itself as being especially for the young, a place for them to gather after school and call into to pick up a warming drink on the way. The Vimto Shop was seen to be a good idea. 5p a cup and 15p for a filled flask, a poster displayed how the shop owners would be happy to fill hot water bottles when the early morning walk to school meant children walking on ice. *'Thoughtful?'* What was heated in the winter, contained added ice come summertime

Not crowded like the city, busy enough, the villagers they met, agreed the place they worked and lived within provided everything anyone could need. A community spirit neither Lloyd or Martha had experienced before. *'Something had to be wrong?'* In the same way the happy couple knew they should never have trusted what sounded too good to be true, the wandering pair reminded one another to be wary of what, if put on paper; would sound like paradise. *'Where was the sting in the tail?'* Aware of all the things they and their children would need to put right, overcome and adapt both wondered what it was their children found not to like when exploring the surroundings. A doctors and a dentist, popping in to each to register their intent to become full-time residence, the couple agreed to fill in what they could and return with all official documents needed as soon as possible. *'Back the next day.'* Agreeing to liking what they saw, when stopping by her place of employment and introducing her husband to her employees, both were encouraged to call into Tinkers Tavern if wanting a meal before heading home

The oldest building in the area, it was when told the large establishment was always looking for staff that Lloyd said they should call in. Not afternoon drinkers, the truth was, the two rarely drank anything stronger than coffee. *'No money?'* Using the line of having to speculate to aciculate, Martha apologised when she laughed at the thought of her husband working behind a bar. *'Any job was better than no job.'* The couple together since they were at school, knew they would always be there for one another in everything each chose, or needed to do. *'Sorry,'* Only the tea shop served breakfast which finished at eleven. The fish and chips shop only opened twelve to seven Tuesday and Thursday and three to ten Fridays. *'Sorry,'* The village bakery said it was usual for them to be sold out of everything by noon. Home to see what they could find, or lunch inside Tinkers Tavern? Spending a little could be worth much, both adults agreed the local drinking place was quite often the font of all knowledge.

Only the one public house, having wandered and looked around, having spoken and listened to those they met, it soon became apparent there was an unwritten rule stating that no moneymaking establishment should hinder another. No duplication; those selling what was similar sold at different times of the night or day. Not ignored, the two knowing others would have questions, couldn't help but notice how some shied away. *'The strangers in town?'* Newcomers? Never having visited or seen what was rural, didn't mean Martha and Lloyd not knowing their acceptance and trust would need to be earned.

Witch

"Hope we don't sit at somebodies table." Lloyd agreed it would take as much time for others to get use to them as it would for them to settle in and become part of what was different. Without work or more money, Martha said them upsetting people wouldn't matter if they had to leave. *'Close nit & caring.'* Yes, his wife agreed to what they could see, being perfect. *'Too wonderful for words.'* Whatever their personal thoughts, the couple knew their fingers and toes were crossed when looking to find what they needed to enable them to stay. *'Where were the jobs?'*

Traditional and oldie worldie, what was needed to assist with the running of the local tavern had been made to blend in with how it had always been. Never had either ventured into a place which sold alcohol unless to attend the occasional celebration. *'An afternoon tipple,'* Mr. and Mrs. Scott admitted to feeling like they were being naughty; when entering what on the inside Lloyd described as an architects dream. *'A drink & something to eat?'* Both worried the money they would need to spend, would be money lost on what they saw as being a treat.

"Welcome, of course sir, you and your good lady wife are free to sit wherever you like." The welcoming barman smiled while encouraging those he saw as visiting for the first time to checkout the main attraction.

The mural wall displaying the history of what surrounded where they were, was large, bright and information filled.

"Thank you." Martha said they were there to discover everything they could, while remembering the main job in hand, Lloyd asked if the one happy to serve knew of any paid work in the area. *'Glass collecting & pot washing?'* Martha apologised for smiling when the helpful male introducing himself as manager Mr. Joey Derwent; brought them a copy of the daily menu along with the requested application form. *'Better than nothing?'* When checking the terms and times of employment, the couple agreed they may have to invest in a much brighter torch.

Oldie worldie, welcoming, clean and spacious, the vast scattering of framed photographs alongside artist impressions, shown how little, things had changed. A coachhouse with stables, Tinkers Tavern was a place proud to advertise the fact it supplied a place of rest and refreshment for many a weary traveler throughout the years. Equip to cater for the needs of many a tired, hungry and thirsty visitor, the tavern had been the main stop for those wanting to rest themselves and their horses. The neighbouring stable block still retained a section which displayed how things were, whilst its' solid structure was extended to create extra accommodation and function room for hire. History blended within what was the present? Interested, Martha and Lloyd struggled to hide how them knowing little, meant them wanting to see everything.

"From the city?" Joey said he use to look at what they were seeing with the same questioning eyes. Guilty of making the same blank expressions when he first arrived. "Now, I love the place." Holding the position of live in manager, the middleaged male admitted that unlike the late Lord Sapphire, his marrying a local girl helped his seeing the village as home.
"Sapphire?" Martha questioned. "Did you say Lord Sapphire?" she asked what it was she heard and was told to checkout on the wall. *'Strange?'* Left to make their food choice, Lloyd told his wife they shouldn't go shouting about what they didn't understand. His true family name? Someone with the name Sapphire had been a Lord? Laughing, Lloyd told his wife he could see himself as Lord of the trees.

Homemade, the choice of food wasn't extensive, plain and wholesome, what was on offer smelt delicious, and those with simple tastes felt spoilt for choice. Noticing the couples indecisiveness, Joey returned to suggest they try the pie. Half a pint of the local ale, Joey couldn't have read his customers better; when realising they weren't where they were to splash the cash. Treated like VIP's regardless of whether they drank one, or a dozen drinks, the professional barman knew to treat others how he would want to be treated; if there was any chance of them spreading good word and coming back. A good meal, within what was comfortable and welcoming gave time to talk away from what the family were struggling to be inside, due to the improvements needed proving slow to reach completion.

Historical, local history, his families history? Having only recently learned the truth about his biological heritage, with much to discover and lots to do, Lloyd hadn't yet found the time to look into what had been the lives of his true ancestors. *'Interesting?'* Finishing their meal, the exploring couple wandered over to the wall seen to be a crowd pleaser. A large wall filled with pictures, poems, scripts, scribbled notes and official papers, tapestries, portraits, prints, photographs, handwritten notes, official letters, newspaper cuttings and photocopies of legal documents. An interwoven family tree, decorative and informative, the tale of two families coming together and creating a mingled maze of linked, broken and confusing branches to form the most amazing of blended family trees under the heading. The First Witch of Ebony Wood: Shocked, when reading what was written and chasing the pathway of names from the top Lord Ray Richard Sapphire to the bottom Miss Raven Rose Sapphire. Noticing the same news article found when Lloyd went searching for what was his official birth certificate and taking a deep breath before reading more. Could it be true, it seemed typical to see how the Lord had lost his fortune and abandoned the manor house but neither was concentrating or concerned with what was written in the middle, for Lloyd it was the bottom and for Martha it was the heading at the top causing her to tell her husband they may have inherited more than the land filled with trees when being given Ebony Wood. *'Who?'* Gasping, reading and re-reading what was before her, Martha questioned them having inherited the local witch?

The End

5

Come Alive

When all shades of grey turn black, it's time for a woman to take control back, Erotic, at times horrific enter if you dare The Tales of a witch in the in Ebony Wood.

Transforming the unbelievable into what is easier to perceive

- Witch
- Witch Way
- Witch Family
- Witch Woman
- Witch One

Read, Alone or follow what through the generations causes those seen to be different, to encounter what no one should endure.

They say success is the best revenge.

Living a life within the shadows of the trees, is it the witch in Ebony Wood, or Ebony Wood the witch lives in to hold the power seen to be magical?

A mystical adventure of lust & loyalty, where only the brave

SURVIVE

J Orton

5
Witch Books
Erotic Adult Adventure

Enter if you dare, into the witches lair
When all shades of grey turn black
She takes control Back
Wanting revenge, without repercussions
That is when we ask, if being a witch?
Is being Human?

Rosa never asked to be what others turned her into. Not the Bride of Satan, her only crime was to marry the man she fell in love with Chased into the shadows, standing back to evaluate ones misfortune is bound to change the fate of those to come after. A myth? A Legend ? A story to be told. Some stories never grow old. A family estate? His not knowing who he was, meant what he saw to be an inherited blessing being seen by others to be his all part of The Witches Curse: We all grow up, growing up different meant being feared & being feared led to being bullied Easier to attack than it is be understanding. Revenge didn't hurt, how could it, when she was getting what she Wanted?

How could someone with everything, be left with nothing & nowhere to be? Can a happy ending be found, when all around, believe you to be The Witch in Ebony Wood?

READ

Take a Selfie

READ

Post your Selfie

READ

Review

READ

Thank You

Note to Reader

Forgive the writer who will have sinned by making mistakes in this self published story. Future editions will be corrected as this dyslexic author continues to release what haunts their imagination.

Thank you for your time Share.

Signed by original author when visiting Derry 25th Oct - 2nd Nov 2024

Printed in Great Britain
by Amazon